# CORPSE IN WAITING

*The brand-new Patrick Gillard
and Ingrid Langley mystery*

Ingrid Langley and her husband and colleague
Patrick Gillard, late of M15 and now working
for the Serious and Organized Crime Agency,
decide to holiday in Bath. It may be close to
home, but they both badly need a break. The
holiday proceeds sedately enough, but trouble –
their old friend – is never far away. Ingrid tries
not to feel jealous when they bump into Patrick's
old flame, the beautiful Alexandra Nightingale,
and he agrees to help her house-hunt. But when
Ingrid joins them on a viewing, she makes a very
gruesome discovery indeed...

# CORPSE IN WAITING

## Margaret Duffy

**Severn House Large Print**
London & New York

This first large print edition published 2012
in Great Britain and the USA by
SEVERN HOUSE PUBLISHERS LTD of
9-15 High Street, Sutton, Surrey, SM1 1DF.
First world regular print edition published 2010 by
Severn House Publishers Ltd., London and New York.

British Library Cataloguing in Publication Data

Duffy, Margaret.
  Corpse in waiting. -- (A Patrick Gillard and Ingrid Langley
  mystery)
  1. Gillard, Patrick (Fictitious character)--Fiction.
  2. Langley, Ingrid (Fictitious character)--Fiction.
  3. Vacations--England--Bath--Fiction. 4. House buying--
  England--Bath--Fiction. 5. Murder--Investigation--
  England--Bath--Fiction. 6. Detective and mystery stories.
  7. Large type books.
  I. Title II. Series
  823.9'14-dc23

  ISBN-13: 978-0-7278-9840-1

Severn House Publishers support The Forest Stewardship Council
[FSC], the leading international forest certification organisation. All
our titles that are printed on Greenpeace-approved FSC-certified paper
carry the FSC logo.

MIX
Paper from
responsible sources
FSC® C018575

Printed and bound in Great Britain by the
MPG Books Group, Bodmin, Cornwall.

*No nightingale singeth too sweetly*
*not to grace a king's table.*

Anon. 16th Century

# ONE

It was waiting. For us. But not, obviously, in any sense that it could do anything for us: *to* us perhaps, the discovery of bodies not being an everyday occurrence, even for members of the Serious Organized Crime Agency. And because of the circumstances I came to feel that the responsibility was ours, to help find out who had killed her.

If the above seems fanciful it is because words are my business: I am a writer by trade. Patrick, my husband, a very pragmatic soul, is sometimes exasperated by my flights of fancy, especially when I apply them to my other job as 'consultant' to his position of 'adviser' to SOCA. The inverted commas are deliberate as he usually goes to work armed to the teeth. My role is usually confined to that of being prepared to provide a sympathetic ear together with, hopefully, creative suggestions to help solve problems. But sometimes I slip into my bag the Smith and Wesson that he has never quite returned to MI5 when he left and we work closely together. Not that I hand over the gun should his ammo run out, I'm a pretty good shot.

To decide to holiday in Bath when you live not ten miles down the road might be regarded as eccentric but after Patrick was fairly seriously ill, the after-effects of having been drugged during our previous case, and I was getting over having a baby at a time of life that could not be described as 'spring chicken', we both badly needed a break. Long flights, protracted car journeys, the whole business of actually getting somewhere else did not appeal to either of us.

'No, to hell with it,' Patrick had said suddenly. 'We've only just moved to this neck of the woods. I've another week left of my leave so let's make like tourists and stay at the best hotel in Bath. Have you ever been to the Roman Baths?'

'Years ago,' I had replied. 'When I was a child.'

Patrick had stretched back in his chair. 'I quite fancy feasts and orgies, slave girls and that kind of thing.'

'The theatre, museums, art galleries, meals out and shopping,' I had amended.

'Not one smallest orgy?'

'Not a chance.'

He had chuckled and gone back to the book he was reading.

'You could seduce me quite a lot instead.'

A dirty chuckle this time.

The weather could not have been better, a surprise after weeks of cold winds, sleet and snow. So, several days later we were on an open-top bus taking a tour of Bath, our guide with a strong American accent, those around us talking excitedly in Japanese, French and German, to name but three languages that I could recognize. With the hot sun beating down on us and the city's famous flower displays in every direction it was exactly like being abroad.

'You know, this is actually rather pleasant,' Patrick commented, gazing in admiration at Royal Crescent. 'We must walk the route afterwards to give us a good appetite for dinner.'

I took a deep breath of the scents of spring blossoms and said, 'Have you told James what we're doing? I haven't.'

This was Detective Chief Inspector James Carrick of Bath CID, who is a friend of ours.

'No, I thought it best not to. He always says that trouble follows us around and I should hate it if he lost any sleep over it. If we bump into him it can't be helped.'

Over the following couple of days we went on a boat trip on the River Avon, visited several museums, had tea in the Pump Room, having toured the Roman Baths, sampled the spring waters and wandered around the Assembly Rooms. Tonight after we had eaten there was a concert in Parade Gardens and the following evening I was vaguely thinking we could go to the theatre.

It was obvious though that the man in my life was getting a little restless.

'You're bored?' I enquired gently, realizing that *Lady Windermere's Fan* might not be quite Patrick's thing.

We were in Sally Lunn's on the fourth day of our break, sharing one of the large brioche-style buns with morning coffee.

'Not ex–act–ly,' he said slowly. 'I suppose it's just that I'm used to *doing* – what Katie would call "stuff" most of the time.'

'You mean you'd far rather be engaged in shoot-'em-up sessions at that SOCA training place in Hammersmith,' I remarked, straight-faced.

He merely smiled. Ye gods, he would.

We had talked of taking our two eldest children out of school for part of the week to give them what would be an educational as well as a fun experience but had decided against it as they were both sitting exams soon and had been away for a few days in London with us at half term. Matthew and Katie are actually Patrick's brother Larry's children whom we adopted when he was killed a while ago. Justin, Victoria and baby Mark are ours and that is quite enough, thank you. I often marvel at our family: after serious injuries in his army days Patrick was told it was unlikely, nay almost impossible, that he would ever be able to father children. At that time we were actually divorced, oddly, one of the things we had profoundly disagreed upon having been my reluctance to start a family.

I daydreamed, thinking back to when he had returned to my life; maimed, mentally iffy because of it and desperate to make a new career for himself, to be *useful*, with a job offer from D12, a department of MI5. Still a serving army officer, a major in those days, he had been ordered to find a working partner, female, as socializing would be required and official opinion held that lone men, especially somewhat saturnine, if not downright dangerous-looking ones, were conspicuous. He had arrived on the doorstep of the only woman on the planet, or so he had thought, who would not want to go to bed with him, self-confidence in that direction not so much being low as having crashed. I supposed I had dreamed of this arrogant, self-satisfied, frankly insufferable, man my husband had become turning up, and briskly sending him away without a qualm, but suffering had stripped all that from him. I am one of those people who can never walk past a lost kitten, or a dog with a thorn in its paw, and rejecting him in the state he was in would have been unbearable. There was also the matter of my guilty conscience.

For some amazing reason the old magic had worked again and we had discovered that we both still loved and now also badly needed one another. Looking back with the benefit of hindsight I suppose that if we had had a period of separation we might never have divorced in the first place. After a short time we had remarried. I can still vividly remember that ceremony in a stiflingly hot registry office but not exactly where it was – just some god-awful part of London – the hapless plants on the window ledges bracing themselves for another day of suffocation from fumes from the gas fire and the Registrar's pipe. Both witnesses had coughed so horribly I had wondered if they would survive to the end of the ceremony without oxygen.

'Would you rather go home tomorrow then?' I asked.

Patrick refilled our coffee cups. 'No, not at all.

11

Have you planned anything special?'

'Not yet.'

'We haven't been to the Industrial Heritage Centre. That would be interesting.' Here he shot me a mischievous look. 'And in the evening the Roman Baths is holding something called a Roman Experience, togas provided. A feast, wine and a wallow in the waters. I asked and there are still tickets available.'

It transpired that there was a tour of the Roman Baths first, which we had already done, of course, but this was after normal opening hours with the promise of being able to look into nooks, crannies and crypts not usually seen by the public. Then we would decamp to the nearby modern spa complex where we would indulge in our wallowing and feasting. Later we would return to the ancient baths where we could lounge around in togas, if we wished, sampling Roman-style wine – which turned out to be Prosecco – and listening to the kind of music that might have been played at the time.

Not quite sure why I had a sense of despondency about the plan I nevertheless went along with it. I did not want to be a wet blanket, or rather towel. Hot baths and jacuzzis have never been my idea of fun and I could see the whole evening turning into some kind of alcohol-fuelled soggy riot because of the presence of teenagers who had wealthy parents – for this was by no means a cheap exercise – ruining it for everyone else.

If Patrick noticed my long face he had said

nothing and I have to confess that I was pleasantly surprised when, after the tour and a very short walk, my head still stuffed full of details of hypocausts, the *apodyterium*, *calderium* and *tepidarium*, we found ourselves floating gently, amid gorgeous surroundings, in a circular pool filled with the famed hot waters and wearing the swimsuits we had brought with us. There were only just over a dozen people present and plenty of room for all. A live string quartet quietly played Mozart.

'You're staying with SOCA I take it?' I enquired lightly after a short while had elapsed during which we had wallowed in silence, relaxing.

'Do you want me to?' he asked. 'It's your job, on and off, as well.'

'But it's not the same for me. It's your decision and if you want to carry on then I'm there if you need me. I have my writing; SOCA's not my number one thing.'

'The last assignment was pretty bloody.'

'In every way.'

'You were hinting recently that I had lost my edge a bit, from the MI5 days.'

'You weren't well.'

'Now you're being kind. Please be honest.'

'You *weren't* well and I think what made me say it was that you were relying on me rather a lot. That's probably my fault. But, on reflection you're not the professionally hard man you once were. I don't know if that's good or bad now you're with SOCA.'

'It's bad. Really bad. I know Mike's got some-

13

thing fairly ordinary and desk-driven for me when I go back. He's insisting I stick to something quiet and not too demanding for a bit. I probably need something with a bit more of a personal challenge.'

Commander Michael Greenway is Patrick's boss.

'And I can't keep swapping jobs,' Patrick went on. 'Not with the sprogs to feed.'

'Katie asked me if it would help if she got a weekend job and Matthew had a newspaper round,' I said. 'She wondered if it would save you from having to undertake such dangerous work.'

'That's amazingly thoughtful for someone of her age even though she's far too young to have a job.'

'When you're hurt we can't hide it from the family.'

'And she and Matthew have both lost one Dad already.'

'Exactly.'

'We must discuss it again later.'

This pool was not designed for strenuous exercise being only five feet deep but Patrick is a good swimmer despite the lower part of his right leg now being of man-made construction. He doesn't get it wet if he can help it though and jokes that if he wants to attain around fifteen knots he straps on the lid of the laundry basket instead. Not tonight, however. At the time I had not noticed any odd looks from our companions when he had lowered himself into the water, no diving allowed. But now...

14

She had bright blue eyes like the beam from some kind of alien weapon in a sci-fi movie, the simile jumping into my mind with an alacrity that was startling given that she was looking at us from the other side of the pool. Or rather she was looking at Patrick. I had not noticed her on the tour of the Roman Baths so could only assume that she had been late.

She was now making her way over to us.

'It's not Patrick Gillard, is it?' she called when still a little way off, her voice mellifluous, like that of an actress.

He turned and I saw the shock of recognition.

'It is you,' she trilled. 'Darling, how are you after all this time?'

I felt she was avoiding making eye contact with me although her gaze had swept fleetingly in my direction on her approach.

The two came face to face and gazed at one another.

'Such a long time,' the woman said softly. 'Well? You haven't answered my question.'

'I'm fine,' Patrick told her.

'But such *ghastly* injuries, darling. I never thought...' She broke off and gave me her full attention. 'You *are* with this lovely man here?' And before either of us could speak, swept on with, 'But there are always sweet souls in this world who have the time to cherish and nurture.' A girlish giggle escaped her. 'Unlike me – always dashing off somewhere or the other.'

'This is my wife, Ingrid,' Patrick said to her. 'Ingrid, meet Alexandra Nightingale. We met up when I came back from being blown up in the

15

South Atlantic.'

Did one shake her hand or merely dunk her perfect blonde hair, swept up into what I could only call Roman goddess style – which unlike mine she had kept dry – beneath the waves?

We shook hands and bared our teeth at one another.

'Your parents lived in such a charming rectory in Somerset,' Alexandra recalled, frowning in exaggerated fashion. 'I shall always remember that weekend. The weather was boiling hot and your mother had made some wonderful ice cream. I'm not a country girl, you know,' she said in an aside to me. 'Hate all the bugs and creepy-crawlies. And the cow poo everywhere – you simply can't wear anything nice.'

I was about to say that we now lived at the rectory with Patrick's parents and sometimes managed to change out of dungarees and wellies when there was an announcement over the public address system that our feast – a buffet – would soon be served. It was time to dry off and get dressed.

'Such a tragedy,' Alexandra said in a loud whisper that Patrick probably heard as he sprang up to sit on the side of the pool, using his arms, as anyone might have done, to lift himself. 'Oh, he did finally have to lose his leg below the knee then, poor man. How on earth does he manage?'

'Well, as you can see,' I snapped. 'Perfectly.'

I left the pool and hurried away from her, hoping that she would leave us alone from now on.

Fat chance.

An excellent spread was laid out for us in a

16

room with a bar off to the side of the pool and therapy rooms. Patrick had struck up a conversation with an elderly man whom he later told me was ex-Royal Engineers. This meant that when Alexandra appeared, wearing a floaty black and cream full-length dress and sparkly sandals, I had her all to myself.

'On your own then?' I asked, aware that my hair looked a real bird's nest after a gale-force blow from one of the establishment's dryers as I had forgotten to bring a hair brush.

She pulled a face, piling her plate high from the buffet. 'As of last week, yes. The rat went and found someone else.' She turned to me with wide-eyed interest. 'Tell me, how long have you known Patrick?'

'We were at school together.'

'How romantic,' she crooned. 'And you're *married*?' She made it sound as though this had surmounted all the odds.

I was determined not to lose my cool. 'Where did you meet him?'

'He was with someone else, some girl or other who'd dragged him off to a fashion show I was in. He was convalescing then, on crutches. I spotted him straight away but not because of that. *So* good looking. I have to say he never mentioned you.'

'We were divorced for a while. Round about then, obviously.'

Elspeth, Patrick's mother, had told me when Patrick and I got back together again that there had been a few 'girlfriends' during the interregnum, as she had smilingly referred to our

17

separation, a couple of whom he had brought to stay for the occasional weekend.

'So I take it he was invalided out of the army and—'

I carved her up. 'No, Patrick was promoted to Lieutenant-Colonel after working for MI5 for a while and then resigned his commission. He's now with the Serious Organized Crime Agency as an adviser.'

'So what does that make him?' she wanted to know.

'Mostly a policeman.'

'Oh.'

I had chosen what I wanted from the buffet and now went over to a table near a window. She followed and seated herself with a satisfied sigh, her gaze going across to Patrick. I took a good look at her. She was older than I had first thought, perhaps mid-forties, and I had to admit was attractive – in a hard sort of way.

'Is he going to stand talking to that old bore all night or join us?' she said. 'He trapped me earlier as we were waiting to go into the Roman Baths, telling me how his wife had recently died. I was forced to abandon – I simply can't stand other people's hard-luck stories.'

Fortunately, or not, Patrick ended his chat and, after helping himself to something to eat, came over. He then went away again to fetch a couple of glasses of wine from the bar – he had not yet been cleared by his specialist to drink alcohol after being drugged. Watching him carefully I noted that he was not exactly devastated by the arrival of Alexandra, giving her a broad smile.

18

'It's lovely to see you again,' she said, turning in her chair so as to slightly have her back to me. 'You haven't aged at all really, just a few grey hairs. Men who have a good head of hair always look distinguished when it starts to go grey.'

The man in my life happily soaked this up, smiling at her again before saying, 'You haven't changed either. I seem to remember we met in a pub in Plymouth.'

'No, that must have been someone else, darling. Perhaps it was that little brunette you were with. No, I found you at the Savoy. There was a charity fashion show – royalty and all – and there you were.'

'That's right. I remember now.'

He didn't.

There was a little silence and then Alexandra said, 'Is your brother – Harry, is it? – well?'

'Larry. No, he's dead.'

'Oh, I'm terribly sorry.'

'He was killed a while back. We adopted his two children, Matthew and Katherine, Katie.'

She nodded understandingly. 'Yes, of course.'

'And we've three of our own,' I said brightly before the bloody woman could say anything that might embarrass him.

Elspeth, having mentioned the 'girlfriends' had also said that there had been no creaking floorboards after lights out. Clergy family or no she had not fixed the sleeping arrangements so they shared a room having thought that the divorce was mostly Patrick's fault, actually not true. She had nevertheless been hoping and praying that we would get back together again.

19

But she had been concerned for him too having been informed by the army medics that his injuries included the genital region. So the no creaking floorboards situation had probably not eased her mind at all. The catalyst had been the arrival on the scene of the patient's ex-wife, the magic boosted by the spell-maker preparing a camp-bed for him in a cobweb-loaded box room with no heating, the spare bedroom unaccountably being 'not in use', while I was given his. And no, I had not run in to him with twigs in my beak, the man had finally cracked, carted me off into the warm and practically raped me.

All he had needed was practice.

'Are you still working as a PA?' Patrick asked.

'I was *never* a PA, darling. You're mixing me up with someone else again. I was a model – that's how we met at the fashion show – but not now. God, no, I'd had more than enough of the catwalk. I run an agency now which I'm transferring down here. London's a truly ghastly place these days.' She was drinking her wine rather quickly.

'A modelling agency?' I said, thinking perhaps I ought to take a bit more interest.

She rounded on me. 'No, haven't I just said I was sick of that life?' She did not quite add, 'stupid'.

'So you're living in Bath now?' Patrick said quickly.

'Not yet, I'm house-hunting, right here in the city,' Alexandra replied. 'I've just decided that's where you come in, darling. Someone to tell me about the pitfalls, what to look out for. I mean,

I've always rented before and wouldn't have the first idea what dry rot looks like but you must have had lots of experience with your parents living round here.'

'You can get dry rot everywhere,' Patrick pointed out. 'In cities and the countryside. I take it you want an old house then?'

'Ancient and with *masses* of character,' she cried triumphantly, causing a few heads to turn.

Rising damp, I thought gleefully, wet as well as dry rot, woodworm, death-watch beetle, bats, spiders, woodlice, rats, mice...

'D'you remember that old place that was for sale in the village wherever the rectory was that we went and had a look at? Like that.'

I willed him not to tell her.

'Hinton Littlemoor. We're living there as well now,' Patrick said. 'It was the old mill cottage and well on the way to falling down if I remember rightly. You wouldn't recognize it now – they had to spend a fortune to get it right.'

'Oh, I've got money. That's no problem. I just need a guiding hand.' Here the woman simpered at him in little-girl fashion that caused my hands to clench into tight fists.

'I'm afraid I work in London. This is just a week's break Ingrid and I are having.'

'I've arranged to see several places tomorrow. Or have you made other plans?'

Patrick looked across at me and I remained as inscrutable as a herd of sphinxes.

'Yes, it would be interesting,' he said thoughtfully. 'Would you rather go shopping while we do that, Ingrid?'

'No, I love looking round houses,' I replied, quite truthfully as it happened. But was I going to leave him alone with this harpy? No.

Alexandra pouted but made no comment. Then she said, 'D'you remember on that weekend when we went to Bath races and that enormously fat woman sat down in a plastic café chair and it collapsed and she went hurtling backwards into a flower bed? I don't think I've laughed so much in my life, although you got annoyed with me and said we ought to try not to let her see us.'

Patrick grinned reflectively and then uttered a hoot of amusement. 'No, what really made us laugh was the owner of the café rushing out, demanding they pay for it and the woman's husband punching him on the nose so he ended up in the flower bed too.'

The pair howled with laughter.

We had not brought our car with us – with Bath's traffic it made no sense to do so – but Alexandra had hired one and we arranged that she would pick us up outside our hotel at nine thirty the next morning. She apparently 'didn't do mornings' but her first property appointment was at ten, a flat somewhere on Lansdown Hill. I was hoping she would be fit to drive by then as the wine had flowed freely at the Roman Baths afterwards and she had taken full advantage of it.

I was still doing my sphinx thing.

'Fancy seeing her again after all this time,' Patrick said musingly as we went up to our hotel room.

'Yes, fancy,' I heard myself respond, graven image-like.

I felt, rather than saw, the sideways look he gave me.

'Surely you don't blame me for having girl-friends while we were apart.'

I looked him right in the eye. 'No, of course not. I just don't like women who call a man darling in public when they haven't seen him in years and he's obviously with someone else. It's just plain bad manners.' Even uttering the words made me feel an old fogey.

'Alex is like that,' Patrick said with a reflective smile.

'As well as being a binge drinker?'

'That's not like you, and cruel,' he shot back at me.

'No, actually this is me being your consultant,' I countered. 'You know, the one on the other end of the phone when things go a bit tits-up for you? Dispassionately, and I might add soberly, I'm telling you that that woman will make trouble for you.'

'Look, I'm only going to look round some houses with her.'

'She's well on the way to ending up a booze-soaked old buzzard.'

'Now you're being ridiculous.'

'Did you sleep with her?'

'Yes.'

I was being ridiculous and I knew he was lying, a shock in itself, and it came to me a little later that we had not had an exchange of words like this since just before we were divorced.

23

# TWO

The morning brought a murky sky with darker, thunder-grey clouds on the horizon. Later, as we stood on the pavement outside the hotel I heard the first rumbles and, cursed with flippancy even in bad moments, it occurred to me that this could be the backdrop for a scene in a rather tacky movie. Even our surroundings, one of the finer terraces in Bath, would have had a locations manager bouncing up and down with joy.

And here stood the hero and heroine, I thought glumly, still not at ease with one another, he thinking she was silent on account of the presence of an old flame, or damp squib, whichever way you looked at it, she desperately wondering how to break the stalemate.

We were still standing there fifteen minutes later, getting restless, the storm coming closer, when Patrick's mobile rang. It soon became obvious that it was Commander Michael Greenway, his boss. Nothing too exciting by the sound of it, just making contact. The call ended.

'Good of him to ring,' I commented.

'Yes.'

'Did he say anything about any job he might have for you?'

'No.'

24

'How long do you think we ought to wait here?'

'I don't know.'

'She's probably still asleep.'

A grunt.

We lapsed into silence again.

At seven minutes past ten, large spots of rain beginning to thunk on to the pavement, I was just about to give up when a Ford estate car roared up to us and screeched to a halt.

'Morning!' Alexandra shrieked out of the driver's window, following this with 'Shit!' as she stalled the engine.

I was directed to the back seat, 'So Patrick can show me the way,' and duly shifted various items to make space for myself; a thin leather document case, open and stuffed full with papers that were spilling out everywhere, road maps, two umbrellas and a large make-up bag. The car jerked away before I had settled, throwing me into the seat. I mulled over how I would be safest; with my seat belt fastened or not, and then discovered that they all appeared to be trapped behind the upholstery where the seats had been folded down to make room for carrying a bigger load in the rear.

'You need a left here,' Patrick was saying, having to raise his voice above a downpour as the storm arrived.

A horn blared and the car slewed to a standstill. I had just prevented myself from being thrown forward when Alexandra delivered, full volume, an amazing string of obscenities at someone through her hastily opened window.

She then swore again as she got wet.

'But you do have to give way,' Patrick added, and then laughed.

Never having been a very good traveller I fought down nausea.

We rolled back a little, someone behind us leaned on their horn in panic and then we rocketed off again.

'This is a horrible little car!' Alexandra raved. 'I have a Porsche at home, you know.'

'Did I hear you say you were being given the keys to one of the houses?' Patrick asked.

'The second place we're looking at. I called in for them on the way over to pick you up. Where to now?'

'Just bear left and follow the main road. What's the address?'

'God knows but it's on the particulars. They're in the left hand pocket of my jacket. Have a rummage.'

The female then commenced to wriggle, uttering little giggles, as he put a hand in her pocket and truly, if she had not been driving I would have battered her over the head with anything heavy that was to hand.

He found the folded sheet of paper.

'Nineteen, King's Court,' he read out.

'That's just along from where James Carrick used to live,' I said. 'Up here, on the left.'

Lightning zipped and thunder cracked and we had to pull over for a couple of minutes as it was impossible to see clearly for the rain even with the wipers going flat out. Finally, when it was easing off, we found the place, actually a large mansion that had been converted into flats. Someone from the estate agent's was waiting to show us around, the owners being abroad.

The flat was on the ground floor, spacious but in need of decoration. Alexandra studiously ignored my presence, asking Patrick about paint, wallpaper, plumbing, heating; subjects about which he has never had time to acquaint himself having been content to leave all that kind of thing to his wife. I could have answered most of her questions but neither of them bothered to consult me so I am afraid Patrick had to flounder. As it was I thought the flat a fair price and with quite a lot to recommend it being quiet, very private and with rooms that had lovely proportions.

'Even if you tore the whole place apart there'd still be a bad feel to it,' Alexandra was saying in ringing tones when I returned from a quick tour of my own, the estate agent, also finding himself superfluous, waiting patiently for us in the hall. 'I mean, their taste is *execrable*. I'd never be able to get things like those bloody awful curtains out of my mind. No, this isn't the home for me.'

We left.

The next property was empty and because of this we were going to be permitted to look at it on our own, the other appointments Alexandra had during the afternoon. It turned out to be a small terraced Georgian house of some charm, clematis coming into bud around the front door, a narrow front garden overgrown and neglected. The building had been on the market for a long

27

time, over a year, and was in a dire state; peeling paint, cracked glass in some of the rotten sash windows, slipping slates. It would cost a fair bit to restore but I reckoned that if it was done properly one would end up with a real gem.

'I'd concrete over all this and park the car off the road,' said Alexandra as we walked up the path, waving one elegant hand in the direction of the dripping garden.

'You wouldn't be allowed to,' I told her. 'These old properties are almost all Grade One or Two listed.'

'Oh, I'd soon see to that. Money talks, you know.'

The old-fashioned keys grated in the locks of the front door and we went in. It was gloomy inside and smelt of damp. Alexandra grabbed Patrick by the hand and towed him off towards the rear of the house leaving me to wander into the gloomy living room to the left of the narrow hallway.

It was obvious that no one had lived here for a long time either. The lack of light was due to plants having grown across the windows, which were thick with dirt. I gazed around, trying to work out how much this room alone would cost to restore. I thought not a huge sum even though the floorboards appeared to be rotten along one side and there was a crack in the wall over the fireplace, suggesting a one-time chimney fire. On the positive side there was a very attractive fireplace, which no doubt Alexandra would have removed, and what looked like the original cornices and central ceiling rose. A long and narrow cupboard to one side of the hearth was locked but there were several small keys on the ring still in the lock of the front door, one of which, I quickly discovered, fitted.

There were only two shelves, towards the top, which held dust and dead spiders, plus one large and very alive one which, upon seeing daylight for the first time since heaven alone knew when, raced out of confinement at my nose height startling me before tumbling down on to the floor and rattling off into the grate. It had probably survived by sucking the life out of the others and then become too fat to get through the crack in the door. I'm not a fan of big spiders, nor anything on this planet, come to think of it, with attitude and that number of legs.

I could hear Patrick telling Alexandra about dry rot and so forth and all at once felt depressed and even more superfluous, just as she had intended. To join them and start throwing my weight about seemed juvenile in the extreme, to stay where I was might be construed as sulking. I left that room, crossed the hall and went into the front room on the other side. This was virtually a mirror image of the first but with window seats in the bay and no cupboard.

'Don't you want to see the back?' Alexandra called, appearing and sounding offended.

'In a minute,' I answered.

'There is dry rot in the kitchen,' Patrick reported, his voice sounding muffled as though he was half inside a cupboard under the sink. 'Probably mushrooms of it under the floorboards.'

'We could always have them on toast for

lunch,' I murmured and went up the stairs.

It was much brighter and lighter here, the two bedrooms and tiny box room charming with faded flowery wallpaper. There was a distant view of hills. I began to fall in love with the place. My imagination blossomed and created a staggeringly wonderful idea. This was a perfect writer's retreat, a winter snug or summer garden cottage where I would not be constantly having to share my workspace with up to nine other people. The box room was just about large enough for a corner shower, hand basin and toilet, one of the living rooms on the ground floor could be made into a study and a simple but modern kitchen installed at the rear.

I went off into a world of my own for a while, gazing out of a window that overlooked the small overgrown back garden, redesigning it in my mind's-eye and for some reason feeling really happy for the first time in ages. Finding my mobile phone I decided to take a photo of it but just as I pressed the button Alexandra walked into shot. She did not see me and I withdrew a little and waited until she went back indoors before taking another. Then I heard footsteps behind me.

'We wondered where you'd got to,' Patrick said.

'This is a lovely little house.'

'Alex is thinking of buying it. But I've told her she'll have a full-scale war with the planners on her hands over what she wants to do with it.'

'She can't have it,' I heard myself say.

'Why not?' Patrick asked blankly.

I turned to face him. 'Because *I'm* buying it.'

'Eh?'

'So I can escape when I want to, to write. I've lost my writing room since we moved and have to make do with my desk in the dining room. I've discovered that I can't work like that.'

'But...' Words didn't often fail him. He tried again. 'Look, I know you—'

A deep resentment that I thought I had emotionally dealt with surfaced. 'All the time I was site-managing the building work being done on the rectory just before and after I'd had Mark I knew that there would be nowhere for me to write. Frankly, no one seemed to care despite the fact that the cottage we'd just sold in Devon had been *mine*. And if you're thinking that I'd use the money we're putting aside for the children's university education that's not the case at all. Besides which, this place'll be worth a lot when it's been done up and is a good investment. Even in this financial climate an historic house in Bath, albeit a very small one, is never going to lose its value.'

Patrick nodded briskly. 'I already knew there might be a problem with the present writing arrangements and I'm sure we can find a way round it.'

I had already racked my brains but could think of no way round it. I was hanged if I was going to have one of those studio sheds in the garden either. There was nowhere to hide away anything like that and I would have a constant stream of little visitors who would think it was a playhouse just for them and would then raise hell when I tried to explain that it was not.

'I wasn't thinking about money,' Patrick went on. 'Although you ought to know that even in this condition it's on the market for just over three hundred thousand pounds.'

The man had not the first clue about Bath property prices. This place was a gift. I said, 'As I told you the other day, Berkley's just sold the TV rights for ten of my novels. That will pay for it.'

Berkley Morton is my agent.

Patrick did not appear to hear. I had not thought he had really hoisted in my good news at the first telling. 'But, Ingrid, the rectory at Hinton Littlemoor is your home.'

'Of course it is. I shall only be here sometimes. Probably mostly when you're in London.'

'So you're no longer going to—'

'There's no question that I won't be there for you if you want my help.'

With a set look on his face Patrick said, 'So how many pieces are you going to try to cut yourself into?'

'Sufficient,' I replied. Then added, 'Look, it'll be no different to the way I used to go to my writing room at Lydtor and shut the door. Everyone used to be quite happy about that.'

'Do as you please,' he said and went away.

The phone number of the estate agent was on the board outside, which I could see from the front bedroom window. I rang, explained I was with Ms Nightingale but acting independently and put in an offer twenty thousand pounds below the asking price. They said they would contact the vendor and ring me back.

I went back downstairs, pausing on the way to note that there was a built-in cupboard in the passageway by the box room door. I knew that what I was doing looked very bad but consoled myself with the knowledge that I did not want this house just because *she* did. The pair of them were in the room to the left of the front door and I estimated that I turned up the very second that Alexandra realized something was going on.

'Have you two had words?' she asked, failing to hide her smile.

'Not really,' Patrick said. 'But I think Ingrid's fallen in love with it too.'

'What, this house?' she cried. 'But it's mine!'

'Not yet,' I pointed out.

'That's what you think!' Alexandra stamped out and up the stairs while I drifted off to have a look at the kitchen and downstairs bathroom.

The former was larger than I had expected with a scullery leading off to the rear from which the damp, mouldy smell seemed to be emanating. One would have to knock the whole thing through into one and hope to be allowed to create another window. I went down the step into the scullery, opened the cupboard beneath the Belfast sink and there indeed were some very rotten floorboards and strange white fungus-looking growths with tendrils going up the wall. There did not seem to be any sign of it elsewhere. The tiny bathroom was hardly worthy of the name, with rusting and stained fittings: this room could also be incorporated into a new kitchen. It appeared the lavatory was an outside one.

As I made my way over to the door to the garden my phone rang and it was the woman from the estate agency.

I had myself a house.

Imparting the news had two immediate effects. The first was Alexandra raging off yelling, 'You weren't brought along to bugger things up for me!' and then, to Patrick, 'Well, are you going to stand there and abandon me now she's got what she wants?' The second being that he didn't. Coolly telling me that he'd see me later, Patrick followed her to her car.

'The harridan gave him no choice,' I said aloud. 'But he could have arranged to meet her after lunch and we could have walked back into the city.'

Actually a little shocked by his reaction, I wandered, bemused, into the back of the house and stared around the kitchen. There were horrible, cheap DIY store cupboards and worktops here, all seemingly holding one another up, but the old scullery beyond had what looked like an original walk-in larder. I went over to it and turned the knob on the door but it appeared to be locked. One of the keys on the ring fitted and turned but it still would not open.

'Stuck,' I muttered. 'Oh, well.'

Forcing myself to concentrate I rang the agents and made an appointment that afternoon to sort out the details of my purchase. Then I went back upstairs, still, frankly, in a bit of a daze. I could not understand why Patrick still felt obliged to help her. Surely it was obvious, even to someone other than this wildly biased observer, that she was ghastly.

Perhaps they had had a worthwhile relationship all that time ago, perhaps he had loved her and was blinded by the kind of person, possibly a better one, she had been. Perhaps there had been some terrible tragedy in her past that he knew about and felt sorry for her.

The cupboard in the upstairs passageway was locked, or stuck, as well.

So whose fault *was* this mess? I inwardly raged.

It might just be mine, was my miserable conclusion. Why did I feel so insecure about Alexandra? Why *should* I regard her as a threat to my relationship with Patrick? I could only put it down to what my father had called my 'cat's' whiskers, the intuition that has helped solve quite a few of Patrick's, and, come to think of it, James Carrick's cases for them.

I got annoyed about the door, wondering if the cupboard would be worth retaining, marched downstairs and raided the kitchen drawers. Amongst rubbish, old newspapers, string, rusting cutlery, and other sundry items I found some old fire tongs and what looked like half an iron poker. It was still quite long, around fourteen inches and I discovered when I hauled it out, everything shedding mouse droppings, that someone had flattened the end a bit like a screwdriver. (I found out at a later date that it was one of the tools for a Victorian kitchen range.)

Absolutely perfect.

The cupboard door was only stuck seemingly in a couple of places, at the top and towards the bottom on the side of the lock. But the wood was not in good condition and there were ominous crunching noises when, crouching down, I had inserted my weapon into the gap – the door did not fit very well – and applied a little leverage. I did not want to do any damage to something that was not yet mine so proceeded gently. At last, the door yielded, leaving a thick layer of paint on the inside of the door frame. No, not paint, I saw when I looked more closely, the deposit was what appeared to be glue.

I stood up, opened the door wide and found myself eyeball to partially empty sockets with someone's head.

My back slammed into the wall behind me and there was a bang as the tool I had been using landed on the floor. I suppose I must have stopped breathing for a moment from shock for I then heard myself gasp for air, inhaling the stink of putrefaction. The head on its shelf just grinned back at me.

It was not a joke one made of some kind of resin that smelt horrible, I ascertained, making myself go closer again. This was real. It was only halfway to being a skull as the shrivelled lips were still there and thick black hair tumbled down from what remained of the scalp. Those eyes...

Feeling sick, I walked away for a short distance, surprised to find that I was a little unsteady on my feet.

Then I rang the police.

# THREE

'You've found a *heid*?' James Carrick exclaimed, his Scottish accent more pronounced then usual.

'In a house I'm hoping to buy,' I elaborated.

There was a pause and then he said, 'I'm not sure which is the more surprising statement. Are you *sure*?'

'I'm looking at it now,' I said. 'It's on the top shelf of an upstairs cupboard. The cupboard had been glued shut and there's another one similarly sealed in the scullery. Perhaps that's where the rest is.'

'Is Patrick with you?'

'No, he's gone house-hunting with some blonde trollop.'

'Bloody hell,' he responded morosely. 'Give me the address and I'll be with you as quickly as I can.'

Cautious as ever, Carrick, fair-haired, in his late thirties, a Scot to the core, and once described by a friend of mine as wall-to-wall crumpet, arrived on his own, had a look for himself and *then* called out the troops.

'Are you all right?' he asked.

We were standing in the scullery, waiting for his team to arrive, gazing at the larder door.

'Yes, I'm OK,' I replied, actually wishing Patrick was here too.

'You're not going to want to live here now, surely,' he said, giving me a sober look.

'I don't know,' I replied. 'I think it would ... depend.' At least Alexandra would be unlikely to want it now.

'You could sweep the cupboards away when you modernize the place,' he suggested. 'Had I told you Joanna's pregnant?'

'No! Congratulations!'

'Well, as you know, she's had two miscarriages. She's taking things very easy.' Awkwardly, he went on, 'Look— er – excuse me for asking but what did you mean when you said Patrick had gone house-hunting with some – er – woman?'

'Trollop,' I corrected before explaining.

His brow cleared. 'You had me worried for a minute. I thought—'

'*I'm* worried,' I interrupted. 'She might have some kind of hold over him.'

'Who – *Patrick*? Surely not!'

'Not the sort of hold you might be thinking of. She might represent ... you know ... his youth, fun times before he had any responsibilities and was still an army officer in a regiment that hadn't been amalgamated with others. Oh, I don't know, James. You're a bloke. You ought to be able to explain it to me. I mean, she used some really filthy language and he *laughed*! Now if there's one thing he hates it's me swearing.'

'But he cares about you, doesn't he? She might

38

have been just a one-night stand – history.'

'And if you met a bloke with whom Joanna had had a one-night stand and he started chatting her up and calling her darling how would you react?'

'I'd kill him,' James responded grimly. 'Oh – right, I see what you mean.'

All discussion on the matter then had to cease as Carrick's team, led by his assistant, DS Lynn Outhwaite, arrived in a blare of sirens and other police designed-to-intimidate sound-effects. Carrick immediately sent the scenes of crime people upstairs to examine the head, directed a photographer to take pictures of the scullery and its larder door, in painstaking detail and close-up, before he too went upstairs and then, personally, set about opening it using the thing I had found in the drawer. This door was more firmly stuck but after about ten minutes of careful diligence on the DCI's part it yielded.

'My prints are already on it, I'm afraid,' I said as he grasped the door knob with a gloved hand.

'No point it having mine as well,' he muttered.

The glue's sealing effect had kept in the stench. Everyone – there was quite an audience by this time – involuntarily jumped back as it hit us. This was just as well because the thing that toppled out and hit the floor with a sickening squelching thud landed on the spot where the toes of Carrick's shoes had been a second earlier. The next few moments were only memorable for the reason that one of those watching from the back ran into the kitchen and threw up noisily into the sink.

'Oh, God,' Carrick said thickly as dark-coloured fluids began to trickle across the ancient lino in our direction.

The body, presumably headless, was wrapped in what appeared to be bedding; sheets and perhaps some kind of thin bedspread but the material was so stained it was almost impossible to tell exactly what it was. The feet stuck out from the bottom of the revolting parcel and were bare, bones and sinews visible through grey, oozing flesh. There were flakes of red polish still on the toe nails.

I was absolutely sure about one thing: I did not want to be around when this nightmare was unwrapped.

'You needn't stay,' Carrick turned to me to say as though reading my thoughts. 'I can catch up with you at home later.'

'We're on holiday,' I told him, forced to smile. 'Come round to the hotel.' I gave him the name of it and left, aware of his baffled gaze on me.

House-buying now being on hold I walked back into the city centre, called in to the estate agents to tell them that that particular property was now a crime scene but I would proceed as soon as was possible. I then bought myself a sandwich and a small carton of fruit juice. Sitting in Queen's Square to have my lunch I did a bit of thinking.

I had to admit that my behaviour as far as Patrick was concerned had been a bit over the top. It was perfectly possible that because of recently having Mark my hormones were still all to hell. Did I have a horror of being no longer attractive, more like a milch cow than anything else? Of losing my figure and turning into ''er indoors', a wife who was a fetter for, as that wretched woman had said, 'a good-looking man'?

'Yes,' I muttered. 'That's about the truth of it. I behaved like a cast iron fetter. A jealous and—'

Patrick has never been to a fashion show in his life. This fact sort of clattered into my brain as I sat there, in truth everything in my mind overlaid with those images of putrescent flesh, bared teeth in rotting gums, the stinking remains in the two cupboards. Was it my imagination or had the stench got into my clothes and hair? I tried to repress the memories and concentrate on what had suddenly occurred to me but this somehow seemed wrong as the horror had once been a living human being.

I could not. Suddenly I did not want anything to eat either.

'Boo,' said a well-remembered voice, its owner seating himself at my side.

'How on earth did you know I was here?' I asked.

'I've a thermal-imaging wife-seeking device on my mobile,' Patrick said, jokey but still cool. 'And I thought you were likely to be in a quarter of a mile radius of the estate agents.' He eyed the sandwiches. 'Have you put those in the sun deliberately?'

I just looked at him and he looked at me, the temperature going down a few more degrees.

Then he gave me one of his stock-in-trade penetrating stares. 'Ingrid, what's *wrong*?'

'A body's been found at the house,' I whispered.

'A *person*, you mean?'

'A woman. The head was in a cupboard upstairs and the rest in the scullery. It was ghastly. Do you want the sandwiches? I'm not hungry.'

Virtually shockproof after his service days, he pounced on them but presented me with the carton of juice. 'Don't get dehydrated – you've had a nasty experience. Would you like something stronger? I know of a nice little pub nearby.'

'No, I'm all right, thank you.'

'Is James on the case?'

'Yes. He's going to call round at our hotel later. Where's Alexandra?'

The chilly barrier between us reappeared. 'Gone off with a headache. She asked me to tell the estate agent that she wouldn't look at any more houses today.' A pause. 'She's really mad with you.'

'It's irrelevant – she won't want the place now.'

'Do *you*?'

'James asked me that. I don't know.'

'It seems to me you'll do anything to stop Alex having it.'

'No, it's not like that at all. And frankly, you ought to know me better than that after all this time. I fell in love with it. But you might be partly right – perhaps I don't want it to fall into

42

the hands of someone I know will tear it to pieces.'

I thought he would carry on with that subject of conversation but he tackled the sandwiches instead, staring into space, munching with a slight frown.

I drank the juice, not knowing what to say, and for a while there was silence.

'I'm almost sure I met Alex in a pub in Plymouth,' Patrick said, finally.

'And I'm quite sure you've never been to a fashion show,' I responded, speaking more curtly than I had intended.

'Your very good health,' James Carrick said, raising the tot of single malt that Patrick had just given him. And then, exasperated, 'Out of all the houses for sale in the world you could have looked at you had to choose that one.'

'Just think of it from the point of view that someone else who found it might be in hospital right now having suffered a heart attack brought on by the shock,' I said, again finding myself speaking more sharply than the occasion demanded.

Patrick said. 'Do you have an identity for the body yet?'

Carrick shook his head. 'No. It was naked under the wrappings – no personal effects. I'm bracing myself to attend the PM tomorrow afternoon. First thoughts are that she was bludgeoned to death. But then to...' He broke off.

'It might have been meant for a specific person to find,' I suggested. 'Some kind of horrible revenge.'

'That's a possible explanation. The house belongs to an old lady who's now in a nursing home, away with the birds. Apparently it had been rented to a nephew, who may or may not be her next of kin – we don't yet know. Lynn's been at the home for most of the afternoon trying to get some answers, but without success. But at least we have the address of a firm of solicitors who are acting for the owner from the estate agent so we're working from there.'

'Do you want me to come to the nick and make a statement?' I asked.

'If you could call in for a wee while tomorrow morning...'

'It wouldn't appear that she was killed at the property,' Patrick said. 'Otherwise, surely, we would have noticed bloodstains.'

'Aye,' Carrick said on a gusty sigh. 'But who knows what went on in the garden? It's pretty secluded because of the trees. Scenes-of-crime are going to rig up lights and work through the night on the entire property.'

'There's a blackbird's nest in the white lilac,' I told him.

'I doubt they'll need to actually fell anything,' he pointed out.

'I wouldn't mind having another look round when they've finished,' Patrick said.

'I expect that could be arranged,' James said, albeit guardedly. 'But—'

Patrick spread his hands, palms out. 'Peace, Oh, son of the North. I have no intention of interfering with your case. Just professional

44

interest.' He gave the other a sunny smile.

James did not appear to be reassured.

'But I've never stuck my nose into his investigations – unless invited to,' Patrick said later that night.

'It's just his natural caution,' I said. The atmosphere was still strained. I knew that Alexandra had phoned him earlier but he had not disclosed anything about their conversation.

The story of the body's discovery had been all over the evening papers with a photograph of Carrick, looking stern, making a statement to the media outside the house. Seemingly unaware that the property would be out of bounds to everyone but the police for at least a week someone at the estate agency, obviously with a bad case of jitters, had rung me to ask if I wanted to carry on with the purchase. I had told them I would let them know the next morning.

Did I really want to go ahead?

I could not sleep, seeing those rotting eyes, smelling death and decay that still seemed to linger around me even though I had showered and washed my hair. And that other thing; Patrick saying that he had slept with Alexandra, almost certainly not true after what he had related to me when we got back together again. Even if it was not there was no point in my getting upset about it as we had been divorced at the time.

But I was.

For several restless hours my thoughts went uselessly round and round. When I did at last sleep it was to dream that several Alexandras

45

with empty eye sockets were chasing me around the house waving large knives. They all cornered me in the scullery and the blades were raised, glittering.

'God, you gave me a shock!' Patrick exclaimed in the pale light of early dawn.

I had woken with a start, sweating, wrapped tightly, like the corpse, in the duvet. 'What?' I muttered.

'You screamed.'

'I had a nightmare.'

'And you have all the bedclothes.'

This matter was grimly dealt with and he promptly went back to sleep.

I surveyed him, his body as lean and sinewy as the day I had fallen in love with him on that summer's day on Dartmoor. We had been as children then in those more innocent times, he eighteen, I fifteen, when my parents had not been concerned that their daughter was walking in wild places with the clergyman's son. Why should they have been? Patrick's interests were well known to be singing in the church choir and going fishing in the River Tamar. So that afternoon when we had eaten our picnic and Patrick had made us laugh until we cried – he is still a brilliant mimic – hugging one another in the hot sunshine and I felt the way his body moved under the thin material of his shirt...

Children one moment and as close as human beings can become the next. A crash course in adulthood. I had decided, there and then, that here was the man I wanted, for ever and ever.

And now?

Patrick announced at breakfast that he was fulfilling the rest of his promise to accompany Alexandra on her house-hunting. I could not remember his making any promises but was reluctant to start an argument in the hotel restaurant so told him to carry on. There seemed to be no point in remaining at the hotel so I went back to our room, packed and left, leaving him either to stay for the rest of the time we had booked, another night, or check out. Then I took a taxi to Bath's Manvers Street police station.

At least, that was what I had intended to do. But, for a reason that I was not too sure about until I actually arrived, I changed my mind.

'SOCA,' I said to the constable on guard outside the property now cordoned off with incident tape, showing him my ID card. I had asked the taxi driver to wait and had already spotted Carrick's car.

'The DCI's in the back garden,' he told me, perhaps not daring to enquire what the hell the case had to do with that particular crime fighting agency.

The front and back doors were wide open, which was wonderful, given the lingering smell. I paused in the downstairs doorways but knew better than to enter, a solitary scenes of crime officer, in a white anti-contamination suit, still working in the living room to the right of the front door. Some of the floor boards had been taken up but otherwise it did not seem that forensics had burrowed too deeply into the fabric of the house. My house.

Part of the back garden had been forked or raked over, which I knew was necessary – I told myself it would take care of a lot of the weeds – and the blackbird was having a ball hauling out a large worm from the disturbed earth to feed to its young. It paid no heed to the man standing quietly surveying a medium-sized hole in the ground that I only noticed as I got closer.

'We found her clothes and bag but not anything that might have been used to decapitate the body,' Carrick said after a quick glance in my direction and not appearing to find my presence surprising or out of order.

'The murderer buried them?' I mused aloud. 'I wonder why?'

'God knows when all he had to do was burn them or chuck them in the river. A small bush of some kind had obviously been dug out and then stamped back in any which way – that's where they started digging.'

'Oh, the dead forsythia. I noticed that.' I eyed the sad bundle of twigs with just a few tiny green shoots that had been put on one side. 'That was done *last* year – it's still struggling to grow.'

'Aye, the pathologist thinks she's been dead a good twelve months.'

'So who was she?'

'The bag was plastic, thank God, so hadn't rotted. The driving licence inside is in the name of Imelda Burnside. The address on it is here in Bath, in the London Road but it turns out she wasn't living there then as she'd been evicted for not paying the rent. There was no money but her credit cards were still in the purse. The inter-

48

esting thing is that there's a set of car keys, plus a couple more that fit the doors to this house.'

'She must have been living here then.'

'Looks like it. Lynn's talking to the neighbours and checking up on things like council tax and with the DVLA. If her killer had another set of car keys he might have sold it or used it for his getaway.'

'I was on my way to the nick when I thought I'd come here to ask myself if I still wanted to buy the place.'

'Did you come by taxi?'

I nodded.

'I can give you a lift. I'm going back shortly.'

As I went back through the house to pay off the taxi my phone rang. It was the estate agent, in panic mode. We had a short conversation.

'I've just received an amazing offer if I carry on with the sale,' I said to James when I returned to the garden. 'Although a price of twenty thousand pounds below what had originally been asked was agreed yesterday I've just been told I can have the place for fifty thousand below if I don't now pull out because of what's happened. I'm only human and I've jumped at it as it's a wonderful investment even if I don't ever live here. But, being suspicious, I'm wondering if the owners' solicitors really have their client's interest at heart or someone else has their finger on the pulse and wants to get shot of the place, fast.'

'The nephew,' Carrick murmured. 'That's my priority already, to find and talk to him.'

'Any other leads?'

'Not yet.'

We bought the rectory at Hinton Littlemoor when the diocese planned to put it on the market having rehoused Patrick's parents, John and Elspeth, in a rabbit hutch of a bungalow on a cheap little development where the railway station and goods yard had once been. Neither Patrick nor I had found this at all acceptable. A lot of alterations to what was already quite a large house later they have their own private annex where an old stable and garage used to be and the new rooms above are for our and our family's use. John still has his study, sacrosanct, in the main house and they are welcome to use the living rooms there too if they wish. It is a very nice arrangement – but for the lack of an author's workstation – with everyone respecting others' privacy although I do have to rake the children out of their grandparents' accommodation occasionally when I feel they are practically living there.

Elspeth, still slim and elegant, was in her own kitchen, preparing her and John's lunch.

'Do you remember anyone by the name of Alexandra Nightingale?' I asked.

'You're back early,' she commented, as usual getting right to the heart of any situation. 'Is everything all right?'

'I *think* so. It's just that this woman's popped out of the woodwork and Patrick's helping her look at houses for sale.'

'*Really?*'

'Umm.'

'I take it this would be someone he knew when

he came home badly injured.'

'That's right.'

Elspeth paused in grating cheese. 'What does she look like?'

'Around five feet six inches tall, blonde hair – although it might not be natural – bright blue eyes.'

'Really piercing blue eyes?'

'Yes.'

'Well, I can remember a girl like that but I think she had dark hair. Let me think a minute ... That's right. He brought her here one weekend. I didn't like her at all, mainly because she was rude and patronizing. She put John's back up straight away by saying that only people like country yokels still went to church. And now she's turned up, you say?'

'Moving some kind of agency down here from London and buying a house. Apparently she used to be a model.'

'I'd be surprised if she was, unless I'm thinking of a different girl. She didn't have the deportment of any kind of model.'

'Patrick thinks he met her in a pub in Plymouth.'

'That sounds more like it.' Elspeth went back to grating. 'What do you think of her?'

'Not much. She's all over him.'

'And flattering him silly, I suppose.'

'Yes, but – Elspeth, please don't say anything to him.'

After taking a glance at an opened recipe book she shot me a look over her reading glasses. 'No, of course not. Not unless he mentions it to me.'

'And you mustn't think it's anything to do with it but I'm buying a small house.'

She did not turn a hair. 'You don't have anywhere quiet to work now, do you?'

'No.'

'Someone found a head and some poor woman's body in a house in Bath yesterday.'

'That's the one.'

A little later James Carrick rang. 'Beaten around the head with some kind of blunt instrument and knocked about generally,' he reported tersely. 'We've checked the neighbours at the address on the driving licence but no one can remember a woman by the name of Imelda Burnside. It's hardly surprising with such a fluid population. The nephew's address is in this area, at Claverton. He's abroad, New Zealand according to his neighbours, but due back at any time. He'll find me, camping on his doorstep.'

I thanked James, who had no requirement to update me like this, and went into the hall just as Patrick came through the front door.

'Any luck?' I asked when, as usual, he dumped everything he was carrying either on to the hall table or the floor.

'No, Alex didn't like any of them. She still wants the one you've set your heart on and is going to put in a higher offer.'

'What, even though a corpse was found there?'

'She doesn't seem to care about that.' Patrick gave me a humourless smile and went in the direction of the stairs, saying over his shoulder, 'May the best woman win.'

# FOUR

Michael Greenway rang Patrick at seven thirty the next morning and I took the call as he was in the shower.

'That find of a body in Bath yesterday...' he began.

'No names were mentioned in the papers but it was me who found it,' I interrupted.

'Why didn't I guess that? Well, we've done our usual trawl through records and it would appear that a woman by the name of Irma, not Imelda, Burnside was known to have lived in Bath for a short while. She is, or was, the girl-friend of a man I'll describe as a crime lord who right now is behind bars. You may know how they're getting messages to their cronies by using code words on Internet chat lines and by utilizing PlayStations. The Prison Service insists that inmates are not permitted to have consoles with Internet access but, believe me, it's hap-pening. Now whether this is the same woman or not I don't know but it's a coincidence and in my experience coincidences sometimes have a habit of delivering the goods.'

'Did this Irma have a criminal record?'

'Yes, for handling stolen property and drugs dealing. I was wondering if Patrick wanted a quiet little number when he returns to work next week and without him having to come to London by tracking down any dental records or other stuff on this woman that might be knocking around down there so we can compare them with those of the remains. I'm very keen to keep tabs on sonny boy in the slammer – who is a sort of refugee from the Italian Mafia as someone out there wants to put a bullet between his eyes – as I think he, and others, are planning something big.'

'What's his name?'

'Martino Capelli.'

'We've come across a Capelli before – when we were with D12. Tony Capelli. It'll be somewhere in the records that Patrick gave you but was sort of unofficial because it was James Carrick who stumbled across a case when he was on holiday in Scotland involving Kimberley Devlin, the opera singer, and Patrick gave him a hand. But Capelli has to be a common Italian name.'

Not all the records had been handed over; only those involving ordinary criminals. The sensitive MI5 information, some of it State secrets, is either locked up in a government strongroom or inside Patrick's head.

'Do you know any more about him?'

'Only that he was the bona fide agent for several top opera singers and in his spare time endeavoured to import crooks into the UK for profit. Someone cut his throat when he forgot about a family feud and returned to Italy.'

'Thanks, I'll look into it and see if there's any

connection.'

'And we're back at home, by the way.'

'Oh, perhaps you'll get Patrick to give me a ring.'

Fortunately, Greenway and James Carrick had met and were on good terms so the former was keen that we did not tread on the latter's toes. In fact it was impressed on Patrick that he should share any gleaned information about the murder victim with Bath CID.

'I don't have a problem with that,' Patrick said after the two had spoken. 'I'm a cop now, not a spook.'

I had never heard him describe himself thus and smiled. Then I said, 'But James might.'

'I'll tell him I'll treat him to haggis and bashed neeps next Burn's Night.'

'So what would have been on your agenda today if you weren't starting this job?' I hazarded. 'More house-hunting with Alexandra?'

'No, she's really fixed her mind on the place with the corpse.'

'She'll rip it apart, do it up and then sell it.'

'Yes, I think that's the general idea.'

'But—'

'Look, I don't want to talk about it any more. All right?'

'No, it's not all right! Just because she was once your girlfriend it doesn't mean I have to treat her like some kind of Holy Grail. She's only going ahead because I've set my heart on it. The woman's a grade one bitch!'

I found myself looking at empty space and

when I got downstairs I discovered that Patrick had gone off without having any breakfast.

Later, when the bedlam of getting children ready for school had abated and little ones had been fed and were asleep or otherwise engaged, I sat down at what I still thought of as Elspeth's kitchen table, an historic chunk of oak farmhouse furniture that was far too large to go in their new living quarters, and poured myself a cup of strong coffee. This was worrying. What was the man *on*? Had Alexandra put something in *his* coffee?

With foreboding, I rang the specialist at the clinic at which Patrick had first been treated when he had been heavily drugged during our previous assignment. I got a very sympathetic ear. Indeed, I was told, what had occurred could temporarily affect judgement and could last for as long as a few months. I pointed out that so far Patrick had shown no sign that anything was wrong but it seemed to have been triggered off by the appearance of a woman from his past. It was then gently pointed out to me that it was quite normal for men to have yearnings for their youth when they were in their mid to late forties, and even older, and I should not read anything sinister into it. He finished by saying that if things took a turn for the worse I was to ring him again immediately.

'Perhaps he took my wanting my own house as some kind of rejection,' I said to the four walls of the kitchen after the call.

There was something in me that prevented me from ringing the agents and calling the whole thing off. An independent streak? Bloody-mindedness? But if Alexandra had put in a higher offer and the vendors had come to their senses I might have already lost it anyway.

I was still sitting there, agonizing, when my phone rang.

'I'm at the nick,' Patrick's voice said. 'D'you want to join us?'

'You have the car but I think there's a bus in a couple of hours' time,' I replied, not about to be anybody's right now.

'I'm sure Mother'll lend you hers.'

'I happen to know that she needs it to go shopping, your father's off to a meeting of some kind and Carrie'll be using hers to take Vicki, plus Mark of course, to Toddlers' Club in Wellow.'

'Then call a taxi and charge it to expenses.'

'I'm not optimistic – all the local ones are on school runs at this time of the morning.'

I distinctly heard Carrick say something in the background.

'OK, James is sending a car for you,' Patrick reported briskly. 'See you later.'

Why did I get the distinct impression that it had been James's idea I should join the team?

'We have no idea if it's the same woman but I'd like you to take a look at this,' the DCI said, pushing a photograph across his desk in my direction. And then to Patrick, 'I'll be delighted if you'll dig around the district for dental records and so forth. It'll save us work and it's imperative we discover who this woman really was. If

57

you get the dental records we'll know straight away.'

I gazed at the picture. It was a mugshot of Irma Burnside provided by the Criminal Records Bureau. She had brown eyes and dark wavy hair just short of shoulder-length, the jaw square and determined-looking. The accompanying notes indicated that now she would be thirty-eight years of age, was five feet four inches in height and of medium build. There were no birthmarks or scars.

Was this the woman whose head I had found in the cupboard? The hair was similar but I had felt no frisson of horror upon first seeing this photograph.

'So far, there's no trace of her around here now,' Carrick said to me.

'Where did she come from originally?' I asked. 'Was Bath a bolt-hole?'

'Bath is often a bolt-hole,' he answered with a rueful grin. 'Yes, lover-boy Capelli was based in Romford, Essex and that's where she'd been in trouble with the law. She served eight months for supplying drugs having been given a suspended sentence two years earlier for handling stolen property.'

'She might have gone back there.'

'You don't think she's the dead woman then?'

'I'm not sure. Commander Greenway has an idea that Martino Capelli is planning something from inside prison. She could be involved, acting for him on the outside.'

'He's Tony Capelli's cousin,' Patrick said. 'Mike rang me a few minutes ago.'

58

I did not comment on that particular gangster further. As well as Carrick, Joanna, his one-time sergeant, had been involved at a time before they were married and Joanna had been shot and seriously wounded by Capelli's henchman, Luigi. Patrick, acquiring a sniper's rifle, had ensured that he had not fired again. I had not been present.

'You can use my office,' Carrick said, rising to his feet. 'I have to go out.'

'Strange though to change your name from Irma to Imelda,' I murmured to myself, still looking at the mugshot. 'They could be sisters.'

'Or sisters-in-law if one married the other's brother,' Patrick said. He had already found a phone book. 'Dentists, loads of 'em.'

'I'm going to take another look at the crime scene,' James said to me. 'D'you want to see if your famous intuition comes up with anything?'

Alexandra Nightingale was arguing with the constable on duty outside the house, her hired car and a police van parked nearby.

'What's going on?' Carrick asked.

'This lady—' the man began.

Alexandra butted in with, 'This will shortly be my house and I demand to be allowed inside.'

'The property is a crime scene, madam,' Carrick told her, having introduced himself. 'I can't believe that you're not aware of that.'

She caught sight of me. 'You! Sticking your nose in again?'

It occurred to me that she had been drinking. I said nothing and neither did Carrick, just regarded her steadily until she got the message and departed, violently slamming the door of her car and then, with a blare on her horn, swerving to miss a cyclist, just, whom she had not previously noticed.

'She's over the limit,' I said helpfully.

'I think you're right,' James said and found his mobile. 'That's *her*?' he enquired, having given Traffic the car's registration number.

'Too right.'

All was quiet within the house. Motes of dust were floating, moving serenely with the air currents in thin beams of sunlight that were finding their way between the leaves of the plants growing across the living rooms' windows. The big spider in the grate came out to investigate our vibrations and then shot back in again as I walked closer to the fireplace. I resolved that it, or more likely she, would not die when the place was renovated. It deserved to live.

But then I had to remind myself that it wasn't my house. Alexandra would get it.

'Was any evidence found in the garden other than the stuff that had been buried?' I called across to Carrick, who had gone into the other front room.

'No.'

'Not even anything that might suggest she was killed out there?'

'Nothing. But don't forget, quite a lot of time's gone by since the crime was committed.'

'Has any soil been taken away for testing?'

'I understand a few samples were taken. But where do you start?'

'There's a patch of herbs growing almost obscenely well close to the back door where it hasn't been dug over.'

Across the hallway, our eyes met.

'Really?'

'Haven't you heard the old but true story about the mortuary that had huge and wonderful tomatoes for sale?'

'No,' he replied. 'Are you saying what I think you're saying?'

'Yes, blood. Blood and bone fertilizer. One of the best.'

Without another word he went out to his car, found an evidence bag and gloves and went into the garden, reappearing almost immediately. 'You'll have to show me.'

Ye gods, didn't the man know what rampant golden marjoram, mint and thyme looked like?

To prevent any contamination from tools Carrick dug down with his gloved hands, having hauled out some long grass, while I held the bag open. The earth was dark and rich-looking here.

'This could have been where the head was severed,' he said, eyeing our surroundings when the sample was safely in the bag. 'None of the neighbours could have seen a thing with all the trees.'

'So she was knocked around with what?'

'The pathologist reckons it was something like a pickaxe handle. There are several broken bones in the hands and arms.'

'She tried to ward off the blows. How ghastly.'

'Murder's always revolting.'

'But surely she would have screamed.'

61

'Aye. But if folk have their TVs turned up loud...'

'Which is all about people screaming and car chases and explosions...'

'Life's a bastard sometimes.'

I left him outside and went back into the house, paused in the kitchen, where the sink was still disgusting, looked into the scullery, where the stench still persisted – perhaps from my point of view it would have been a good idea to let Alexandra have another look round after all – and then slowly mounted the stairs. During the past few years I have been in several houses where murders had taken place and there is invariably a nasty resonance. People pooh-pooh this but to me it is real. This little house had no unsavoury echoes, if it had I would not want to buy it. The garden could take care of itself: nature is a great healer.

'I don't think she was killed indoors,' I said out loud, wandering into the other bedroom.

'No?' James said, obviously not too far away.

'I have no evidence of course, just ... intuition.' I went to the head of the stairs and he was standing at the bottom. 'Thank you for involving me.'

'I value your thoughts.'

'Would you check that woman's name in records for me?'

His eyes widened. 'You reckon she's dodgy?'

'Just ... intuition.'

'I think we're good enough friends for me to ask if you're sure that's all it is.'

'I'm sure,' I said with a smile.

62

'As a consultant for SOCA you must have all the CRB computer codes.'

'Patrick has. I'm not good with figures and have enough bother remembering my pin numbers. And ... I don't want Patrick to know I'm checking up on her.'

There was a little silence during which Carrick regarded me with steady gaze. 'You say he met her when the pair of you were divorced and he'd just come home with his legs pretty badly smashed up.'

'That's right.'

'It would be quite something for him then, to have a woman fancy him when he was on crutches.'

As a student of human nature I should have seen that it would have to be a special relationship, an important 'something' that even now drew him to her. The woman had found him attractive despite the fact that he had been barely mobile and, having once regarded himself, as do so many young men, as invincible, had been left a little bit crazy by the sheer unfairness of having been rendered permanently crippled, or so he had thought at the time, following an accident with a hand grenade. There was no glory, no honourable wounds, no tales of heroism, no medals, even though he had not been the one who had thrown it. His wife had chucked him out, smashing his classical guitar in the process – has since buying him another, I wondered, a much better one, mended that hurt? – because she found him insufferably superior, a perfectionist who tried to show her how to cook a soufflé that did not sink and that, for her, as well as the business of children, had been the last straw. His wife had not been there for him when he had returned, had not bothered to keep in touch with his parents, with whom she had previously got on well, had not troubled herself to ask how their eldest son had faired on the battlefield.

I had remarried instead, a policeman colleague of Patrick's, Peter Clyde. A little under twelve months later I was a widow as well as divorced, Peter having been killed in a shoot-out in Plymouth. Realizing he was being followed by criminal suspects he had gone to where he knew Patrick had a flat in the Barbican. Still on crutches and too slow because of it, Patrick – newly issued with a firearm by MI5 – had shot the armed intruders who had burst in on them but Peter had been killed in the crossfire. He had actually used his body as a shield to save his friend's life. Ever the romantic, he had made Patrick promise to look after me before he died.

And now I wanted to buy the house this one-time woman in Patrick's life had set her heart on, for whatever reason, and was checking up – out of spite? – to see whether she had a criminal record. Who was the grade one bitch now?

This, mostly unwelcome, retrospection had continued while Carrick was driving us both back to the nick. He had planned to take a longer look at the garden, and the small one at the front, but had received a call that he was needed as the local crime prevention officer wanted to talk to him.

Patrick was in the canteen, finishing off a very late breakfast. I fetched myself coffee and a bun and pulled out a chair at his table.

'I've tracked down Imelda Burnside but not Irma,' he said, mopping up the last of the egg yolk with a piece of fried bread.

'So you have her records?'

'The dentist is putting them on disc for me – it's all digitalized these days – and I'm collecting them in about half an hour.'

'Is this an NHS dentist?'

'He takes national health and private patients.'

'Find out. It'll tell us a bit about her financial situation.'

'That's a good point.' He glanced at me. 'Find anything interesting?'

'Not really. We took some samples of earth where the body might have been decapitated. I don't think she was killed in the house.'

'Your cat's whiskers?'

I nodded. 'And...'

'And?' he queried when I paused.

'I'm going to pull out of the sale.'

'I can understand that. The place does have an unpleasant history now.'

'It's not that. It's causing ... difficulties between us. I don't want that. I've behaved badly over it really.'

Perhaps my unsettled hormones cut in then again or it was the fact that it then came home to me that I still had no writing room, and perhaps never would, and the tears took me completely by surprise. I sobbed into my paper napkin, just managing to get out, 'When I think about it, I've always behaved badly towards you.'

Patrick replaced the soggy paper relic with his handkerchief and then delved into my bag to answer my mobile, which had just started ringing. Whoever it was rang off as soon as he spoke.

'Look, we can't talk about it now,' he said quietly in my ear. 'I must collect the records and then tackle doctors' surgeries and see if I can find out more about this woman.'

'OK,' I gulped. 'Is there anything you'd like me to do?'

'No, not really.'

I did not ring the estate agency, there seemed little point. Alexandra's higher offer would be accepted: it was her house now. Fine, I thought, I have no writing room: I would just have to get on with it in the dining room. Either that or give up writing altogether. Telling myself sternly that most authors would exchange their back teeth for a beautiful old room like this to work in, with the French doors giving a view into Elspeth's garden – it was her creation and I could never lay claim to it while she lived – I sat behind the antique desk that we had brought from Devon and switched on my computer. Yes, this was the situation I would have to get used to, to expect anything else was shirking my family responsibilities.

I dealt with a few emails, one from the fiction editor of my publisher asking how the latest novel was progressing. I told her absolutely fine but without going into details. I had a contract for this one and the deadline was the end of September: I had hardly started it. OK, dig it out and remind myself what I had written.

The doorbell rang and it was a man who had come to repair Elspeth's brand new cooker.

'The Reverend and Mrs Gillard live in the annex,' I told him. 'That's what the address says and there's a notice on the wall outside which clearly indicates you have to go round to the back of the house to reach it.'

'Can't I come through this way?' he enquired, all ready to do just that, huge tool box and all.

'Sorry, no.' I shut the door in his face.

Right, the story so far...

I read it through, made a few small changes, added a little more but still had no real idea how it would progress, or for that matter, end.

There was a tap at the door and Elspeth opened it sufficiently to put her head round.

'Elspeth, you don't have to knock!' I exclaimed.

'Yes – or rather no – but I'm sure you're working. It's just that I'm making sandwiches for a rather late lunch as the cooker repairman's only just gone, John's come in and I wondered if you'd like some.'

I glanced at the clock: an hour and a half had gone by.

I ended up by having lunch with them as it had seemed positively churlish to take mine away and eat it on my own. Carrie then found me to say that the school had rung with the news that Katie was not very well and could someone go and fetch her? Vicky would enjoy the ride but would I mind watching over Mark for a while as he had only just gone to sleep and it seemed a shame to disturb him? I could hardly refuse to look after my own son.

Mark decided to wake up and grizzle as soon as she had gone out so I took him downstairs and carried him around the garden; for some reason he loves looking at trees and leaves moving in the breeze. My mobile rang and I sat down in a little arbour to answer it.

Whoever it was hung up as soon as I spoke.

'That's the second time it's happened today,' I told Mark. I gazed down at him and he looked up at me. 'So you're going to be a garden designer one day? A landscape painter? Or just a man who cuts people's grass?'

I could not get the little house in Bath out of my mind. Despite all the horror surrounding it, it just cried out to be restored. I had worked out colour schemes and renovation ideas for the interior as well as plans for both the front and back gardens.

My mobile rang again.

'The dental records are a positive match,' James Carrick said. 'Imelda Burnside. The dentist told us that she's been his patient, on the NHS, for around two years. He thinks she worked as a carer for the elderly. The checking goes on, of course – Patrick's doing that – but it doesn't appear, unless it is the same woman and she lived a double life, that this is anything to do with serious criminals. Only the bastard who killed her, of course.'

I had only just put the phone back in my

pocket when it rang yet again.

'Whatever Alex takes a fancy to, she gets,' a man's voice rasped. 'Remember that.' The line went dead.

# FIVE

It appeared that while the house was still a crime scene all matters concerning its sale were definitely frozen. I confirmed this when I rang the agents to impress on them that I was still interested in purchasing it. Polite persistence on my part elicited the information that a higher offer had been received but, as before, matters were on hold. I was desperate to know whether it was the owner's solicitor who had panicked when the price had been dropped so drastically in an effort to get a sale or whether they had been acting on the instructions of someone else – the nephew who might be due to inherit? – as surely the owner, the old lady, was incapable.

Carrie returned, we established that Katie had a slight temperature and some of the other children were away from school with bad colds so she was popped into bed and instantly went to sleep. TLC and something tempting to eat would be administered later. The youngest, also fast asleep by now, was laid in his pram in the garden. Their mother, actually feeling light-hearted, happy even, that she had established a link between Alexandra and someone who was nasty enough to make veiled threats, went back to work.

I sobered up, fast. This woman knew where I, we, lived. Did one confront her with what had happened? No, she would deny any involvement and accuse me of making yet more trouble. She would insist that she did not know my mobile number. How had she got hold of it? Had Patrick given it to her for some reason? At least that could quickly be established.

There was one completely unbiased element in all this: James Carrick.

'You'll have to get Patrick on board,' was his advice. 'I haven't had time to do any checking on her – as usual I'm up to my ears in work. Sorry to be a bit blunt but you are folk also with the means of finding out such things. But I promise I'll get back to you, Ingrid, when things aren't so manic here and help if I can. And please be careful.'

I then called Michael Greenway only to be told by his deputy, Andrew Bayley, that he had taken a two days' well-earned leave. He went on to ask if he himself could help. I decided not to involve him: he worked mostly in the main office and I did not want to risk my worries being aired to all and sundry. Men gossip.

Patrick rang.

'I might be a bit late. I'm going to give James a hand for a while longer but with something that isn't really anything to do with the case as he's snowed under. And Alex has had some photos she took when we first met emailed from

70

London by a friend. As they include some of the rectory and Mum and Dad I thought I'd take a look at them with a view to having them ourselves.'

'That's fine. You and I can eat later,' I said.

'No, it's all right. You have yours with the family. I'll have a pie and a pint, or something.'

I was stung to say, 'But surely she could email them to *you*.'

'She says she doesn't know how to. See you later.'

I did not throw my mobile across the room after this conversation, it doesn't like it.

'But she runs an agency of some kind,' I heard myself say out loud. 'A *business*. How can she not know...?'

'The house owner's nephew's name is David Bennett,' Patrick said, coming into the kitchen where I was having an early breakfast. 'He was due back from New Zealand last week but for some reason hasn't shown up.'

'How did you find that out?' I enquired.

'I leaned on the solicitors handling the sale. The SOCA ID card seemed to do the trick.'

He had arrived home at a little after ten the previous night, apparently looking very tired – I was writing, or trying to, and had not seen him come in – had not had his usual chat with his father, and then gone to bed. By the time I had gone up he had been fast asleep.

'Did you find out anything else about him?' I asked. 'D'you want toast?'

'Please. Yes, he has dual British and New

71

Zealand nationality and goes out there quite a lot where it would appear he has business interests.'

I fixed the toast.

Buttering busily Patrick then went on to say, 'While it's still iffy whether Irma and Imelda Burnside are the same person or not I think I'll go up to London later this morning and work from HQ. Carrick's happy for me to meet this man at the airport and interview him there if I can find out when he plans to return to the UK. It will be easier to do that checking from London too.'

'Better intelligence?'

'Of course. Provincial forces simply don't have the resources SOCA does.'

'You won't be able to arrest him though.'

'No, unless he refuses to answer questions.'

I sat down at the kitchen table opposite to him and regarded him steadily. Then I said, 'What were the photos like?'

He looked a bit blank for a few seconds. 'Oh, those. They're not very good. She takes lousy pictures, chopping off people's feet and heads. I don't think I'll bother with them.'

'It was all a bit of a con then.'

He loaded on marmalade. 'No, not really. There were a couple of good ones of the village street.'

I carried on gazing at him. It was a bit like having a remote control with flat batteries and the TV channel would not change.

He glanced up, mid-spread and our eyes locked.

I said, 'You know, up until now I really thought

72

you weren't like other men. Silly of me.'

'What d'you mean?'

'I'd thought you were of above average intelligence too.'

He dropped his gaze and shrugged.

'Where are you, Patrick?' I asked softly.

He said nothing.

'She's reduced you to this,' I said. 'She's taken my husband, the man I love more than anyone in the world and brought him down to this level; ordinary, sheepish, just any old bloke in the street. It's a disease. It's a kind of character POX!'

I had bellowed the last word and he actually jumped.

I went on, 'I don't know whether we were talking about houses, or husbands, but you're really the only one I can tell that I had a heavy breathing kind of phone call from a man who told me that whatever Alex takes a fancy to, she gets. I was encouraged to remember that. Any thoughts on the matter?'

'When was this?'

'Yesterday afternoon, around three.'

Patrick put down his knife. 'You should have rung me immediately.'

'I think I got a bit bloody-minded at that moment and there was rather a lot of domestic things going on as well as Katie coming home from school not very well.'

'What's wrong with her?'

'She's only hatching a cold.'

After a pause Patrick said, 'We shall have to look into that call you had.'

73

'Well, Alexandra's obviously taken a fancy to the house. I get the impression she's set her heart on you as well.'

'Oh God,' he muttered. There was another little silence and then he added, 'Confession time. I got a bit sloshed last night.'

'But you're not supposed to drink yet! Not after you were ill. She knows it too.' So that was why he had not said goodnight to me.

'She had some Islay twenty-year-old single malt that's reckoned to be one of the crown jewels of whisky. They only make around two dozen cases a year.'

I said nothing.

'I did tell her, again, that I'd been banned from drinking for a few months but she said a little nip couldn't possibly hurt,' he went on, addressing the opposite wall. 'Even talking about it makes me feel like some pathetic git on a reality TV show.' He gave me a – yes, sheepish – glance. 'I think the idea was to get me into bed.'

'And do I take from the wording of that that she failed?'

'Of course!'

'You said you'd slept with her before,' I said stonily, really needing to know.

'Sorry, that wasn't true.'

'I'm sorry too.'

He looked surprised. 'For what?'

'That we're having this kind of conversation.'

People speak of 'death wish moments' and this was how I felt now. I was the woman with good advice who was usually proved correct, 'er indoors, the mother of his children, the one who

74

represented his responsibilities. Whatever the truth, the magic in our relationship suddenly wasn't there any more.

'Look, I'm in a real quandary here,' Patrick said, finding me a little later in the dining room again failing to concentrate on writing. 'As I said earlier, I think I ought to work on the case from London. But now this has come up. I got clearance from Mike to get the call to your mobile traced and established that it came from another that had been reported stolen from a fourteen-year-old schoolgirl in Hounslow. The poor kid was mugged by a man in broad daylight close to her home as she walked to meet friends. This phone, according to the wizards at GCHQ, is now dead, presumed destroyed. The fact that Alex's name was mentioned rather puts her in the frame. When you chatted with her just after we met at the spa did she say anything about anyone else in her life?'

'She said that as of the previous week she had been on her own,' I recollected. 'In her own words, "the rat went and found himself someone else."'

'Umm.'

'Is there a description of this mugger?'

'A hoodie, that's all. She didn't really get a good look at him as he pushed her over before running off.'

'Did you give Alexandra my mobile number?'

'No, why on earth should I do that?'

'Well, she must have given it to someone else.'

'Not necessarily. It's perfectly possible this

75

originates from someone *you* know.'

'But I haven't discussed any of this business with anyone else. Only your mother.'

'And James?'

'Yes, and James. But he has no axe to grind.'

'No, obviously, it couldn't be him but someone might have overheard the conversation.'

'But who the hell else in this neck of the woods would care a toss about Alexandra Nightingale?'

After an edgy pause Patrick said, 'The quandary's to do with the fact that I shall have to ask her about this. And about this man.'

'Yes, you will.'

'And you must understand that I shall have to carry on being friendly, otherwise I won't get anywhere.'

'You don't usually bother with cosying up to suspects,' I declared. 'I've actually been present when you've mentally, and sometimes physically, taken them apart!'

'Look, I know you're annoyed about this but—'

'No, I'm not annoyed, I'm absolutely furious and also scared. For myself, your parents and for the children.'

'You said you were going to pull out of buying the house. Have you?'

'No, not yet. I'm undecided.'

'Then perhaps you should think of your own priorities.'

I stared disbelievingly at him. 'Are you saying that I ought to call off the sale *because* of the phone call?'

'It might be the sensible thing to do.'

'And you? Shall I give her a ring and say she can have you as well?'

He made no comment and left the room.

He was right up to a point; I had to get my priorities right. I shut down the computer having made a few notes of ideas for the plot that had, oddly, just come into my head, mechanically tidied the desk and then went into the entrance hall in time to see the front door close. A quick peep through a window told me that Patrick was just getting into the Range Rover. Unless he had loaded it earlier he did not appear to have any luggage with him. This suggested he was going to talk to Alexandra, if indeed she was still at her hotel, before returning the vehicle and calling a taxi to take him to the station. Good, not that he usually drove to London.

It was a surprise then when he came into the kitchen a minute or so later.

'I've just had a call from Carrick. David Bennett's due to arrive on a flight from Johannesburg at thirteen hundred hours today. I'll have to talk to Alexandra another time and catch a train.'

'I'll drive you to the station,' I offered.

'Oh, all right.'

Patrick seemed a little surprised when I parked the car on double yellow lines, went right into the station with him and, very shortly, waved him into a first-class carriage. When I got back a traffic warden was just about to write out a parking ticket.

'Serious Organized Crime Agency,' I said,

waving my warrant card beneath his nose. 'Sorry, but it's a top priority case.'

For some reason this worked and I felt even guiltier when he practically bowed me into the car.

Alexandra was staying at the Albany hotel which was in the city centre, not far from the Orange Grove.

'I have an appointment with Miss Nightingale at eleven thirty,' I told one of the young women on the reception desk. 'But I'm dreadfully early. Is it all right if I wait here for her and perhaps order coffee?'

'Yes, of course, madam. I happen to know she's out at the moment. I don't usually remember guests but she has such brilliant blue eyes her name stuck in my mind.'

'She didn't say where she was going, I suppose?' I risked asking. 'Only I've come quite a long way and if she's forgotten...' I assumed a rueful expression.

'No, I'm sorry, she didn't.'

'Excuse me, but are you talking about the lady in Room 354 who went out a little while ago?' said another receptionist.

The girl to whom I was talking said we were.

'I don't think she'll be all that long. She asked me the way to the nearest hairdresser's. Apparently the hairdryer in her room isn't very good so I said I'd attend to it for her.'

From her expression I knew that Alexandra had given her a tongue-lashing about it.

'So would that be the *Fine Cuts* place I noticed?' I asked, the name the first I could

78

remember.

'No, I sent her along to *Lovelocks*. It's a bit more classy and on the right hand side of Milsom Street about halfway up.'

I already knew where *Lovelocks* was, an establishment that positively dripped designer chic. This author has her hair cut in a tiny salon in the village by a Milan-trained and somewhat world-weary gentleman who can nevertheless make you look and feel as though you're heading off to Cannes Film Festival.

It seemed unlikely that even Alexandra would be able to bully her way into such sacred groves without an appointment, but one never knew. I decided to wait for her return, whenever that would be, having no intention of starting a war among potentially dangerous chemicals in case she started throwing them at me.

I had my coffee, pretending to read a newspaper, in a small lounge to one side of the reception area where I had a very good view of all comings and goings. It was fairly quiet. Three-quarters of an hour went by and soon it was almost eleven thirty. Then I saw her, outside, talking to a man. She appeared to have had her hair done somewhere or the other. They parted and she entered the hotel; long strides, body rigid, head held high, eyes flashing, as mad as hell.

By this time I had positioned myself by the reception desk, reckoning that she might not start yelling straight away in front of others.

'Sorry to further ruin your morning,' I said, turning to face her as she approached.

'You!' she hissed.

'That seems to be your usual greeting,' I said, going on to say before she could interrupt, 'Patrick was going to interview you but had to catch a train to London instead. He probably sends his love but I don't yet know that for sure. I suggest we talk down here.'

'I have no intention of talking to you.'

'There's no choice as I work for SOCA too. This is official. So is it here or down at the nick?'

The woman noticed that the receptionists were trying not to look as though they were all ears, gave them a thousand-watt glare and then said to me, 'Five minutes, no longer.'

I led the way to where I had been sitting, making sure that she followed.

'Well?' Alexandra snapped when she had perched herself right on the edge of a chair.

'Who was that man you were talking to outside just now?'

'It's none of your bloody business!'

'Was it the same one who mugged a schoolgirl in Hounslow the day before yesterday, stole her mobile phone and used it to make a threatening call to me?'

'No!'

'Perhaps you'd like to think about it for a moment.'

'I don't know what you're talking about.'

'He told me you always got what you fancied, a fact that I was to remember. He didn't add "or else" but his tone did.'

'I still don't know what you're talking about.'

'Making threatening phone calls is a criminal offence.'

'So?'

'It's obvious that this man is someone you *know*.'

'Well ... perhaps I did sound off to someone about being at risk of losing the house.' Then, with a toss of her head, she added, 'I've hundreds of friends – I talk to them all the time.'

'Did you mention it to the man I saw you talking to outside?'

'No, Stefan's—'

'*What*?' I demanded to know when she stopped speaking, no doubt mentally kicking herself for letting the name slip out.

'Nothing.'

'Look, I do have the power to arrest you.'

'He works for me, that's all – an employee,' she said, none too convincingly. 'He's looking for a business premises for me in this area.'

'What is your business?'

'I've told you already. I run an agency.'

'Yes, but what kind of agency?'

'For domestic staff, nannies, home helps, that sort of thing.' She started to rise. 'I'm going now.'

'Sit down.'

Slowly, she did so.

'How many of your friends are ex-cons?' I enquired.

The woman actually went a little pale. 'Why, none of them, of course!'

'A first offender then, this man who mugged the child. Someone who was described as a hoodie.'

'All this has nothing to do with *me*!'

'Could it be that it's the boyfriend who chucked you over who's trying to get you into trouble?'

Visibly, she thought through the implications of cooperating over this. Then, 'I don't know,' she answered slowly.

'You've spoken to him then.'

'Yes, I had to. I discovered I'd got some of his stuff. I told him I'd bin it all if he didn't collect it.'

'And you shared a few worries at the same time?'

She shrugged. 'Well, you do, don't you?'

'Did you give him my mobile phone number?'

'No.'

'I think you're lying. What's this man's name and address?'

'His name's Alan Kilmartin. He's an architect.' She gave me the address, all the information now coming with an alacrity that made me think that she wanted revenge and also that he probably wasn't the man who had made the call.

'But you did get hold of my mobile number. How?' I asked, trying to keep calmly professional and knowing I was failing, fast.

The lip-glossed mouth formed a little pout. 'OK, I admit I had a little look at Patrick's mobile when he was in the john at a café where we went for coffee. He'd left it on the table.' She smiled in knowing fashion, gazing down at her perfectly manicured fingernails.

'I see,' I said. 'And last night you persuaded

him into drinking alcohol even after he'd told you he was banned.'

'Banned? What's banned?' she muttered. 'Who banned him? You?'

'No, his medical specialist did. He was doped by thugs during his previous case and suffered slight liver damage.'

'Well, I don't suppose a few drinks did him any harm.'

'You don't actually care, do you? You see something and you want it, mostly because someone else already loves it, whether it's a house or a person. You have to have it and then, like the house, make money on it by ripping it apart and getting rid of it. But the real satisfaction is taking it away from someone else.'

Alexandra shot to her feet and I did likewise.

'He's a fine man too,' she said, almost spitting out the words as though they disgusted her. 'I like fine men. They turn out to be quite ordinary in the end when you've stripped them off, layer by layer. For some reason it's something I'm really good at. But don't worry, you'll get him back – eventually.'

And with that she stalked away.

I stood and cursed myself for allowing my feelings to get the better of me.

# SIX

If the address Alexandra had given me was correct Alan Warburton Kilmartin, Dip.Arch. RIBA, lived in Warminster. I wondered, after what she had said, if he really had thrown her over for someone else or merely run like blazes when he realized what she was doing to him. On the other hand, they might have had a fairly normal relationship and he had become fed up with her hobby of hoovering up other, desirable, men mostly on the grounds that they were married, engaged, devoted to, or going out with, someone else.

I could not, of course, investigate further, officially that is, without getting permission. I probably would not get it, no crime having been committed and all that. To carry on privately sleuthing would also involve going behind Patrick's back and that was not right either. All that apart, my cat's whiskers told me that Mr Kilmartin did not come from the kind of background to make such a call – and was hardly a hoodie – and the voice, unless whoever it was had disguised it, had sounded distinctly rough. There was a part of me that wanted to do as Patrick had suggested, let the whole thing drop, the house, that is. Perhaps I should just trust him.

I do trust him, I love him to bits, but I still wanted Alexandra's flesh boiled off her bones and fed to hyenas.

'Bugger everything,' I muttered.

My phone rang and it was James Carrick.

'I thought you'd like to know that the soil sample we took in the back garden is heavily contaminated with human blood,' he informed me. 'It's the same blood group as the murder victim's but, as you know, DNA testing takes a bit longer so we don't yet have a positive match.'

'It has to be almost a foregone conclusion surely,' I commented.

'Looks like it. Are you busy with anything in particular?'

'No, not really.' Only in trying to write a book.

'Are you interested in talking to the owner of the house, Miss Hilda Bennett?'

'If you think it'll do any good.'

'She's suffering from dementia so it'll be hard work. But I know you're good with people.'

'Lynn didn't manage to communicate with her?'

'It didn't go at all well. And I have to say Lynn's brilliant at her job but she can have a rather brusque manner with people who can be described as vulnerable.'

'I'll have a go,' I said. 'She might not get many visitors and enjoy talking to someone.'

'Lynn said she found herself talking to an Easter Island statue.'

'I assume she didn't bring up the subject of the murder.'

85

'Of course not. I told her just to say she was with the police and checking up on empty properties. The last thing I wanted to do was distress her. What I could really do with is knowing whether her nephew was living there around the time we think the woman was killed.'

'I'll have a go.'

'Shall I arrange it for you?'

This he did and, at just before two thirty that afternoon I walked up the drive to a medium-sized house with a modern extension situated off the Wells Road. Frail and elderly people, some seemingly completely comatose, were being pushed around the garden in wheelchairs by relatives or uniformed carers and not for the first time I came to the conclusion that I would rather end up beneath the wheels of a large, red London bus than like this.

'Another police person?' sniffed the woman on the reception desk.

'Miss Langley'll do fine,' I assured her. I write under my maiden name.

Miss Bennett was one of those remaining indoors. She sat, apparently dozing, in a chair in a corner of a lounge. A few other residents were also in the room, but not sitting close to her, some asleep, others staring blankly at a television screen, the set switched on but with the sound turned almost right down.

'Miss Bennett?' I said softly, pulling up a chair. 'My name's Ingrid Langley. May I speak to you for a few minutes?'

There was a slight start so at least she was not hard of hearing.

86

'How are you?' I asked.

There was no response.

'You may or may not remember Sergeant Lynn Outhwaite coming to see you to ask you a few questions about your house.'

I was slightly shocked for she was not an old woman, surely she could not be much more than fifty-five to sixty. Her dark-brown hair was lank and tied back with a weary-looking piece of green ribbon but her face was practically unlined.

I continued, 'I'm here because I'm thinking of buying it and wondered if you knew anything about its history. Such an attractive little house – I've really fallen in love with it. It's a happy sort of place.' All this sounded horribly banal to me but what on earth *did* one say?

She raised her head and looked at me and for some reason a shudder went through me. She had not been happy there.

'The garden's got plenty of potential,' I said. 'I should imagine that at one time it was really pretty. Do you enjoy the gardens here?'

There was no response.

'I understand that your nephew's on his way back from New Zealand,' I went on chattily. 'David, isn't it? He must be your brother's son as you've the same surname. I expect he'll come and see you when he gets home.'

Again there was something in her look that told me I was wrong. They were not close and he would not be coming to visit her.

I asked the important question. 'Was he living at the house before he went away?'

87

She still said nothing and I felt as though her dark, unsettling eyes were burning holes in me.

I tried to get a response for one last time, risking, 'Don't you like him?'

She closed her eyes, rejecting me utterly, and returned to her own world.

'She don't say nothin',' hissed the old man sitting in the chair nearest to me. He peered searchingly at Miss Bennett for a few moments and then jerked his head in the direction of a door on the far side of the room that led into a large conservatory. I made my way there and he followed me, slowly and painfully, half a minute or so later.

'I wish you hadn't suggested struggling so far,' I said.

'If you don't bloody struggle you may as well go outside and shoot yourself,' he declared. 'Besides, that woman has long ears.'

'It doesn't sound as though you like her very much.'

He flopped down on to a padded bench. 'I don't like people who can't even spare you a smile – no matter how ga-ga they are. Sit down, gal, so I can see you better.'

I sat.

'Thought so. I've seen your face somewhere before. Been on the box, have yer?'

'A few times,' I replied. 'In books programmes.'

'That's it then. Sorry, my ears are too long too and I heard you say you were buying her house. I'm not too daft to read the papers and I know a police sergeant came to talk to her the other day.

Is this the place where they found the body?'

'Yes, it is.'

'P'raps it's just as well that she's here then, not knowing, like.'

'You're probably right. How long has she been here?'

'Around a year. I know that because she came two days after my birthday last year and it's next week. I overheard someone say that she'd been in another home but had got worse.'

'D'you happen to know which home that was?'

'No, but a green people-carrier with some kind of gold-coloured logo on the side brought her. I didn't pay much attention.'

'Does she have any visitors?'

'No one that I've seen.'

'The police are trying to find out who was living in her house when the murder was committed. Do you know anything about a nephew who sometimes goes to New Zealand?'

'No, sorry, nothin'. As I said, she don't speak.'

'What, to *nobody*?'

'Sort of grunts when the staff ask her things, that's all.'

I thanked him and left. I did not enquire as to which care home Miss Bennett had come from as I knew I would be wasting my time. 'Client confidentiality' would see to that.

At three thirty that afternoon I had a call from Patrick.

'He tried to do a runner so I had to arrest him,' were his first words. 'I'd already got Immigra-

89

tion at the airport involved, of course, and he threw a punch at me and still tried to get away. The man stank of booze so obviously he'd been drinking on the plane.'

'That's a hell of a lot of drinking, from across the other side of the world,' I commented.

'Too right. As far as the rest of it goes Mike's still working on the theory that Irma and Imelda are, or were, the same woman and there's a connection with organized crime. At least, he's keeping an open mind about it until it's proved otherwise. As you know, this Martino Capelli is bad news and Mike really wants to know what he, and others, are planning. It's been near the top of his priorities list for months. The underworld grapevine's humming with all kinds of plots but that could be gossip or deliberate red herrings.'

'You're at HQ then?'

'Yes. D'you want to come up? Mike reckons it might be useful for you to be in on the interview with David Bennett.'

'He could be a Capelli minion, you mean?'

'We don't know, do we? He does have a previous conviction for assault. And we really do need to know why this woman was murdered.'

'Was this conviction in the UK?'

'No, New Zealand.'

'Look, I might be being naive here, but I've never associated New Zealand with the likes of the Capellis.'

'That's what they hope everyone thinks though, isn't it? These people are branching out everywhere.'

'Sorry, I can't come up tonight. Matthew's playing in the school concert.'

'That's OK. Bennett's being detained overnight and brought here for ten thirty tomorrow morning.'

'What shall I tell him about your absence?' I asked evenly.

'Oh God, I'd promised to be there, hadn't I? You'll just have to tell him the truth, that I'm working. I'd actually forgotten all about it.'

'There's time if you got a train soon. Why don't you come home and we could both travel up early tomorrow morning?'

'No, sorry. I'd like to but I've arranged to meet an old army chum for dinner.'

Why was I doubting his word? Why did I wonder if Alexandra had checked out of the hotel in Bath and was heading back to her flat in town?

David Bennett was furious. Livid. He was a big man with a florid complexion, untidy fair hair and was, I guessed, in possession of a bullish demeanour normally, never mind his present anger. He occupied a chair in the interview room but gave every impression of being about to detonate from it at any moment. It was probably only the presence of Patrick, who had positioned himself between Bennett and the door, that kept the man from raging around the room, the interviewer exuding a healthy menace.

'Right,' Patrick said, shooting me what I shall describe as a brief professional smile, this nothing to do with any difficulties that might exist

91

between us, but to make it appear that I was merely one of the tiny cogs in SOCA's machine and not his wife, current squeeze, or whatever. This was normal practice with potentially serious criminals to prevent any possible revenge being visited upon me should he happen to half screw their heads off. 'This is Miss Langley. With your permission she will take notes. You may object if you wish.'

Bennett just scowled at me which I interpreted as a 'that's fine by me.'

I knew that Michael Greenway was listening to the interview in an adjoining room and watching through the one-way glass window that gave every appearance of being a large mirror on the wall of the room we were in.

As I had entered I had assessed Patrick very quickly but carefully. There did not appear to be any signs of post-coital bliss but then again he is a master of the art of schooling his facial expression.

He formally opened the interview and started the recording machine. 'Let's be quite clear on this,' he opened the proceedings with, 'When you've been questioned here, and whatever our conclusions are, you'll be taken to Bath and handed over to Detective Chief Inspector Carrick who is heading the investigation into the discovery of the body of a murdered woman at 3, Cherry Tree Row, Lansdown Hill, Bath. Is that understood?'

'I've been abroad for months,' Bennett grated. 'Which could have been proved if you'd bothered to go to the trouble. This isn't anything to do with me.'

'And I'd like to remind you that there's already a charge of resisting arrest and striking a police officer.'

'I'd been drinking. And anyway, I hit your shoulder – no harm done.'

'That's only because I have good reflexes,' he was told with a nasty smile. 'To resume,' Patrick continued, 'I received an email from the DCI early this morning to the effect that you were the registered occupant of the house, both for council tax purposes and on the voting register, for a period of three years up until thirteen months ago.'

Bennett took a deep breath, stared at the ceiling for a moment and then decided to cooperate. 'I was listed as the occupant, but I wasn't. At least, only for a short while. The place was a tip, unfit to live in. I kept an eye on it because I knew it would be mine one day as my aunt's leaving it to me in her will.'

'Where did you live?'

'I rented a small flat in Claverton, little more than a cupboard really. You haven't even told me who's been killed.'

'Her name was Imelda Burnside.'

Bennett's eyes narrowed. *'Imelda!'*

'She was known to you then.'

'We went out for a short time.'

He did not seem to be at all upset.

'She lived with you when you were at the house?'

'Yes, for a bit.'

'Did you break up?'

'No, I got fed up with the conditions there – Imelda wasn't too keen on housework either – and rented the flat at Claverton because it was all I could afford at the time. It wasn't big enough for both of us.'

'Did you let her stay on at your aunt's house?'

'Yes, she'd lost her job.'

'And?'

'She got another one quite quickly and said she'd pay the utilities so I let her stay on for a little longer. Then I got a letter from her to say that she hated the new job and was moving, going to live with her sister.'

'When was this?'

'About a year ago – not all that long after I'd moved out.'

'Do you know the sister's name?'

'If I remember rightly it was Irma.'

'Where did she live?'

'She didn't say.'

I said, 'Was your aunt aware that she was living at her house?'

'I didn't bother her with it.' He added, but openly resenting my interjection, 'She probably wouldn't have approved.'

'But you don't go to see her now.'

'How do you know that?'

'Please answer the question.'

'No,' Bennett said after a pause. 'What the hell's the point? The woman's just a cabbage now – finished.'

'Would you say that your aunt's fond of you?'

'What a stupid question,' the man said scornfully. 'Yes, very – or she used to be when her

94

brain was all right. Otherwise she wouldn't be leaving me her house, would she?'

'What is your business, Mr Bennett?' Patrick asked.

'I do a bit of this and that. I've a couple of properties in Christchurch that are rented out. My mother was of New Zealand nationality so I've a dual passport. Over here I own three flats over shops in Bearflat, Bath. Sometimes I take a temporary job or buy and sell stuff on the Internet – if I want extra cash.'

'And yet you say you rented a "cupboard" as times were hard. How was that with rent money coming in?'

Bennett grimaced. 'The tenants of two of the flats over here stopped paying the rent saying I hadn't done any repairs. It wasn't true and I had an idea they were in the plot together. It took months to get them out and one of the flats was trashed. Cost me a couple of thousand to put it right.'

'That must have made you pretty angry.'

'Oh, I know who they are.' He realized that statement could be misconstrued. 'I mean, I'll not have them as tenants again.'

'Let's return to Imelda. Was she close to her sister?'

'God knows. She didn't really mention her.'

'So you don't know anything about her at all.'

'No.'

'Is there any doubt in your mind that Irma actually existed? Could they have been one and the same woman?'

'I haven't the first bloody clue.'

95

'Did she ever mention a man by the name of Martino Capelli?'

'No. Look, what is all this about? I only went out with the woman for a short while and—'

'You don't seem remotely upset about the fact that she's been murdered,' I fired at him, loathing him for his general callousness. 'Her decapitated and badly decomposed body was found in the larder of the house and her head was in a cupboard upstairs. Did she actually lose her job again and couldn't carry on paying the bills? Did she refuse to move out as she had nowhere else to go? Did you get drunk again and go round there to chuck her out only for everything to get out of hand?'

'No!' Bennett gasped.

'Tell us what happened in New Zealand when you were convicted of assault,' Patrick asked silkily.

'I – er – I—'

'I already know. You got drunk and beat up your girlfriend who suffered extensive bruising, contusions and a broken jaw. You were sent to prison for six months, a sentence shorter than it might have been because, according to witnesses, she was blind drunk as well and had come at you with a broken bottle.'

Bennett sullenly remained silent.

'It's DCI Carrick's job to find out if you're guilty of Imelda's murder,' Patrick continued. 'My interest is with the victim herself in case she did lead a double life. Where did you meet her?'

'In a pub somewhere.'

'Think!'

'In Bristol.'

'You picked her up.'

'She wasn't a tart!'

'No, of course she wasn't,' I said. 'You got talking, she was flat broke and desperate and you offered her money for sex. She turned out to be quite useful along those lines but you fell out when she got fed up with clearing up after you, cooking your meals and washing your socks because actually you're a complete slob!'

'It wasn't like that!' Bennett bellowed.

'What did she do for a living?' Patrick said quickly, in a tone that represented a slapped wristie for me. Throwing any petrol on to the flames would be his prerogative.

'I'll tell you that only when you've had that woman removed from the room!' A quivering forefinger was pointed in my direction.

'Oh, good, we're getting somewhere,' Patrick murmured. 'She stays. Answer the question.' He gave the man a freezing stare. 'Otherwise ... I shall find it difficult to remain ... patient.'

'She worked in retirement and nursing homes,' Bennett muttered after a long pause.

'I would have thought there was a constant demand for people like that in the Bath area with so many retired folk living there. And yet from what you say it seems she was often out of work.'

'Imelda could be a bit stroppy,' Bennett said after consideration. 'If she didn't like someone she told them so. Perhaps it didn't go down too well.'

No doubt he had had first hand experience of that.

'You mean she was rude to the clients?'

'Oh, no. To the staff. If she thought they weren't treating people right. They don't you know, they drug 'em up if they get difficult and slap them around. She used to tell me about it.'

'What else did she tell you?'

Bennett shrugged. 'Well, I don't know. I didn't pay much attention, did I?'

'Think.' The word dropped into the room like molten lead.

'Well – well, about her day really. She didn't talk about her past, if that's what you mean.'

'What, not about her childhood, parents, friends?'

'No.'

'Didn't you find that a bit strange?'

'I can't say I was that interested.'

'Although this might have been at a time before such stringent checks were made on people who work with the vulnerable, do you think it's remotely possible that she kept losing her job because they discovered she had a criminal record? I want you to think very carefully about that.'

'She did hate the cops. One cautioned her in Union Street once when she called him a bastard. No reason for her to do that really.' He chuckled humourlessly. 'Except that you are – all of you.'

# SEVEN

'He could easily have killed her,' I said later.
'The man *is* a complete slob.'

'I agree, but whether he did or not is for James
Carrick to find out,' Michael Greenway said.
'Thanks for coming, by the way.'

Patrick said, 'She and Irma could have been
one and the same woman. She had a criminal
record and moved to the West Country to start a
new life, changing her first name. But I do have
to ask myself why she didn't change her surname as well.'

'We must be very careful here,' the commander said to him. 'There might be a sister. If not
and it is the same person it doesn't appear that
Bennett's aware of, or been involved with, her
past life. But I still have to have the true state of
affairs confirmed.'

'Are there no DNA samples of Irma in view of
the fact that she has a record?' Patrick wanted to
know.

'No, it happened quite a while ago when she
was in her late teens and before the technology
really kicked off. Since then, other than having a
dodgy boyfriend, she seems to have stayed out
of trouble. There are fingerprints, yes. But we
can't compare those with the body as it was too

99

badly decomposed.'

'Do I get the feeling you want me to go and find out if Irma still exists?' Patrick queried.

'Yes, but don't make a career out of it and leave no trace if you get into her last known address in Romford, Martino's flat. I don't want there to be any suspicion that it's being watched. Is that clear?'

'Of course.'

'It's a nice quiet little number for you while you're still off main ops, but three days, no longer. I can't throw any more money at it than that on the strength of snouts' gossip.' He gave us one of his big smiles, which suited him perfectly as he was a big man, around six foot five. 'Take Ingrid. She can watch out for Capelli honchos for you.' He chuckled.

I was last out of the room and he called me back.

'Is that OK?' he whispered a little anxiously.

'You have a woman's intuition,' I said, no louder.

'Coming from you I'll take that as a compliment. What's the problem?'

'A woman.'

'God, have I made things worse?'

'Not at all, but you might look up the name Alexandra Nightingale in records for me.'

Shortly afterwards I received a phone call from the estate agency repeating the news that a higher offer, above the original asking price and surely emanating from Alexandra, had been made. I reminded them that my offer had already been accepted but was told that it was not legally binding and the solicitors representing the owner had made no final decision. Other prospective buyers had looked at the property. I immediately put in an offer of twenty thousand pounds over the original price.

We had just checked into an hotel. Patrick, who was unpacking clothes and tossing them on to the bed, glanced up as I finished the call but made no comment.

'This is about more than just a house,' I observed quietly.

He still said nothing.

'After I'd taken you to the station I went to see Alexandra at her hotel,' I went on to say. 'She admitted that she'd obtained my mobile number from your phone, which you'd left on the table in a café when you went to the loo. She's been complaining to any number of friends about my wanting to buy what she regards as her house, including her ex, one Alan Kilmartin. She seemed quite ready to drop him in it.'

'You should have let me talk to her. I said I would.'

'I saw her with a man just outside the hotel entrance. She was very angry, upset really. He was of medium height, dark, ugly and wearing a single but quite large, gold earring. He looked distinctly snaky. Alexandra told me that he was an employee and was looking for a commercial property for her. I'm not too sure that was the truth.'

'And your point in all this?'

'I asked her what sort of agency she had and

she told me it was to do with domestic staff, home helps, nannies and so forth. When—'

Patrick butted in with, 'It seems it's a perfectly innocent business then.'

'When you have that kind of agency you build up a huge client base. If she shifts down to Bath she'll have to start all over again, from scratch.'

'So?'

'Then she told me that you were a fine man. She likes fine men, she said. But they turn out to be quite ordinary after she's stripped them off, layer by layer, something that she's discovered she's good at. But I was assured I'd get you back – eventually.'

'Ingrid, she was just winding you up.'

'That's exactly what took place, what she said, practically word for word, no bias on my part, no bitching. I've edited out the superior smirks and the odd drops of spit. As I said the other day, it seems to me that one of your layers has gone already. I think the stripper she's using is called infatuation.'

Patrick flopped down on the bed. 'Look, this is a real distraction from the job.'

'I'm aware of that. Would you rather I went home?'

He looked at me, alarm writ large as though if I did I would head straight off to see a solicitor. 'No. I didn't mean it like that.'

I opened my travel bag and started to unpack. 'OK.'

'We're a great team,' Patrick said.

'I know. We'd better get on with the job then.'

102

'Look, I am *not* having an affair with this woman.'

'Fine,' I replied, giving him one his own shark's smiles.

As we knew already, Martino Capelli had run his crime empire from his home, a flat in Romford, before being sent to prison and this was, according to criminal records, the last known address of Irma Burnside. A cross reference to information about him listed any number of others known to have worked for, consorted with, or be related to him, one of the names in the latter category being that of his cousin, the late but not remotely lamented Tony. It would be naive of us to assume that the business was defunct while he was inside. Not at all: it would be ticking away quietly under the care of some of these people until such time he was released. Or, as we had now been told, was rumoured to be functioning with orders being issued by him from inside prison.

That was the background and it was not our brief to infiltrate the gang, merely to try to track down the woman, if indeed she still existed and had not come to a horrible end in Bath under a different name. One of Michael Greenway's team had suggested a trawl through dental records in the area as a quick way of establishing the truth as then we would have instant identification material. But for practical purposes Romford can be regarded as part of Greater London and the number of dentists runs into dozens. We had already established that the practice where

103

the woman who had called herself Imelda Burnside had been registered had no previous history of her, this blamed on a one-time inept employee who had somehow caused their computer to crash, destroying all the records.

The address was a flat that turned out to be over a fish and chip shop in a busy road near the High Street. If no one was in we were going to break in, completely off the record and leaving no trace of our entry.

'Even if Irma had abandoned her home it wouldn't have stayed empty all this time,' I said when we had found somewhere to park the car and were walking back. 'I should think the place was rented.'

I had driven up from the West Country as the Range Rover has its uses – not being referred to as the 'battle bus' for nothing – and, most importantly, it has been adapted so Patrick can drive it. Having a right foot with no sensation does not make for good control and he only gets behind the wheel of conventional cars if he has to and then only for short distances.

He said, 'That's something we shall have to discover because if it wasn't and she owned it that rather strengthens the case for there having been two women. Otherwise she wouldn't have been flat broke in Bath and had to live at the house in Cherry Tree Row.'

'Unless it didn't sell for ages.'

'And David Bennett was telling the truth when he said Imelda had written to him saying she was going to live with her sister. Who had just, presumably, bought somewhere else to live. No more conjecture though. Let's get to the truth.'

We were assiduously 'making a great team' as Patrick had put it. There was no strained atmosphere and we were just being terribly, terribly businesslike. I had made up my mind that I was not going to mention Alexandra's name unless really provoked or she arrived, all poisonous charm, and proceeded to strip a few more veneers off my husband.

A little intelligence gathering was undertaken first. It was now just after four thirty and the fish and chip shop was open and full of noisy children just out of school. We waited on the pavement until the chaos inside had abated and then went in.

'The flat upstairs?' said the man behind the counter who appeared to be in charge in response to Patrick's query, backed up by his warrant card. 'Yes, a woman lives there. But I don't know who she is.'

'Are you the proprietor?' he was asked.

'I am.'

'Are these properties rented?'

'Yes.'

Patrick then went on to ask him for the name and address of the landlord. The man had to go to a room in the back to get the information and when he returned he said, 'You've missed her. I've just seen her go down the back stairs.'

Patrick shook his head sadly. 'Thanks. We'll have to come back later.'

We did not make the mistake of immediately making our way around to the rear of the building in case anyone's curiosity in the chippy

105

caused them to watch our activities for a while and we ended up by having to break in. There was a café practically opposite so we headed for it and spent a short time drinking tea.

'Are you armed?' I asked in casual fashion.

'Just with my knife.'

'We *are* still on certain terrorist organizations' hit-lists.'

'Yes, you're right,' Patrick mused. 'I'll go back to the car and get it. We're possibly dealing with a spin-off from the Mafia here too.'

Patrick is permitted to carry a firearm, for our personal safety and in the course of his present duties. He periodically attends practice sessions at a police weapons training establishment to maintain his standard and is a very, very good shot. The weapon, a Glock 17 pistol which he carries in a shoulder harness, is otherwise kept in a safe at home or in the secure cubby box in the Range Rover that can only be accessed by those in the know, us, and even then we have to enter code numbers, changed once a month, on a key pad. I too have received instruction but stick to the short-barrelled Smith and Wesson as I am used to it. It was in my bag now and my story, if asked, is always that it is for his use, merely back-up. *I'm* the back-up.

I stayed behind to finish my tea. From where I was sitting I could see the fish and chip shop and also an opening that provided access to the rear of the various premises by delivery vehicles. There appeared to be a private car park in there too. People were walking in and out but I was too far away to be able to identify Irma Burnside from the mugshot, a copy of which we had brought with us.

Very shortly afterwards I spotted Patrick on the other side of the road. He paused, glanced across in my direction and then disappeared into the entry. I paid the bill and went outside. When I caught up with him he was standing at the bottom of what looked like a fire escape, and probably was, that was used to provide access to the first-floor flats. We went up and rang the appropriate bell. There was no reply.

Patrick's 'burglars" keys quickly dealt with the somewhat dated door locks and we went in. As we had already ascertained from the exterior of the building there appeared to be no conventional alarm system fitted.

I stayed by the front door while Patrick performed a swift check that the flat was otherwise unoccupied. I had half expected in this somewhat lacklustre area that the interior would be the same but from what I could see from where I was standing this was far from the truth. There was a huge Chinese carpet in the living room off to the left of me, silk probably, and the oriental theme was continued with tasselled lamps and a carved wooden dragon painted green and gold, also a lamp, that must have stood over five feet high.

'Whoever lives here doesn't struggle for money,' Patrick said, echoing my own conclusions. 'Plasma screen TV, designer kitchen, ditto bathroom, king-sized bed.'

'All a bit tacky though.'

'I've never met a so-called crime lord who had

good taste – not that we know he still rents the place.'

We both moved into the living room where my working partner, who had donned gloves, rapidly and carefully went through the drawers of a Chinese lacquer cabinet, leaving everything exactly as he had found it. This kind of searching is not part of my role, unless he requests my help, so I touched nothing, walking around the flat to assimilate detail, looking at photographs and pictures, trying to find something that would help us. Well, she obviously liked dragons, as I had already seen. There were luridly coloured wooden ones, also china ones, silver metallic ones, on shelves, in pictures on the walls and, like the large one I had spotted first, standing on the floor.

I was looking for photos of Irma, as we knew what she looked like, and also anyone who might be Imelda. There were none that could be described as family pictures, just a couple of framed snaps of temples. Then I discovered a professional portrait of a small group of young people taken on their graduation day but it was impossible to identify any of them as the women in whom we were interested.

In the bedroom the bed was as good as a four-poster, only eastern-style, the whole thing swathed, festooned and swagged in heavy gold and crimson brocade that must have necessitated the wearing of dark glasses when the sun was shining on it. I had an idea this would never be allowed as the curtains, also heavy fabric, were almost closed giving the room a kind of phoney exotic feel like the inside of a fortune-teller's tent. I was still looking for photographs and found one on a bedside table.

'Here's something,' I called, only quietly. And, when Patrick had arrived, 'I only had a quick look at the mugshot of Martino Capelli but if this man isn't him I'll take up knitting dishcloths for a living.'

And with that, the dragon breathing red- and yellow-painted wooden flames in one corner of the room fired a shot at us.

It missed, the bullet thunking into the padded headboard of the bed. It is unnecessary to report that we had both dived to the floor.

'I did wonder about the apparent absence of a security system,' Patrick muttered from somewhere on the other side of the king-sized monstrosity. 'Silenced too. Please stay completely still where you are while I take a look at it.'

Scuffling noises followed as he wriggled across the floor. Then, after a minute or two, there was a click and a soft thud.

'Come and look at this.'

The firing mechanism lay on the carpet, Patrick examining the inside of the carved figure, a section of the lower part of the neck of which was open like a small door.

'Very crude but effective,' he said over his shoulder. 'An illegal booby-trap device armed with a low calibre firearm married to a domestic infrared sensor that's been adapted to have a fixed beam. Thank God neither of us crossed it when we first entered the room. Where's that photo?'

I retrieved it from where it had been knocked off the table.

'That's him,' Patrick said succinctly. 'Right, I suggest we wait until this female returns.'

'SOCA isn't supposed to be here,' I reminded him.

'SOCA isn't going to be here,' he replied and commenced to dig the bullet out of the headboard with one of the tiny tools on the ring with his set of lock-picking keys. 'And please don't roam around until I've given the rest of this place a proper once-over.'

In this ex-soldier's mind, of course, we were now on a war footing, and, the tiny missile soon consigned to an evidence bag in his pocket, Patrick commenced to prowl around the flat to look for evidence as well as more booby-traps. I did as instructed and stayed where I was. Having removed the rest of the live ammunition he had replaced the dragon's innards but, glancing at it, I was half expecting it to do something else distinctly unfriendly. It had that look about it.

'I've only got as far as the kitchen,' he reported, coming back. 'Five thousand US dollars in a drawer, six thousand euros in the fridge, all new, plus some small packets of what are probably drugs hidden under the rubbish bag in the bin. I'll have a quick look in—'

He stopped speaking when there was the sound of a key turning in a lock of the front door. Patrick immediately exited, motioning to me to follow and we went into the living room. This now being war I saw that his knife was now in his hand. With people who keep live-firing

110

dragons you never know what to expect.

A woman who must be Irma Burnside became framed in the doorway. In the split second before she saw us she had been smiling, the reason for this probably because she had company; two men of Italian appearance, one of whom, on seeing Patrick stopped dead, an expression of shocked recognition on his face.

'I know you!' he blared, pointing an accusing finger. 'You were Kimberley Devlin's body-guard!'

'So I was,' Patrick said. 'A little business I used to have. But I thought someone had done the planet a favour, Tony, and cut your throat.'

Whether the man nudged the one with him I do not know but this individual made a grab under his jacket. He froze into stillness when Patrick sprang the blade of his knife, that ghastly metallic slicing sound.

'You're some kind of cop,' said Capelli, eyeing Patrick warily. He gave his minder a murderous look that said too slow, too stupid, consider yourself fired. The man put the weapon away.

'Don't insult me,' Patrick said heavily.

'I saw you in the company of a man called Carrick in Scotland. He was a cop.'

'Carrick was investigating you and your scam. I was looking after the Devlin woman and as you were her agent it was hardly surprising that we were all in the same place at the same time.'

Capelli seemed to accept this explanation. He was a fat little man with smooth brown hair that looked as though it had been painted on. His

111

face was lined where it was fixed into a permanent scowl and he had the shiftiest eyes I had ever seen this side of reptiles.

I was sure Patrick would stir things up a little and did not have long to wait. In conversational tones he said, 'Why do you employ such crap to protect you?'

That was what he actually said. But I could only assume from the minder's reaction to the remark that it was accompanied by another look intended for him alone that spoke reams about his parentage, sexual inclinations of the unspeakable variety plus anything else unspeakably insulting Patrick could think of, and knowing him, lots. A second later the gun was in the man's hand, in another it was falling to the floor, the room resounding with screams of pain, the knife blade embedded in his hand.

Patrick walked forward and, having applied a thoughtful general anaesthetic in the form of a swift chop to the side of the neck, pulled out the knife.

'I am minded of Luigi,' he said in a deathly whisper to Tony Capelli. 'One of your previous minders. He was crap too. Remember him?'

'You humiliated him,' said Capelli through his teeth. 'You trussed him up like a pig ready for the oven.'

'He was lucky just to get an apple between his teeth instead of being roasted. I told you that if you sent him in my direction again I would kill him. So you sent him after Carrick and his fiancée was shot instead. I killed him before he could fire again – and hit me.'

'The police shot him.'

'Wrong. *I* shot him. I took a police rifle and killed him before making my escape. The police were stupid and hadn't set up road blocks and that was how Luigi had got through.'

The woman found her voice. 'What the *hell* are you doing in my home?' she yelled furiously.

Patrick looked her up and down. 'I take it you're Irma Burnside.'

'I am.'

'I've a contract to take out Martino and decided to look you up first to get any information about him you might have.'

Irma, who had gone blonde since her mugshot was taken, did not appear to find this strange, transferring her attention to me. 'And *her*?'

Busy looking stupid, I was given a leery smile. 'She brings me luck.'

'She must do. I don't know why you didn't trigger any of the security devices.'

'Darling, I'm *hungry*,' I whined. 'And these people are so *boring*.'

'Shut up,' said my husband peaceably. The blooded knife blade was pointed in Irma's direction with a gesture that was more than faintly obscene. 'When's Martino due out then?'

'Soon,' she replied scornfully. 'But I don't care. Kill him if you want to. He means nothing to me now I have Tony.'

Patrick beamed upon Capelli, who was simmering gently. 'Pinched your cousin's girl then? That's no surprise.' And to the woman, 'Will he come here?'

'God knows. Now get out.'

'All the usual networks are buzzing with news of a big job planned from inside. What's that all about then?'

Irma hesitated and glanced across at Capelli causing me to wonder whether there was no love lost between the two cousins and one would be only too ready to sell the other down the river.

Having received no guidance, Irma shrugged. 'I don't know.'

'You're lying.'

'I'd rather stay alive, thank you.'

'It must be going to happen soon if he's due to be released before too long and the idea is that whatever it is it can't possibly be his fault as he's still banged up. Actually, that's pretty naive – the cops aren't stupid. Everyone knows that big-time crooks are using smuggled interactive games consoles to get coded messages out in chat room facilities.'

The two exchanged worried glances.

'You're a marked man,' Capelli said to Patrick.

'You always did sound like a Mafia B-movie,' he was told as we took the opportunity to leave.

# EIGHT

'That was pure revenge,' I admonished gently when we were on our way back to SOCA's HQ. 'Although I know you needed to keep the upper hand.'

I was given a cool smile. 'Thicko won't be handling any kind of weapon for a while though, will he?'

And I had accused him of losing his edge. Perhaps I was losing mine. 'I reckon Capelli swallowed your story.'

'Yes, we might be lucky there. But surely the man's assumed a new identity or he wouldn't have been able to get back into the UK. He's still wanted in connection with the Scottish case. I must phone James and give him the good news.'

'Otherwise though...'

'Yes, I've done what I was ordered to. Irma exists. She's hanging out with those who ought to be detained, helping with enquiries, but aren't. End of story. You know,' Patrick went on reflectively. 'I might just take out Martino anyway.'

I knew from the way he spoke that he was only joking. But there was a trace of wistfulness in there somewhere.

'You don't enjoy killing people,' I probed.

'No, of course not. It's the planning, the track-ing down, the fine weapon to hand, the out-witting of someone who employs vigilant and vicious armed minders and is responsible for the murders of innocent people and for various reasons has never been brought to court.'

'You've done it!' I gasped.

'In Northern Ireland and elsewhere,' Patrick admitted. 'I've never quite got round to telling you. Forbidden ever to talk about it actually.'

I knew it had gone on but...

'We didn't find out about this big job, which is a pity,' I said, changing the subject.

'D'you feel badly about me because of it?'

I risked taking my eyes off the traffic for a quick glance in his direction. 'No. Soldiers are ordered to do all kinds of things.'

'They are.'

'Have you told your father?'

'I had to. Because of—'

'You don't have to explain to me. What did he say?'

'Almost exactly the same as you just have.'

'I think because of what he is we must regard him as the protector of your conscience.'

'Thank you,' Patrick whispered.

Commander Greenway was just leaving his outer office but did an abrupt U-turn when he saw us. 'Well?' he barked when the three of us were in the room and the door behind us was still shivering in its frame.

No doubt all army officers are familiar with having to present a thirty-word report to grumpy

116

superiors with catastrophically low blood-sugar. Patrick rattled one off now, standing to attention and providing the full stop by clicking his heels together. It had the desired effect: Greenway roared with laughter.

Patrick took the evidence bag with the tiny bullet in it from his pocket. 'I don't know what you're going to do with this but I've brought it anyway. Plenty of money and packets of what are probably drugs in the flat. I'd like to know what Tony Capelli's game is and how long he's been in this country. Irma's not a particularly attractive woman so I can only assume that he's using her to close in on his cousin's empire with a view to taking that over as well. I'm afraid we didn't manage to find out what the big job is.'

Greenway brooded for a few seconds and then said, 'I don't really want to disturb that rats' nest until a little more intelligence is forthcoming but I'd dearly like to pick the woman up and try and find out what she knows. It might save lives. Did you tell her that her sister's dead?'

'No. Why would a hit-man care? Besides, reports of such a gruesome killing must have been in all the national media.'

'Good.' With a rueful smile Greenway added, 'I don't usually have time to read the papers or watch television either.'

I wondered, if David Bennett was telling the truth, if Imelda really had sent the letter to inform him that she had gone to live with her sister. What if she had gone off to London and got caught up in her life of crime? Had she threatened to inform the police about something

117

she had discovered and paid a terrible price?

'I'll bring the Met up to date with this first thing tomorrow,' Greenway went on, dashing out a reminder to himself on a pad on his desk and then lobbing the whole thing into a drawer and locking it. 'Now, I'm off home before anyone thinks of anything else I ought to be doing. It's my wife's birthday and I'm taking her out to dinner.'

'I'll report for further orders in the morning then,' Patrick said impassively as we moved to leave.

'Do that. And tonight take Ingrid out too. You can put it on expenses. Oh, which Force wants to get Tony Capelli by the short hairs?'

'Strathclyde police has more than a passing interest but this scam he had of importing foreign hoodlums for cash was actually based at Castle Stalker near Inverness. That's in Northern Constabulary's territory. James Carrick has more info than I do.'

'Thank you, I'll give him a bell. Tomorrow.'

'Capelli's odious,' I said with feeling as we were getting ready to go out, obeying orders, naturally. No doubt Greenway had been delighted that he had the answer to the Irma Burnside question so quickly. 'But you know that, you've met him already.'

Patrick glanced at me knowingly from perfecting the knot in his tie in a mirror. 'I've been a marked man for a large proportion of my life. But I don't think he'll be in any rush to tangle with me again.'

His mobile rang.

'I'm in London,' he said to whoever it was. 'No, you can't, I'm working ... Yes, she is ... No, sorry, it's nothing to do with me, it's DCI Carrick's case ... Yes, I know he's a friend of mine but— No, sorry, I can't do that ... Yes, I know we have ... OK ... Bye.'

'Alex?' I queried.

'Yes. She wants to get into the house on Lansdown with a builder. Carrick won't let her have entry as the place is still a crime scene. She seemed to think I ought to be able to make him change his mind.'

'But it's nothing to do with changes of mind!' I exclaimed. 'The house *is* a crime scene.' The house was hers then.

'I know, but it probably won't be for all that much longer.'

I was pondering the reply, 'No, you can't, I'm working.' She had wanted to come to London and had then asked if I was with him. But what about, 'Yes, I know we have'?

Things in common?

Memories to share?

A date next week?

'You're looking at me as though I'm a slug on one of your plants,' Patrick complained.

'I'm not,' I protested, having been completely unaware of the fact. 'Just ... thinking.'

He trilled, 'Darling, I'm *hungry.* And these people are so *boring.*'

Giggling, we went out.

We had just been shown to a table in an Italian

119

restaurant when Patrick had a call from James Carrick. Despite Patrick insisting that he never minds talking shop their conversation was of short duration when the DCI discovered that we were having an evening out.

'Bennett's admitted that Imelda did stay longer at his aunt's house than he wanted and they had a couple of rows about it but is emphatically denying having anything to do with her death,' Patrick reported. 'There's more James wants to tell me and I'm going to phone him in the morning. But at least he now knows the exact identity of the murder victim.'

'If the woman in Romford really is Irma,' I observed lightly. 'She didn't look much like the mugshot.'

'I shall make sure you have boiled squid with a double helping of eyeballs if you start saying things like that.'

'Perhaps Capelli and Co killed Irma, or Imelda, for whatever reason, then installed another woman in her place.'

'But *why*?'

'Heaven knows. To conceal the murder perhaps. I'm only doing my oracle thing.'

'Please switch it off for a few hours,' he begged.

'Martino will know whether it's her or not when they let him out of prison,' I persisted.

Neither of us spoke for a short time while we perused our menus. Then Patrick said, 'She was quite happy for me to top him.'

'Umm.'

'*They* might be planning to top him when he

gets out and before he discovers the truth.'

'Umm.'

'And scoop all the dosh from this heist, or whatever he's planning from behind bars, having already decided to take over the entire crime empire.'

'Umm.'

'I might trot that theory past Mike.'

The Commander was very interested but restricted in what he could do. As he pointed out, 'It's not as though we can go and visit him in prison and warn him by saying we think something dodgy's going on at home. I didn't mention it before but a lot of work on the Met's and our part has gone into planning to grab this lot red-handed. What used to be called snouts but now have to be referred to as CHIS, Covert Human Intelligence Sources, have been supplying snippets of information for quite a while. This is coming almost entirely from people who are connected in some way to those who work for Martino Capelli on the outside. There's a lot of resentment. They haven't been paid for months, there are violent, and loyal, characters who keep everyone in line with threats and punishment. A lot of people would like to see the big man in a pair of lead-lined Y-fronts being dropped off Tower Bridge.'

'Any hints as to what's being planned?' Patrick asked.

'As of the day before yesterday it would *appear* that it's an armed raid on one of the top London jewellers and then an attack on a central

121

police station as they make their getaway to create a diversion and settle a few old scores by killing as many cops as possible.'

'When?'

'Soon.'

I said, 'Will there be any kind of warning?'

'At the moment that's only in the pipeline.'

I said, 'The London, Paris and Florence Diamond Consortium are holding an international jewellery exhibition at a Kensington hotel next week.'

'That was one of the possibilities mentioned but discounted on the grounds that the security will be really tight.'

'But *armed* security?' Patrick wanted to know.

'Quietly, yes.'

My mobile rang and I apologized, leaving the room to answer it.

'I shall have to go home,' I said, putting my head around the door a couple of minutes later. 'That was Carrie. She sounded awful and thinks she's got the flu. I suggested she went to bed and stayed there in case she gives it to John and Elspeth.'

'Take the car,' Patrick said. 'I don't really need it.'

'We'll work on this with the rest of my team but keep you right in the picture,' Greenway promised. 'And please let me know as soon as you're free to return.'

I drove to Hinton Littlemoor without stopping. There are contingency plans in place if Carrie is suddenly taken ill while Patrick and I are away and I had been wondering on the drive whether she was feeling so dreadful that she had forgotten about them or the people who would have taken over from her were somehow all unavailable. And surely we had mentioned to Elspeth what emergency measures were there for the asking. All she had to do was pick up the phone.

Something wasn't quite right.

This immediately became apparent when the first thing I saw was Carrie playing with Vicky on the rear lawn of the rectory, Mark in his pram nearby. Not wishing to worry anyone I parked the car and went over to tell her that I had just 'popped' home. Mark woke up and welcomed me by filling his nappy so I took him away to change him, meeting Elspeth who had just come out of her own front door.

'Oh, how lovely,' she said. 'Have you had lunch?'

I told her I had not.

'There's a portion of Waldorf salad in the fridge if you'd like it. Is Patrick with you?'

'Yes, please, I'm afraid he isn't and I must deal with this niffy baby before I do anything else,' I said, hastening indoors.

Thirty-five minutes later, everything having been attended to, I had a one-woman council of war. Point one: I had been lured away from London, point two: I had a damned good idea who was responsible, point three: if I now had to go behind Patrick's back so be it, point four: I would talk to Alan Warburton Kilmartin, Alexandra's one-time boyfriend.

It seemed sensible to apprise James Carrick of what had happened in the event of the architect turning out to be a crazed serial killer in his lunch breaks.

'I agree, strange,' said the DCI. 'Do keep me posted. You say you're going to Warminster to see this man?'

'Yes.'

'Be careful. And I'll get an area car to drive occasionally by your place – just to be on the safe side.'

'Thank you. Did Patrick ring you back?'

'He did, and like him I'm very disappointed that Tony Capelli's still in the land of the living. As far as the murder case is concerned I've been given more time to question Bennett. Put politely, he's an unpleasant character and I'm fairly convinced he knocked the woman around even if he didn't kill her. But he might know who did or put out a contract to someone to have her done away with. He's still insisting he got a letter from her to say that she was going to live with her sister.'

'Did Patrick tell you about the dragons?'

'His middle name's George, isn't it?' Carrick responded dryly.

I reached Warminster, in pouring rain, noting carefully the black Merc tailing me: not getting too close, keeping two or three cars between us, but nevertheless present. I had proved quite early in the journey that we were not merely going to the same destination by taking a couple of short unnecessary detours around country lanes. Still the vehicle remained in my rear mirror, but I finally managed to get rid of it by some convoluted driving in side roads on the outskirts of the town.

The address Alexandra had given me was a business one; Kilmartin and Liddlestone-Mitten Associates, so I was hoping that even if the man was not at work they would give me his home address. But I saw when I arrived that the business was run from a private house with a large modern extension, the upper floor of which had the kind of huge windows that denote a drawing office.

'Do you have an appointment?' queried the extremely elegant young woman on the reception desk, the quiet hum of a professional business in the background.

'No, it's a private matter,' I told her. I gave her my card. The words 'author and scriptwriter' usually get me into most places.

After a short wait I was shown into a nearby office and into the presence of surely one of the most gorgeous men in the universe. Besides having green eyes and ash blond hair he virtually dripped elegance, refinement, good taste, polish, culture, plus anything else of that ilk Mr Roget could have listed.

'Miss Langley, how nice to meet you,' he said, voice-of-God. 'I was just about to have some tea. Would you like to join me?'

'That would be lovely,' I replied, hoping he could not hear my heart pounding against my ribs.

I fully expected him to call some minion over an intercom but he went over to a corner cupboard, opened it and thus revealed a mini-kitchen complete with a kettle, tiny fridge, microwave, bone china tea and dinner ware on shelves, the entire thing a dream of a design in toning shades of green.

'Like it?' he asked, giving me a grin over his shoulder that made me feel a bit faint.

'It's super,' I said inanely.

'My own design. I'm in the process of patenting it. There's other storage where you can keep biscuits and non-perishable snacks and stuff like that.' He demonstrated quickly. 'And, this –' he flashed another smile at me that turned my knees to water – 'Is where you wash up.'

The little stainless steel basin, glitteringly clean and complete with taps, had seemingly folded down from an invisible aperture in the wall.

'It's perfect for modern offices and there's a bigger version for bedsits and flats where there's no room for conventional stuff. Comes in several colourways too.'

'I hope you're wildly successful with it,' I said. I had already decided that I must have one but where, exactly, to put it?

'Thanks. China or Earl Grey?'

'Earl Grey please.'

He made the tea, every movement of the tanned slim hands adept and graceful.

'Now, what can I do for you?' Alan Kilmartin said when it was brewing. 'Molly said something about it being a private matter. But have we previously met?'

'No, but it concerns someone we both know,' I

told him. 'Alexandra Nightingale.'

'Alex!' he almost yelped.

'She's not for one second a friend of mine,' I hastened to add.

'I'm really pleased to hear that,' he responded grimly.

'In the smallest of nutshells,' I said. 'My husband works for the Serious Organized Crime Agency and so do I, in an advisory capacity. It appears that he knew Alexandra years ago and she's turned up and—'

'Stolen him from you?' he interrupted.

'It's worse than that. She's—'

'Chewing him up and spitting out the bits?'

'Sort of.'

'It's what she does.'

'Alan ... May I call you Alan?'

'Please do.'

'You're obviously a very intelligent man. So is Patrick. He used to work for an undercover army unit and after that for MI5 and is the kind of person they used to let loose on so-called traitors. He's an expert on people and subversion is one of his specialities. He once subverted a whole bunch of foreign terrorists and they turned against their leader. But now...'

'She's steamrollered all his talents and rendered him blind as to the kind of person she really is.'

'Yes.'

He poured the tea. 'She should have gone on the stage – fantastic actress. Biscuit?'

'Please. But I haven't come here expecting you to sort this out for me. Do you know any-

127

thing about this agency she runs?'

Kilmartin looked surprised. 'Not really. Only that it's in the West End and hires out home helps and nannies in that general area. Why do you ask?'

'Did you ever wonder if she was involved with anything illegal?'

'No! I wouldn't go out with anyone like that.'

I just looked at him.

'Oh, but look, I don't think I was that blind.' He broke off and then said, 'You must understand that Alex and I used to get on really well, at least for a while. We had fun. All quite normal really although she could be very silly sometimes and intolerant of other people. And then she started flashing her big blue eyes at a friend of mine who was engaged to a lovely girl. They had an affair. The poor guy was putty in her hands and the wedding was suddenly all off. As you might imagine, I had words with Alex about it and she swore she was sorry and would never do it again. But she did, she wanted all the blokes who loved someone else, even the married ones. She didn't really want them of course, only to play with them and ruin their relationships. We were living together at the time – before I got this place. I moved out and the last I heard was she'd got a flat in town.'

'She told us you'd found someone else.'

'Not true.'

'She's moving down to Bath – plus the agency.'

'Plus the agency? What, starting all over again, you mean?'

'Presumably.'

Thoughtfully, he sipped his tea. Then he said, 'I really wish I could help you.'

'Is there anything you can remember, or something of hers you still have that would give some kind of insight into what she's up to in her business life? Please think.'

'You really think she's up to something illegal?' he asked dubiously.

'I have what my Dad used to call cat's whiskers, intuition, and no, this isn't me trying to get her out of my marriage by cooking up accusations about her. To give a little weight to what I've already said I feel I ought to tell you that I've had a mildly threatening phone call from someone who said that what Alex wants, she gets and I'm to remember that.'

'She does,' Alan muttered. 'I wouldn't call that *mildly* threatening.'

'I take it you haven't spoken to her lately about me wanting to buy a house she's set her heart on?'

'Have you? No, we haven't exchanged a word since we split up.'

I told him about the non-existent case of flu.

He chewed thoughtfully on a biscuit for a few moments and then said, 'You were lured away from London. That's worrying.'

'Did she never talk about what she did?'

'No, but, be honest, it wouldn't be the kind of thing a mere male would be interested in.'

He had a point. I said, 'Would you say she made a fair living out of it?'

'Oh, yes, a very good living. She bought a

Porsche, cash, just before we split up.' He frowned, thinking. 'I know there's a man who sort of works for her.'

'Medium height, broad shoulders, dark receding hair, swarthy complexion, one gold earring and a bit shifty-looking?'

'Yes, exactly like that. You've obviously seen him.'

'He was talking to her outside the hotel where she was staying in Bath. She said he was looking for a commercial premises for her.'

'If it's the same bloke – and it sounds like him – I doubt that. His name's Stefan and she told me he was the odd-job man at the office block where she had her business. She employed him to do extra things like clean her car or even drive it if she was going out for the evening when she stayed in town and wanted to get plastered. I didn't mention her drinking like a whole shoal of fish, did I? No, Stefan's not very bright. I would not even trust him with buying an evening newspaper.'

'Do you know his surname?'

'Sorry, no.'

'I don't suppose you have the address of this agency.'

'No, not exactly but I know where it is. There's a newish building in what must be the only scruffy street in Kensington. It's in the style someone I know once described as Albanian Slaughterhouse Revival. It's horrible – you can't miss it. Boyles Road.' He smiled and my heart thumped again. 'The name says it all really.'

I thanked him and finished my tea.

'Are you staying in Warminster tonight?' Kilmartin asked.

'No, I'm off home.'

He glanced at my card. 'Hinton Littlemoor. That sounds nice. Only I was wondering if you'd like to have dinner with me. I've never met a writer before.' He laughed. 'No evil designs, I assure you. I don't want to be slowly taken apart by your husband.'

I refused as graciously as I could.

# NINE

On the verge of panic, a youth with red and orange hair and wearing a tee shirt with the words Attack of the Killer Robots printed on the front was staring at me through the opened driver's window. 'You – you all right, like, Mrs?' he stuttered.

I rather thought I wasn't.

The Range Rover was at quite a steep angle pointing downwards and seemed to be partly inside a small tree. I turned my head a little and saw that the jagged end of a broken branch that had come through the windscreen was about six inches in front of my nose. Glass was everywhere. Automatically, I reached out to turn off the ignition but my arm was either trapped or broken: I could not move it. There was blood on my jacket which seemed to be dripping off my chin. Wriggling round carefully despite being tightly braced against my seat belt, my body feeling strangely numb in places, I turned the key with the other hand.

'Has someone called the police?' I asked the youth, who was still gawping at me.

'Dunno.'

'Do you have a mobile?'

'Yeah, but there's no money on it.'

Heaven only knew where my handbag had ended up. 'Please go and find someone who can dial 999,' I asked him, trying to stay calm for his sake.

'I'll go and see the woman whose garden it is.' He scrambled off up a grassy slope.

Garden? What did the stupid boy mean, garden?

What the hell had happened?

I had had an accident, obviously, but could remember nothing about it.

Without warning the car slid a little farther and I flung my upper body towards the driver's door window just in time before being impaled on the branch. I simply dared not undo my seat belt and try to get out in case the inevitable shift in my weight made the vehicle career down into what might be a deep hole, taking the tree with it, or even flip over on to its roof.

Land Rovers aren't cars, someone had once said to me, they're a legend.

'So please stay right where you are,' I said out loud.

It slid a little more and then juddered to a halt again.

Time went by. I might have lost consciousness, or even dozed in some kind of stunned apathy, and when I was again aware of my surroundings the car seemed to have moved again, the branch now pressing into the side of my head, forcing it almost out through the open window. The fact that I prefer to drive with it down on a warm day rather than use the air con was paying off in bizarre fashion.

Sirens.

Then, when I was beginning to think they had gone somewhere else there were voices followed by clanking and clinking noises.

The car jerked slightly.

Several people slithered down to where I was, one of whom I knew.

'Someone said you were *dead!*' James Carrick exclaimed.

'How are you here?' I said.

'Because the registration of this vehicle is in my personal database so that it gets flagged up when anything happens to it that shouldn't. The medics are here, Ingrid, and the fire brigade guys have just fixed a winch-line to the tow bar so you don't finish up in the bottom of the valley. You're going to be fine.'

I wanted to believe him.


I could imagine the comments.

'Women drivers.' *(Sighs all round.)*

'They do get distracted easily and admire the view.'

'Or be busy fiddling around with the CD player.'

133

'Ingrid being a writer does mean she tends to live in her imagination – for days on end actually.'

'Yes, that must have been it; she was working on the plot for her new novel.'

'Shame about the car though. What was it, fifty-odd thousand quid's worth?'

'Nearer sixty by the time we'd had it customized.' (*Groans all round.*)

After the paramedics had established that I had no visible major injuries I had been gently eased out of the car and placed on a stretcher, my head immobilized in case of neck injuries. A large splinter sticking out of my cheek had been removed there and then in case it was accidentally knocked and created a larger wound.

What felt like hours later I was checked over in the A&E department of Bath's Royal United hospital. I was staggered to discover that nothing was broken, and I was suffering only from mild shock. That was it, sent home with some painkillers.

James Carrick had stayed with me and seemed to have abandoned work for the rest of the day, not that there was much of it remaining unless he had planned overtime.

'This is really kind of you,' I said gratefully as he helped me, still shaky, out of his car.

'I've a professional interest in this too,' he said.

'How so?'

'Well, being as the pair of you have worked for state security departments, are on foreign terrorists' hit-lists and you've told me you can't remember what happened *and* no other vehicles were involved I'm regarding your car as a crime scene until I learn otherwise.'

I suppose I gaped at him. 'No one else was involved?'

'No, there was no glass, bits of metal, skid marks or any of the other tell-tale signs you get when vehicles collide. So yours is on its way to be gone over with the proverbial fine tooth comb. I've told them I want a verbal report today.'

'Patrick loved that car,' I said sadly.

'Och, he'd rather you were in one piece.'

I wasn't too sure about that, murmuring, 'I must have dozed off at the wheel. I haven't been sleeping too well lately.'

'Don't beat yourself up about it. I shall want a statement from you if you're feeling up to it.'

We were slowly making our way towards the front door, my arm through his. 'You're triffically senior to do things like statements,' I remarked.

'It gets me out of going to a deadly boring late meeting.'

Our eyes met and we both laughed, the aching ribs of the accident victim instantly making her wish she hadn't.

'You've told Patrick about this, I take it?' Carrick asked casually.

'No, not yet. He'll only come rushing home and I could do without a husbandly hoo-ha right now. I hadn't mentioned I was going to see Alexandra's ex-boyfriend either.' A memory came into my mind. 'Oh, I've just remembered,

I was followed to Warminster by a black Merc. But I managed to lose it.'

I had given James my keys and he paused in unlocking the front door.

'When did you first notice it?'

'Not far from here. Just past the junction with the main road at the top of the village.'

'Did you get any details of this vehicle?'

'No, I was too busy getting rid of it.'

'And where do you reckon you shook it off?'

'On the outskirts of Warminster.'

'If it's relevant and not just a coincidence they might have had a good idea where you were heading to by then. And we mustn't forget that someone pretended to be your nanny saying she was ill. Did this man Kilmartin give you anything to eat or drink?'

'Yes, tea and biscuits. But look—'

Carrick interrupted with, 'Perhaps we ought to get some blood tests done on you.'

'But he was *lovely*. He hates Alexandra now.'

He grunted. 'You did get a threatening phone call from a man.'

'James, he has no *motive*. He said he wished he could help me. But he did give me directions of how to find the office from which the woman runs her agency.'

'OK, BUT DON'T GO THERE ALONE!'

Several small people, plus Carrie and Elspeth, then investigated why a policeman was bawling me out in the hall.

I was putting my feet up having given James his statement – although I could hardly remember

136

anything – aware that Elspeth had asked him to stay to dinner as he had mentioned that Joanna would not be at home, attending her Italian evening class. He had thanked her but said he intended to hoover their old farmhouse home while she was out to save her doing it so would leave straight away. I knew he was worried about her having another miscarriage and fully agreed with his intention for if there is one piece of household equipment born with a wish to kill you it is a vacuum cleaner.

Katie put her head around the open door. 'May I come in, Auntie?'

'Of course.' I patted the space beside me on the bed and she came and sat down.

'Is Uncle Patrick coming home now you're a bit hurt?'

'Probably, but I haven't told him yet.'

'Because he'll be cross about the car?'

'Sort of.'

'He'll be very glad you're not worse though.'

'That's true.'

'Did another car hit you?'

'No, apparently not. I can't remember exactly what happened.'

'That's quite usual. I read it in a book. In detective stories the bad men do something to cars and people go over cliffs. Only no one would want to do that to *you*.'

I wondered what she had been reading. If she was anything like me at that age it would be stuff that was rather ... unsuitable.

'I've been reading your books,' Katie said all at once in the manner of someone keen to get

137

what might be thought of as a transgression off their chest.

'They're not really meant for people quite so young as you,' I pointed out but feeling ridiculously chuffed. Other writers whom I have met have grumbled that their offspring, without even picking up a volume, regard their work as though engraved on stone ·tablets, hopelessly outmoded. Either that or 'difficult'.

'I read *A Man Called Celeste*. Is he Uncle Patrick?'

'Yes, he is – with a few small changes.' Ye gods, what had she made of the somewhat steamy love-making?

This question and answer was having almost the same effect on me as driving the car off a road at Limpley Stoke. *A Man Called Celeste*: a tale written when Patrick and I had got together again and I was very, very much in love with him. I suppose delayed shock caught up with me then because I burst into tears. I became aware of a small arm around me.

'Shall I ask Grandma to phone him?'

I sat up and made a fairish attempt to dry my tears. 'No, I think I'd better do it, thank you.'

'Auntie, I know Mum's still alive but...'

She is, in and out of treatment for her drug addiction in York. We monitor the situation and recently had not been disappointed to discover that she wanted nothing more to do with her children. At one time she had tried to gain custody of them purely in an attempt to get her hands on jewellery and a very valuable old watch left to them by their father.

'What, Katie?'

'Can I, or rather Matthew and I, call you Mum? We feel a bit sort of outside because Justin and Vicky do. And then we'll have a Dad again too. That's if Uncle—'

This was something we had never pushed, not even mentioned, because they had loved their father dearly and his death had been an enormous blow to them.

'Of course you may,' I replied, giving her a big hug and shedding a few more tears.

'I'll ask him though,' Katie said decidedly. 'Not just ... do it.'

The problem with living with both the young and the getting on in life is that they all worry about you far too much. I increased the dose of the painkillers slightly and discovered after a short while that I could move around fairly normally, using the comparative freedom from aches and pains to shower and wash my hair. I still had not told Patrick what had happened, which was daft of course as he rang shortly afterwards to find out how Carrie was. Elspeth, who was cooking everyone's dinner on her beloved Rayburn in the rectory kitchen, took the call.

'Ingrid, I think *you'd* better speak to Patrick,' she called up the stairs as I was preparing to descend.

'What's up?' he asked when I had picked up the phone in the bedroom. 'What's happened? Mum sort of clammed up.'

Pathetically, I was shaking and wanted to cry

139

again. 'Carrie's fine,' I said. 'It was a hoax.'

'And?' he demanded to know, aware that there was more to tell.

'I've pranged the car,' I managed to get out.

'Are you all right?'

'Just a bit bruised.'

'What happened?'

'I don't know. I can't remember. It left the road near Limpley Stoke. I must have dozed off.'

'Is is badly damaged?'

'I only know for sure that the windscreen's broken but it must be. James had it taken away for examination.'

'Why, for God's sake?'

'You're shouting at me.'

'No, I'm not. It's only just been serviced.'

Well, yes, I wanted to say, James knows we look after it and we're careful drivers and have been on all kinds of off-road and handling courses as the vehicle could save our lives in a tight corner. I could have reminded him that I must be the only woman in the world who has driven across a field as fast as a horse gallops and then jumped a three-foot high stone wall, albeit a broken down one, in a Discovery and everything survived. I wanted to say all these things and that Carrick was taking the matter seriously but could not, helplessly weeping instead and quietly putting down the phone.

I was not hungry after all, apologized to Elspeth and went to bed, not to sleep but to torture myself with the thought that Patrick and Alexandra were in a bar somewhere – he had not come home – she commiserating with him over the damage done to his beloved motor by his silly wife, giving him go-to-bed-eyes, turning him into any man in the street.

At nine thirty the phone rang. It was James Carrick.

'You had no brake fluid,' was his opening remark.

'But it's only just been serviced.'

'No, I mean there was none left. The brake pipes had all been holed so it leaked slowly away. And when you got to that steep stretch of road ... I'm surprised they lasted as long as they did.'

'I tend to use the gears to slow vehicles down.'

'That might be why then. You didn't see an oily-looking patch under the vehicle when you got back in it?'

'It was raining buckets. Oh, and there was a drain. I noticed it as I have a horror of dropping my car keys down one.'

'Anyway, we have a crime on our hands. I did look up that female in records, by the way. Nothing.'

'She's probably never actually broken the law then.'

'Except for a drink-driving charge from the time we first met when it hits court,' he re-collected succinctly. 'There's nothing to connect her with what happened to you but bear with me – I'm working on it. Be careful and stick closely with that man of yours. I'll have a word with him if he's handy.'

'Sorry, he isn't.'

'He didn't come home?'

'No.'

He said something vivid-sounding in Gaelic – James nearly always swears in Gaelic – told me to rest and rang off.

I lay there trying to remember what had happened. Although fully aware that it was not unusual for those involved in accidents to suffer from temporary amnesia it made the whole episode all the more upsetting. And all I seemed to have done recently was to get upset.

'No, as I suspected, it's me who's lost their edge,' I whispered into the night. 'I've been raging around, crying all over him and generally behaving like an idiot. Come to think of it, I've almost driven him into her arms.'

OK, I asked myself, what would a newly honed and reborn Ingrid Langley do now then?

Make like Lara Croft and go and blow Alexandra's bloody head off, that's what.

'No, no,' I keened. 'Something *intelligent.*'

At which point I must have fallen asleep for the next thing I knew was someone coming into the bedroom.

'Stop right there!' I ordered.

'It's me,' Patrick's voice said.

I switched on the bedside lamp.

'Please calm down,' he said, eyeing the Glock.

'Sorry, I'm a bit twitched right now.' I shoved it back under the pillow.

He was still gazing at me, appalled, and then remembered to close the door.

'I didn't want to leave it in the vehicle so asked James to fetch it from the cubby box before it was taken away. I had to give him the security code.'

'You look terrible,' he blurted out.

'It's only superficial.'

'But the dressing on the side of your face...'

'Just where a biggish smallish splinter went into my cheek.'

He came to sit on the other side of the bed and in the brighter light I saw that his face was pale and drawn and he was very tired.

'James told me exactly what he thought of me.'

'Oh?'

'Some of it was Gaelic so I guessed there weren't any suitably filthy English equivalents. But I got the general drift.'

This from someone with a Master's degree in Creative Swearing.

'He was right. I should have come home as soon as you'd told me what had happened.'

'Someone had holed the brake pipes. James told me since we spoke.'

He took my right hand, raised it to his lips and kissed it. 'Yes, he told me too. Thank God the vehicle hit the trees.'

'We shall have to go and see the woman who's garden they're in.'

'Yes.' Then, 'I saw Alexandra earlier on tonight.'

I made no comment.

'She rang me to say she was back in London and how about a drink. I told her you'd gone home as the nanny was ill and she said what a shame and we could make it dinner. I played along but suggested something in a pub instead

143

as I was pushed for time. When you and I discussed this before, you remember, I did say I'd have to stay friendly with her if I was to find out anything. We met, had a snack and over coffee I told her about your threatening phone call and she said it must have been Alan Kilmartin who was still madly in love with her after all and was jealous. I got his mobile number from her before I asked her how the hell he knew yours. I knew the answer of course because you'd already told me but wanted to make her admit it. She did and I told her exactly what I thought of her and walked out – leaving her to pay the bill.'

'He loathes her,' I said, inwardly whooping with joy.

'I know. I rang him and said I was checking up on Alex and he told me you'd been to see him. He felt guilty that he hadn't warned you that she could be dangerous if crossed. He sounds a very nice bloke.'

'Plus being the most glorious-looking man imaginable.'

Predictably, this rolled over Patrick's head. 'Then James phoned and gave me an earful, plus the news of the car having been meddled with. I've come home to apologize for being a shit.'

'You're not really a shit.'

'I am.' He kissed my cheek, gingerly, in case everything hurt and then said, 'I've got to go back in the morning as this Capelli thing's really hotting up.'

'What time is it?'

'Just after one thirty. I caught the last train.'

144

'Are you hungry?'

'Starving.'

'So am I. If you hold my hand as we go down the stairs I'll raid the fridge for something.'

'*I'll* raid the fridge. You stay here in the warm.'

'I quite fancy a glass of wine.'

'Do you reckon it would kill me to have a taste?'

'Hardly.'

'I admit I got a bit besotted with her when she turned up again,' Patrick said when we had mostly finished an already opened bottle of Chablis with our cold roast chicken and salad. 'Male pride. She made me feel good when I was as good as crippled.'

'That's not pride,' I told him. 'It's perfectly normal human nature.'

'I simply couldn't see what you were on about. All I could think of was how she'd cheered me up when everything was black, made me feel there was a future for me after all.' He pulled a wry face. 'She didn't used to be a bitch.'

'Why did you break up?'

'Mostly because I hadn't got my confidence back and kept chickening out of sleeping with her. Also, I found out she was seeing a married man.'

I cleared my throat in exaggerated fashion.

'OK, she was a bitch then too.'

'You were on your own though as I'd chucked you out, hadn't I?'

'But that was before I was blown up. You took me back when I was still as good as crippled.

145

Did you feel sorry for me?'

I had, deeply. But that was not the entire reason prior to falling in love with him again. 'No,' I said. 'You were still dead sexy even with a bad limp.'

He poured the rest of the wine into my glass.

# TEN

Michael Greenway called at six forty-five the next morning and asked me how I was.

'Slightly dented in places,' I told him, dying to say that a little more sleep would have been nice.

'Only I was wondering if you were well enough to come up with Patrick and give us the benefit of your expertise. No rushing about,' he added hastily. 'Nothing energetic.'

'Will it be all right if we catch an afternoon train?' I queried, eyeing the normally light-sleeping man at my side who was dead to the world. 'I shall feel stronger by then.'

'Of course. Travel first class if it'll make it easier for you. Have you found out what caused you to leave the road?'

'Yes, someone had messed around with the brakes.'

There was a shocked silence. Then Greenway said, 'That's serious. We must talk about it. Oh, I double-checked that name you gave me. Nothing showed up.'

I thanked him. The sooner someone had a good poke around in that architectural monstrosity in Boyles Road, Kensington, the better.

An hour or so later, when I was dozing, there was a light knock at the door.

'We thought you'd like this,' Katie said, deeply concentrating on a mug of tea.

'If you watch where you're going instead of the mug you won't spill it,' I whispered. 'I hope someone else poured the boiling water into the pot for you.'

She passed it over and then caught sight of Patrick. 'Oh! I didn't know ... Yes, Matthew did. I told him how to.'

Quite right too.

'Shall I get some for ... Uncle as well?'

There were two questions here and one of them was sufficiently important to warrant waking him as Katie would be off to school very shortly and we were returning to London.

I prodded Patrick gently.

'I'm awake,' he said, muffled. 'Yes, please.'

She came straight out with it. 'Can Matthew and I call you Dad? Auntie's said we can call her Mum.'

Patrick surfaced. 'That's a shatteringly splendid kind of present to give someone when they've just woken up,' he said. 'Of course. Thank you.'

Katie wriggled gleefully, was hugged and kissed and went away to fetch the tea. She was yelling the news to her brother before she reached the bottom of the stairs.

Patrick grinned at me. 'I still have to remind

147

myself sometimes that I've *five* children. I really hope you're still on the pill.'

'Absolutely.'

'It might be deliberate smoke and mirrors tactics but it *looks* as though they're aiming to raid a jeweller's in an arcade in Regent Street followed by a lightning strike at West End Central nick on the way out,' Mike Greenway said, before we had even seated ourselves in his office, having caught a train just after midday. And then to me, 'I'm worried about your prang. Is it in connection with this woman you mentioned, do you think?'

'There's a good chance it is,' I replied. 'She has a man called Stefan working for her. I don't know his surname.'

'We're talking about a one-yob female here, I think,' Patrick said.

'What the hell's she after?'

'Me.'

A meaningful forefinger was pointed at Patrick. '*You* sort this out. It's private and the department can't get involved.'

'Yes, sir,' Patrick said. 'Besides which, DCI Carrick is investigating as it happened on his patch. I'll liaise closely with him.'

Which was a neat and tactful way of reminding his boss that a crime had actually been committed.

'Good,' Greenway grunted.

I gathered that there had been some kind of conciliatory phone call between Patrick and James, instigated by the latter, but had not asked

148

for details and the episode was not openly talked about again.

'Now then,' the Commander said, dropping into the leather revolving chair behind his desk, setting it creaking alarmingly. 'As Baldrick says, I have a cunning plan. There are other departments on board as well so I can't take all the credit even though it was my idea. We're going to release Martino Capelli from prison – late this afternoon.'

Patrick whistled softly.

'He was due out soon anyway and I'm delighted to bounce him into it. I'm hoping it'll have the effect of a cat among the pigeons as I'm banking on him not knowing that his dear cousin's arrived in the UK.'

'And who would know the man's real identity anyway?' Patrick commented.

'It might just mean that this plan of theirs is aborted, temporarily anyway.'

I said, 'There's every chance that Martino's stationed someone to keep an eye on Irma though – to see what she gets up to. The rear stairs up to the flat are in full view. Even the man in the chippy below was able to watch her movements.'

'Did he actually used to live there with her or was the flat just for her use?' Patrick asked.

'Yes, according to the Met he seemed to be around for most of the time.'

'I'm surprised he didn't move her out. He must have known the place would be watched by the law.'

'Pass, but some of these people aren't half as

149

clever as they think they are. By the way, about that slug that just missed the pair of you ... It was sent off to NaBIS, the National Ballistics Intelligence Service, which in case you don't know, is—'

'The Met opened the Southern hub fairly recently, I understand,' Patrick smoothly interrupted.

'Right, you do know. It's from some kind of shitty Italian-made weapon. As I'm sure you're also aware the Italians don't normally make anything shitty in that direction but these are thought to be knocked up somewhere like a village garage, possibly by the Mafia, and are used in booby-trap devices such as those carved dragons. Apparently they've been come across before and it's been known for them to be concealed in more ordinary items of furniture. They quite often malfunction and blow apart, doing far more damage than might be expected.'

'We're not exactly sure *who* installed that one in the flat either,' Patrick mused.

'Martino might be in for a few surprises if there are more.'

There was not a lot we could do with this particular case at present – police work always involves a lot of waiting around – so Patrick got on with something else; a few telephone enquiries for Greenway. I am not one to sit around twiddling my thumbs either but the Commander as good as told me to rest in an adjacent room that he uses on rare moments when he can unwind for a few minutes. I decided to find out if there were any developments in the Case of the Body in the House I Dearly Wanted to Buy.

'You must be telepathic!' James exclaimed. 'I was just about to give you a wee phone.'

This always makes me laugh and he had said it deliberately, the pair of us gently amused by the west of Scotland expression; the request in a hairdressers or some other place where one might have to wait for a few minutes invariably being, 'Take a wee seat.'

After asking after my bumps and bruises he went on, 'We've probably found both the murder weapon and the knife used to remove the head.'

'Oh, well done! Where?'

'You may remember that there's a substantial wall at the end of the garden of the property, around seven or eight feet in height. Beyond is the end of another garden belonging to a big house in the next road which until yesterday was very overgrown. This was searched at the time of the discovery of the body and I got permission to clear some of the waist-high weeds over there. We found nothing. Whether this reminded the owner of the place that his patch was in a bit of a mess I don't know but he got some contractors in to do a proper job. After a load of stuff was cleared and they'd exposed the mature trees a plastic bag was spotted hitched in one of the lower branches. In it was a kitchen knife with a twelve-inch serrated blade, the kind I think are used to carve up still-frozen food, that still had visible bloodstains on it, together with an old police truncheon. Really old, I mean, an antique.

151

I've sent the details and a photograph to the Metropolitan Police Historical Collection to see if they can come up with anything about it.'

'It might even have someone's name on it,' I said.

'You're right, not that anything like that was obvious as it was green with mould after all this time.'

'Did you manage to locate the victim's car? You said a set of keys were in her bag.'

'No, but it could be one of any number of burnt-out wrecks that are dealt with every year.'

Then, rightly or wrongly, I told him what was happening at our end.

'You might end up with a large Italian-style turf war on your hands,' he remarked.

'I reckon Mike Greenway thinks that if it prevents the risk of innocent people getting hurt in a jewellery raid and a nick getting shot up then it's worth it.'

'I quite agree. You always want any incidental damage to happen to the mobsters. Let's just hope they hold it indoors.'

That was a good point, one that I raised when I next saw Patrick.

'We can only ring the place with undercover armed police,' he said. 'And I don't think anyone's expecting much to happen for a while. Not only that, Tony Capelli can't have many supporters over here.'

And Martino's followers were unpaid, intimidated, resentful? I was not too sure who they would support when it came to the crunch. Not only that, I had an idea Tony Capelli could

152

charm vultures out of trees and rats out of sewers if he thought he could use them.

'So what's your role in all this?' I wanted to know.

'Chief inquisitor of those left standing,' Patrick answered crisply and went away again.

I decided that I was not needed right now and was suffering from a lack of fresh air. Kensington would do nicely.

Boyles Road was not as bad as Alan Kilmartin had said it was although it might have been smartened up since he was last there, presumably when he was still going out with Alexandra. In light rain I walked up and down it, first on one side and then the other. (The painkillers were working amazingly well provided I took them every three and a bit hours instead of four: I'm convinced pharmaceutical companies build in leeway to their dosage instructions specially for people like me.) There was no doubt in my mind as to which building he had referred, a concrete edifice that resembled a dirty cardboard box that had been stood on end and lightly stamped on.

I glanced down the names of the businesses and so forth listed on a sign by the entrance. There was nothing with the name Nightingale included, which was a nuisance. It was not lost on me that she might be working within the building right now, had already spotted me from a window and sent Stefan down to warn me off. It was a risk I would have to take. The problem was that there were hardly any other people about who *might* come to my aid if things turned nasty. Another snag was the notice that said all visitors must register upon entry and be issued with a pass.

Postponing making a decision about going in through the front entrance I went instead through a wide gateway at the side of the building into a car park. The focal point at the rear, which was, if anything, more hideous than the front, was a row of plastic refuse bins in different colours barely discernible through the dirt on them. By a doorway, I saw when I got closer, were several boxes loaded with empty wine and spirit bottles. Perhaps Alexandra had had a bit of a turn out. Another, wider, entrance seemed to be the one that was mainly used. I went in and found myself at the bottom of a concrete staircase with a couple of lifts on one side. The sheer dreariness of the place seemed to settle around me like a weight in the air.

'Lookin' for someone, luv?' asked a man from a small room, more like a large cupboard really, that appeared to contain cleaning materials.

'Is Stefan here?' I asked, flattening my vowels to fit the part I intended to play.

'Not sure but 'e's so busy running errands for 'er ladyship these days 'e 'ardly ever shows up to do 'is real job. 'E's goin' to git 'is marchin' orders soon, you mark my words. Er – you a friend of 'is?'

I shook my head. 'No.'

The man, who had several days' growth of stubble, bloodshot eyes, not much in the way of teeth, grinned knowingly. 'Like that is it?'

'Like that,' I agreed. 'He owes me money.'

154

'Forget it, luv, ya don't stand a chance. If I was you I'd stay right away from 'im.'

I feigned acute disappointment. 'Is her ladyship here? He calls her that too.'

'We all do. Same place as usual, third floor, room fifteen.'

'Stefan told me she runs a domestic agency.'

'She does. Dodgy though.'

'What's dodgy about it?'

Again the furtive looking around. 'Well, from what people have said, there's ... add-ons,' he whispered hoarsely.

'Add-ons?'

'Just lately. I don't know nuffin', mind.'

'No, of course not.'

'Someone said some of the wimmin do ... other things. Not just cleanin' an' stuff like that.'

'You mean it's some kind of escort agency?'

'Yus, only ... wus.'

'Worse? So, in other words she runs a brothel?'

He turned and gave his attention to a vacuum cleaner in the cupboard. 'Her and others. I'm not sayin' no more. An' you didn't hear it from me. I just told ya to make sure you keep right away from Stefan. He's bad news, all right. To wimmin. You might just get ... drawn in.'

'Where do these women come from?'

A shrug. 'All over.'

The outer door banged and we both started.

'How's life, Fred?' called a well-dressed man before making for the lifts and without waiting for an answer.

'Fine, thanks, sir,' Fred called in response. And then to me in a whisper, 'Forget the money, ya

155

won't get it.'

'Do you know if her ladyship's in the building?'

'No, she ain't. She said sommink about lookin' for an 'ouse.'

I returned to the front and was in luck: quite a large group of women exited the building, the high heels of more inside clattering on the stairs. Most were carrying briefcases and all had in their possession a large red folder. I waited until there was a gap in the egress and went in. There was a security guard, more like a janitor really, in a small office just inside the door, picking his teeth.

'Forgot my folder,' I told him breezily.

He just gave me a sour look.

I took one of the lifts to the third floor. I had not been able to see any CCTV screens in the doorman's office but they could have simply been around a corner somewhere. People came and went in the large open-plan area with seating that I emerged into but no one took any notice of me. Following signs I walked down a corridor, found room fifteen and at that point my cat's whiskers completely freaked out. This was something along the lines of Fred having been bribed, threatened, or cajoled to direct all nosy parkers asking for Alexandra, or Stefan, to the third floor, room fifteen. There, if they broke in, they would be gassed, poisoned, sprayed with acid and/or generally incapacitated, the real business operation being on another floor entirely.

Telling myself that it was merely my writer's

156

imagination going berserk I nevertheless decided against using Patrick's burglars' keys to open the door right then and was just moving away when my mobile rang.

'Where are you?' Patrick said.

'I did leave you a note,' I replied.

'Yes, you intimated that you were popping out but didn't say where.'

'I'm in Kensington.'

'Oh, shopping. There's been a hitch. The prison service won't release Capelli until tomorrow at the earliest. The usual rubbish; haven't received the right forms authorizing it. Mike's chuntering but he can't do anything about it and has told me to knock off for the day. Did you book anywhere to stay?'

'Sorry, no, I forgot.'

'I'll see if I can get us in at the usual place. Shall I meet you there?'

'You know how much you miss the excitement of working for MI5?'

'What's that got to do with anything?'

'And Mike's told you to sort out this business of Alexandra?'

'Yes, but not right *now.*'

'I'm standing outside the office that I've been told she operates from. Only I'm not sure that she does.'

'Where the hell is this?' Patrick asked, in quite a different tone of voice.

'Boyles Road, Kensington. It's actually called Boyles House.'

'Get yourself *out* of the place. Is that understood?' he said furiously.

'OK.' I never argue when he speaks like this.

'If you don't phone me back in under exactly five minutes I shall get the cops over there. Walk to the end of the road nearest to the main shopping centre and I'll meet you there in a taxi.'

The line went dead.

I looked up and a man was striding down the corridor towards me. He was not Stefan but nevertheless had a big bad snarl on his face.

Once upon a time, a long time ago and after I had promised to love, honour and obey, I received, perhaps in late compensation for the last of these vows and as a thank-you for having him back, a self-preservation package from Patrick to use on such occasions as this. The training, deliberately conducted on an afternoon when an elderly and nervous neighbour was out, left the pair of us totally exhausted and not speaking to one another for several hours. On my part this was because I was aching all over, on Patrick's that I had put my all into it and he had gone head over heels into the dining room table, stunning himself.

In a few words, the main idea is this; look terrified, cringe and whimper and then, when they're closing in, the snarl having changed to a relaxed and superior smirk, you hit them with everything you've got, right where they live. Patrick had shown me – and it had probably made him a traitor to his sex – *exactly* how to do this. It is not pretty.

I phoned Patrick in just under the five minutes, by this time walking along Boyles Road towards the junction with what was the far end of Kensington High Street. No, half running actually, convinced that the man could be not far behind me. But, glancing over my shoulder I could not see him. Again, hardly anyone was around, in vehicles, or on foot.

'Is there a pub or shop that's still open?' he asked curtly on receipt of the news that a man had attacked me, obviously speaking, because of the background sounds, in a taxi.

'Not quite at the end of the road yet,' I panted.

'Make for somewhere like that and call me as soon as you arrive.'

Hurrying, desperate to get somewhere where there were plenty of people, I was more than aware of my limitations. I badly needed to take more of the painkillers, the exertion of the past few minutes having reawakened all the reminders of the 'accident'.

I was within fifty yards of the junction when a car roared up behind me and stopped a short distance ahead. A man got out and ran back. This time it was the man I had seen Alexandra with in Bath, Stefan.

'I'll do the same to you as I did to him!' I yelled.

He took no notice and even though I jinked and tried to dodge around him, grabbed me by one arm. He let go when I swung round with the other and hit him, close-fisted, on the side of the nose, following it up with a kick to the kidney region as he half turned away. Then I ran. Feet thumped behind me.

On the corner of the road was a pub. I hurled

159

myself into it, first door, and found myself in the kitchen; blokes, steam, frying, shouts of 'Oi!' Erupting out of this I shot along a passageway. No, don't go into the ladies' or the gents' loos because they are potential dead-ends, traps. Keep moving. Another door and that was where I came face to face with him, he having come in through another entrance.

We faced one another, breathing hard, in the saloon bar.

'You're making a real fool of yourself,' I said. 'All these people watching.'

Well, two men and a fox terrier actually.

The presence of an audience did not appear to put Stefan off and he lunged at me. I jumped to one side, grabbed a full ice bucket from the bar and threw it. It hit him in the chest and ice cubes clattered into everything. I did not stay around to watch the resultant figure skating, just ran like hell through the public bar next door, regrettably jogging one drinker as he raised a full tankard to his lips resulting in him getting a beer tsunami. I thought about diving up a staircase to what was obviously private accommodation to give me a chance to phone but tore on: it was probably the only access and, again, I might become trapped up there.

Outside, the street was busy. I ran on, fuelled by adrenalin alone but rapidly running out of puff. Somewhere in my wake, and even over the traffic I could hear rapid footfalls. Huge office blocks, long boundary walls, churches and flats serenely flowed by while I pounded on. Then I saw an Italian wine bar around a hundred yards ahead and put everything I had into getting there.

Shockingly, I was suddenly grabbed from behind and hauled to a standstill. I screamed when another hand seized me by the hair. Countering this by going completely limp I slid to the ground, my hair being excruciatingly pulled even more but I clutched him round both shins and hung on. He overbalanced and crashed to the pavement.

No passers-by took the slightest notice. Not even when I had extricated myself, scrambled to my feet and aimed a kick at the last place he needed it. He moved and I caught him on the thigh instead. There was nothing for it but to run again, and I swerved through a narrow gap into a tiny tree-lined square praying he had not spotted where I had gone.

The only thing to hide behind was a large bush. It turned out to be several bushes with a gap in the middle that was filled with empty bottles, drinks cans and heaven alone knew what else. I stopped looking too hard but watched out for the used syringes.

Ye gods, if I carried on panting like this, like a steam train, he would hear me.

I found my mobile and rang Patrick's number.

'Where are you?' he asked, not for the first time that afternoon.

'In a bush, in a little park in Kensington High Street,' I whispered. 'Near The Unicorn pub. Stefan's after me.'

'Near The Unicorn? I know it. Stay right where you are!'

'I can't. He's right behind me.'

'I know it!' someone roared in the background. 'Go back there!'

'Go back there,' Patrick repeated.

Fine, go back there.

Someone was quietly patrolling around the outside of the bushes.

I picked up a handy half a brick and peered through the leaves but the greenery was too thick to see anything. So I listened instead, trying to work out where he was. This proved to be fairly impossible too. There was nothing for it but to run and head for an exit I had noticed on the other side of the square and hope to find my way back to the pub using side roads.

At which point Stefan lunged into the bushes hoping to surprise me. Well, he did and because I was holding the brick high all ready to hit him on the head he ran straight into it, getting it right in the mouth, and then floundered over backwards into the vegetation. I flung the brick, hard, with both hands, in his general direction and then bolted.

My legs did not want to run any more but I goaded myself on, not daring to waste time in looking back. There was a maze of roads but I turned right and kept going, following my nose. Before very long this picked up the smell of stale beer. I was down to a walk by now and could hear no one following me although the general hum of traffic and my own gasping for breath made this virtually impossible.

The rear entrance to the pub was on a corner; wooden gates that led into a yard. They were wide open. I hardly noticed the silver-coloured car that was drawn up by the kerb nearby and did a nervous shimmy when a man put his head out of the driver's window and spoke to me.

'Slump down by the gateway,' Michael Greenway said softly. 'Make out you're finished.'

'I am,' I responded, knowing that I was to be the bait in the trap.

It was a huge relief just to flop there.

After a minute or so a woman came from a house across the street and looked down at me. 'Are you all right, dear?'

'It's OK, we're making a film!' Greenway shouted to her from his car.

She went away again.

No Stefan.

At least five minutes went by and then I heard a small movement from behind the other gate. Patrick appeared in my line of vision but not necessarily anyone else's in the road.

'Any sign of him?'

'No.'

'Show me where you last saw him.'

'You'll have to pick me up first.'

# ELEVEN

We were able to go most of the way in the car and found blood and a knocked out front tooth. Enterprisingly, the latter and a sample of the former were popped into an evidence bag by the Commander who then took us back to the pub where Patrick bought the still sopping but not particularly aggrieved imbiber another pint. However, it was Greenway who placed a gin and tonic in front of me, a subtlety that was not lost on the recipient. I asked him to fetch me a glass of water so I could take a couple of painkillers.

'She's a two-yob woman,' I said to Patrick. 'At least.'

He was still annoyed with me. 'Where did you come upon the other one then?'

'In Boyles House. I spoke to a man by the name of Fred who was some kind of cleaner. He either told someone else that I was asking questions or I was spotted.' The G and T was going down a treat.

'And?'

'And nothing. I left him on the floor. Your training and all that.'

Patrick began to thaw. 'What did he look like?'

'Like a smallish pub or club bouncer,' I replied after due thought. 'Broad shoulders, beer belly,

164

around five feet nine, shaven head but, like Fred, several days' growth of beard, dark eyes, bad teeth, piggy eyes. He was wearing dirty jeans and a once-white sweatshirt.'

'God, I wish all witnesses were that observant,' Greenway said under his breath. 'It might pay for you to look at some mugshots.'

Patrick said, 'And perhaps I'd better go and talk to this Fred.'

'He seems to think Alexandra's running a brothel,' I told him.

'We'd better make it a priority then – when I have the time.' He turned to his boss. 'Thank you, sir, for helping out. But as you said, this is nothing to do with SOCA.'

'Well ... no,' Greenway said slowly. 'But something dodgy's going on all right. We could get the Met involved.'

'I'd like to get a little more evidence and then, if it's appropriate, hand everything over to DCI Carrick and he can make that decision – if that's all right with you.'

'Delighted, as long as you don't use SOCA time to do it. It would help if we had a photo of this woman.'

'We have,' I remembered. 'Alexandra walked into shot when I was photographing the garden of the house in Bath from an upstairs window and I haven't deleted it.'

'Deal with it tomorrow,' Greenway decided. 'Can I give you a lift back to HQ so you can pick up your stuff?'

'So does anyone live in this building or is it just

165

offices?' Patrick asked me later when we had had something to eat.

'No idea. Although from the long list of outfits that operate from it I would have thought it is just an office block.'

'I think I'll go and have a look round.'

'I'll come with you.'

'I don't think you should. You're still not well.'

'No, but as you said yourself, I bring you luck.'

He did not appear to have an immediate answer to that.

It was a little after seven thirty as we approached Boyles House. We had taken a taxi to The Unicorn where Patrick had been hoping to ask the barman if he knew Stefan, his friends or anyone with whom he worked. Not surprisingly, different staff were behind the bar, mostly foreign students, so there seemed little point in questioning them.

There were plenty of lights still on in the building and as we got closer several people exited through the main doors. But we did not go in that way, making our way around the side as I had done when I had first arrived earlier that day. The rear door was closed and locked.

'It's a fire door,' Patrick muttered. He shook his head. 'No, my keys are no match for heavy-weights like this – it'll have to be the front. I wonder if there's...' He carried on walking around the outside of the building.

I looked around but there did not seem to be

166

any security cameras, only the things one might expect to find; fire hydrants, utility room-type windows with bars on them and oil tanks, plus a lot of litter that had obviously been blown there and accumulated over the years. Stairs that led down to a basement were noted in passing. Then Patrick stopped, scenting the air like an animal. Even I could smell it; cigarette smoke.

Ahead a short distance away a wall around six feet high jutted out from the building. We silently approached and peered around the corner. It proved to be one of two and actually formed a porch around a doorway. This was ajar, smoke visibly emerging. There was a dim light within and I could hear voices. Patrick jerked his head and we went back to the basement entrance.

His keys soon unlocked it but the door was immovable: it was bolted on the inside.

'Plan Z,' Patrick whispered, locking everything up again.

'Which is?' I asked.

'Bluff our way in through the front.'

'There was a doorman who saw me,' I recollected.

'It might not be the same one now. Can you describe him?'

'Thin, round-shouldered, sallow complexion, dark, greasy, receding hair.'

'I'll go in alone if there's any doubt.'

A large black man wearing a smart uniform was taking the air on the front steps.

'Good evening,' Patrick called. 'Have you seen Stefan?'

167

The security guard nodded with a big smile on his face. 'You want him?'

'Yes, I was hoping to knock his block off, actually.'

A bigger grin. 'Someone already has, man.'

'D'you know where he is now?'

'He said something about getting his teeth fixed.'

'D'you know where he lives?'

'No, sorry.'

We went up the steps and Patrick said, 'My wife was visiting an office on the third floor this afternoon when she was attacked by a man whom it would appear is a friend of Stefan's. Although we both work for the Serious Organized Crime Agency,' and here he produced his warrant card, 'I can't investigate this officially as it is, at present anyway, outside our remit. But as you might imagine, I'm as mad as hell about it and I would very much like to have a look around up there.'

The man shrugged. 'If you've got an ID card that says you're anything to do with the police, mister, then as far as I'm concerned you can have a nose round the whole place. Help yourself. But please don't tell anyone I said that.'

'And I'd appreciate your not saying a word either.'

'What did this character look like?' asked the guard.

I gave him the man's description.

He pondered. 'Can't say as I know him. But there's hundreds of folk here during the day and I'm only around at night.'

We thanked him and went in. While this conversation was taking place I had again scanned the list of companies and organizations with offices in the building but nothing had been listed as located in room fifteen on the third floor. This was not in itself suspicious but did suggest a desire to keep a low profile.

We went up in the lift, the thought going through my mind that all security staff might have been bribed or threatened to report to certain people the presence of strangers asking questions. It had probably occurred to Patrick too, a swift glance in his direction revealing that he had tensed, his jaw taut, ready for anything.

Nothing appeared to be amiss as we emerged from the lift. Without speaking, I indicated which way we should go and we made our way across the open space and along the corridor. Other than for the hum of distant machinery it was quiet: this floor, at least, appeared to be unoccupied. We reached room fifteen.

'I think Fred was lying,' I said. 'Sorry, I should have mentioned this before.'

Patrick was eyeing up the door locks. 'Nothing too complicated here – very cheap and nasty actually. Lying?'

'Yes, well, he must have told someone I was around, mustn't he? I don't think she operates from here.'

'It might have been a coincidence and that bloke was merely checking in at HQ.'

'And this room might be a cupboardful of nasty surprises.'

Patrick straightened and gazed at me but did

not deride the suggestion, gently remarking, 'What with gun-carrying dragons and people messing with the car you've had more than your fair share of nasty surprises lately. But I doubt she has the wherewithal for that kind of thing.'

'No, but she employs pretty revolting blokes,' I pointed out.

He smiled. 'Do I up the security level to Red Alert then?'

'Don't say I didn't warn you,' I retorted primly.

With his keys he opened the door, turned the handle and pushed the door back as far as it would go. It was dark inside: there did not appear to be any windows in the room. Patrick carefully felt around for light switches, found one, and stood back quickly after he had clicked it down.

The room, around twelve feet square, was completely empty, not even a waste-paper basket. There was another door in the opposite wall. We went into the first room after Patrick had checked behind the door and looked around but there was absolutely nothing to see. He then walked round it tapping the walls, some of which sounded hollow.

'This is just a thin partition, little more than hardboard,' he said, standing over by the wall with the door in it. 'And so is that.' He waved in the direction of the one on his left.

'Perhaps that's how the place is divided up,' I said.

'You should have stud walls, proper wooden frames with plasterboard nailed to them. Let's see what's...'

Strong wrists wielded the keys again. The second room was in darkness as well: no daylight whatsoever. An unpleasant stale smell, like drains, only worse, wafted out. Patrick could find no light switch so he dug in his pocket for his torch. It is not designed for large-scale illumination but by the tiny beam we could see that the room was quite large and fitted out with several bunk beds.

'Stay there,' Patrick said and went in.

He roamed around for a couple of minutes, tapping on the walls in here too.

'The window's been boarded over,' he called across to me. 'I think you can come in but please don't touch anything. I must be getting it from you but there's a bad feeling in here.'

It was a horrible feeling. The little pencil of light picked out the soiled bedding, discarded bloodstained clothing, other filthy strips of cloth, scraps of food, rubbish everywhere. The stench right inside the room was ghastly.

'This is a prison,' I said.

'You may well be right.'

'There only seems to be women's clothing.'

'People trafficking?'

I felt sick. Why did I think women had been raped in here?

Patrick swung the torch around. There was a side room. This was not locked and the source of most of the smell; at least seven buckets filled with human excrement.

I fled for the outer door, retching.

'To the fag smokers,' Patrick said grimly,

171

catching up with me after relocking both doors. 'No, on second thoughts, I'll go alone as Fred's seen you before and he might be one of them. If I end up pulverizing him I don't want you involved.'

'I'd rather be in scream-shot, if you don't mind,' I told him. 'It's not as though we have the car here and I don't want to hang around outside.'

'OK, just stay out of sight.'

We exited the building, waving to the security guard and went round the back again. By this time it was getting dark and I reckoned myself just about invisible if I waited behind one of the malodorous rubbish bins. Patrick went on ahead with the air of a man with a real grievance. All was quiet for a couple of minutes and then I heard him shouting.

'Health and Safety at Work Executive!' he yelled. 'It's been reported that people are smoking within this prohibited area!'

There was a muted crash as though someone's chair had fallen over backwards, taking them with it, not surprising as when Patrick really shouts everything within a fifty-yard radius tends to judder. He went on talking, speaking a little more quietly but not much. I could tell that he was taking names and addresses interspersed with dire warnings of prosecution.

After all had gone quiet I peeped around my bin and saw him coming back, putting his notebook back in his jacket pocket.

'There's no guarantee they gave me their genuine details,' he said, unerringly coming to where I was. 'But they can all be put in the file. There was no one who fitted Fred's description there.'

'That was a good move,' I said. 'We don't want anyone involved with whatever's going on in that room to know we're on to them.'

'But they're aware that you were sniffing around and they failed to catch you. If Alex has anything to do with it she already knows we're with SOCA so for God's sake don't do any more lone sleuthing. OK?'

'OK. But it served its purpose, didn't it? – getting you to take my suspicions seriously.'

'I'm sure I don't have to tell you that there's absolutely no evidence to connect what you found to Alexandra Nightingale,' James Carrick pointed out. 'Having said that, there would appear to be some connection in that the man by the name of Fred told Ingrid that's where the woman has her office, which is where you discovered the room that sounds as though it's been used as a prison.'

It was the next morning, we were at SOCA's HQ in the office Patrick uses when he is there, sometimes having to share it with someone else, and he was talking to the DCI on his mobile. I had my head on his shoulder, eavesdropping.

He said, 'Fred's not very bright and probably should have kept his trap shut but I would guess that the first room is kept empty as a ploy to make people think nothing's going on there. It's actually rather feeble but might work with casual enquirers. What do you want me to do

173

with the names and addresses I took?'

'This is a real can of worms and I'm very concerned that young women might have been removed from the place and are being held somewhere else,' Carrick replied. 'Since you rang me last night I've been on to a couple of ex-colleagues in the Met who deal with people trafficking and prostitution and they told me that most of that kind of thing, especially where it's regarded as being big organized crime, is handed over to your lot. Otherwise it'll have to be reported to the Met. I suggest you sound out Mike Greenway and give him your info before I do anything else in case connections can be made with stuff people are already working on. My bit of it's really only involved with Ingrid's incident at Limpley Stoke. Oh, by the way, you can have the car back.'

'It must be a write-off surely,' Patrick said in surprise.

'I doubt it. The windscreen's smashed and there are a couple of small dents on the wings but otherwise, other than the damaged brakes, it seems OK. D'you want me to get a Land Rover expert to give it the once-over?'

It was agreed that Patrick would arrange with the garage where the vehicle is serviced, not far from home, that they would collect it thus freeing James from any further bother.

Greenway was deeply involved with the Capelli case but receptive to what Patrick had to say; that is, he gave him ten minutes. I stayed in the office, calling the garage, updating our insurance company and checking that all was well at home: just because I am a consultant it does not mean I have to be in on everything.

I felt better today. A few bruises, mostly hidden by my clothes, had ripened nicely but the wound on my cheek was healing well and I had been able to leave off the dressing. Otherwise I was still relying on the painkillers, but at least was down to a 'legal' dose. Other ills, my marriage, could be described as no longer 'dangerously ill' and now 'stable'.

Greenway referred the information Patrick had given him, plus the names and addresses, to his second-in-command, Andrew Bayley, who undertook to deal with it as soon as he possibly could. There were certain parallels to cases already being investigated, he said; young women lured to this country with offers of good jobs in domestic service and similar, only to be imprisoned in inner city apartment blocks and other such buildings. Gang-raped and forced to become drug addicts they were then sold into prostitution. Bayley also said that he would contact James Carrick.

At present anyway, this was as far as Patrick's and my responsibility lay as the Capelli business had to be given absolute priority.

Martino Capelli left prison and, twenty-four hours later, nothing had happened. I knew that Patrick, for one, was keen to stir the brew gently, famous, or otherwise, in our MI5 days for 'making things happen'. Greenway was impatient too and at five in the afternoon on the second day of Capelli's freedom he called a meeting.

175

'Any suggestions?' he asked, having briefly run though events so far and after there had been some general discussion.

I gazed around the room, the one adjacent to the Commander's office. Other than Greenway, Patrick and I there were present a trio from the Met I had not met before, the man running the surveillance on the flat in Romford and another two involved with the operation to thwart Martino Capelli's jewellery raid and subsequent strike on West End Central police station. There was one development in connection with this; the jewellery shop to be targeted was heavily rumoured to be Hinchcliffe and Atterberry's, in an arcade off Regent Street.

Patrick asked, 'Is it known where Martino Capelli's mob keep their weapons?'

Without looking up, the man in charge of the surveillance team, DCI Leyland, muttered something to the effect that it was not.

'Would you like me to find out for you?' the adviser, who did not like being muttered at, then went on to enquire coolly.

'No, thank you,' was the grating answer. Leyland added, reluctantly, 'They use a lock-up garage not far away but we don't think there are any weapons or explosives stored there.'

'How's that?'

'Intelligence.'

'What intelligence?'

Leyland sighed with exaggerated patience. 'Mobsters don't usually use lock-ups to conceal valuable stuff or weapons and explosives as they're so easily broken into and people are always hanging around such places hoping to do just that. And they're scared stiff of sniffer dogs.'

'Italians probably don't come under the heading of usual mobsters,' Patrick argued.

Before there could be any local explosions, controlled or otherwise, Greenway said, 'Gentlemen, I asked for *suggestions*. Please stick to the point.'

'It is the point,' Patrick persisted. 'We locate their weapons, stake out wherever it is and grab them when they collect them. No raid, no risk of the general public getting hurt.'

'But we want to arrest these people when they're on a big job,' one of the other two said.

'So they get banged up for ever,' his chum added.

Patrick said, 'But most of these men are wanted for serious crimes already – they can be arrested anyway for firearms offences and will be banged up just about for ever.'

Leyland said, 'There's a lot of meticulous planning already gone into this. We need to scoop up even more mobsters, already wanted or not, whose role in the job is further down the line, when the gang's actually carrying out the raid and when they're making their getaway – drivers, heavies, people like that.'

'You'll need to have top-quality armed personnel right in the jewellery shop.'

'We *are* putting armed personnel right in the jewellery shop. But only to protect the staff if necessary. We don't want to start a firefight there and the idea is that the gang'll be allowed to

177

steal some stuff and we'll pick them up with it on them.'

'I should very much like to be permitted to be in the area of these premises,' Patrick said.

'No,' Greenway said. 'If Tony Capelli's wheedled his way into the outfit he'll know your face.'

'He wouldn't know me at all. I'd be the bloke with the squint mumbling to himself while cleaning the windows – anything.'

I have noticed that sometimes when men are together, especially those very tired with brain-storming, the testosterone level seems to have the effect of diluting the sum of their collective intelligence causing them merely to snipe at one another.

'*When* is this supposed to happen?' I enquired heavily.

They all looked at me.

'We don't know,' Greenway admitted.

'As you yourself said you'd like to, you could risk everything and have Irma Burnside brought in for questioning. Quietly, while she's out on her own so anyone'll think she's still out shopping. Tell her that she might be in serious danger as her sister's been murdered and the police still don't know the motive behind the crime. That could be perfectly true. If Tony Capelli kills his cousin in order to take over the crime syndicate, he'll probably get rid of her as well as she will have fulfilled her purpose. We haven't a clue what yarn he's spun her although the little shit must have promised her loads of money.'

My turn of phrase seemed to sharpen them up

a bit.

'I like that,' Greenway said. 'But what happens when she doesn't return? We daren't risk her telling them where she's been.'

'No, you send a cop round to the flat crying his eyes out to tell whoever's there that she's been run over,' I said much more sarcastically than I should have done. 'Come on, will they care? She's quite likely an inconvenience anyway. The fact that she's missing might even force their hand. I'm sure the woman will cooperate and opt for police protection if it's impressed on her that all she's likely to get is a bullet from Tony if she doesn't.'

'Right,' Greenway said decisively. 'We do it now.'

'But there's no knowing whether she'll go out on her own again today,' I warned.

Leyland grabbed for his mobile and contacted someone on watch. It was possible to discover from overhearing the one-sided conversation that Irma Burnside had already left home, at around four fifteen that afternoon and driven off in her car, a Vauxhall estate.

'Did she have any luggage with her to suggest she was bailing out?' Leyland asked. 'No? Did anyone follow her?'

I guessed, from the nervous way that he was drumming his fingers on the arm of his chair and the worried look he shot in Greenway's direction that the reply was something along the lines of there being not enough personnel to tail everyone who could be regarded as a bit-player who might only be going to Sainsbury's. Sir.

It was arranged that a comprehensive lookout would be kept for her return and that she would be stopped, if possible, before she came within sight of the building where she lived.

We all hung around, waiting for news.

Nothing happened.

'She's done a runner and it's all my fault for acting the hit-man,' Patrick said unhappily when we were both in the canteen a little later drinking coffee and eating fruit cake, in-flight re-fuelling really as neither of us was hungry.

I could see some truth in this as Patrick is potentially far more intimidating than any Tony Capelli clone on a bad day. Recollecting what had taken place though there had been every impression that Irma had been more impressed by him than scared, together with having the exciting prospect of the intruder blowing Martino's brains out and thus smoothing out her love life for her.

I said as much, with little effect on Patrick's mood.

'Look, bringing her in for questioning was originally on Greenway's wish-list,' I reminded him. 'And don't forget, things change from minute to minute.'

They changed: Irma Burnside was picked up half an hour later, her car loaded with shopping, and weapons, having collected them from the lock-up garage on her way back from Sainsbury's.

# TWELVE

Obviously, this complicated matters because the gang would be wondering where their guns and Jammie Dodgers were. Both Patrick and I knew that it was no use praying that they would think Irma had done the dirty on them, something had to be done, quickly.

'Will you trust me on this?' Patrick asked Greenway when the meeting was immediately reconvened.

'What do you want to do?'

'Get some results by talking to her, with Ingrid.'

'Explain to me why I should hazard the entire operation by placing it in your hands.'

'Because it's what the pair of us are bloody good at.'

Greenway looked at him stonily as if trying to read his mind.

'You can confirm what I've just said by speaking to Richard Daws,' Patrick added.

Colonel Daws, Patrick's one-time boss in MI5, was now somewhere in the upper echelons of SOCA. He recommended him for the job.

'There's no time for that,' Greenway said roughly. He turned to the others. 'What does everyone else think?'

181

'I don't,' Leyland said with a shrug. 'If it's screwed, it's screwed.'

The other two had nothing positive to offer either.

'They're backing you to the hilt,' Greenway said to us with a fierce grin. 'Off you go then.'

He at least, would be watching and listening.

Irma Burnside had been escorted into the same interview room in which we had questioned David Bennett. She was almost as furious as he had been.

'I thought you were supposed to be an effin' crook!' she bawled at Patrick when we entered.

'It's just one of my hobbies,' he said with a smile, seating himself.

The baleful glance landed on me. 'And who's she – really?'

'We go around together. And if you don't object she'll take notes.'

'I don't suppose I have much choice in the matter, do I?'

'Miss Burnside, despite driving a car carrying weapons of various kinds and egging me on to murder Martino Capelli you have not yet been arrested or charged with any crime, but are here mostly for your own safety.' He then went on to formally introduce himself, and, as before, giving the impression that I was just one of his not-really-worth-introducing assistants.

'I'm not saying anything,' Irma announced, crossing her arms defiantly.

'At least we know where we are then,' Patrick murmured. 'I take it these weapons were concealed in the lock-up garage which the various gangsters you're harbouring use for precisely that.'

'Go to hell!'

'And you were told to collect them as they were to be used very shortly in a raid on a West End jewellers. *After* which, as a diversion and a two-finger salute, an attack was to have been made on a central London police station.'

'You're talking as though—' She stopped herself just in time.

'It's not going to happen?' Patrick said softly. 'It's not, it's history, Irma. You've been watched for months.'

'I – I wasn't going to say anything like that! And what's all this about me being brought here for my own safety? More lies?'

'No. Tony Capelli is fairly stupid but greedy for power and although police informers are silent as to whether he's out to take over his cousin's criminal empire we think he is. You won't be part of that plan.'

'Yes, I am. He loves me. He said so. He told me he's over here on business – he's nothing to do with crime now – and then he's going to take me back to Italy where he's got a lovely villa.' Irma stopped speaking abruptly but then added, 'I'm not saying one word more. Take me home.'

'He has a wife and family in Italy,' Patrick said.

I looked at him quickly but his expression betrayed nothing. I was aware that he had been on the phone to James Carrick within the past hour but knew nothing about this revelation. He does not normally lie about this kind of thing

183

though, not even to criminals.

Silence.

'I don't believe you,' Irma Burnside said at last.

'The Italian police seem perfectly clear on the matter.'

'Why should they know about him?'

Patrick sat back in his chair. 'You didn't notice the armed thug who acts as his minder? Were you asleep when I had a conversation with him recently at your flat? It's never occurred to you that both of these men belong to the Mafia?' And without waiting for a reply, 'Where is Martino, by the way?'

The woman gaped at him. 'Why – why he's inside! You know that!'

'He was released yesterday.'

'Released? But no one's seen him. He hasn't been back to my place.'

'He's probably been given the news that Tony's around and might just be planning to kill him. What did they tell you they were going to do with the firearms?'

'I didn't know it was guns I had to fetch.'

'You must have done. Together with semi-automatic pistols in a cardboard box and another box containing ammunition in the boot of your car there was a sub-machine gun on the back seat that only had a length of old curtain wrapped around it.'

'Bugger off,' Irma muttered.

'You're in this up to your neck and will go to prison for a very long time. Worse, and as I said just now, your life is very likely in grave danger.

Have you never asked yourself why your sister died?'

There was immediate alarm. 'Imelda? What's happened to her then?'

'I'm afraid she's dead. Murdered.'

'You're lying to me again!' the woman cried in real distress.

Patrick switched off the tape machine after saying that he would not continue the questioning until the witness had recovered.

This was risky and not like him at all. If the person being interviewed had been male he would have taken full advantage of the shock and carried on battering him down until he confessed and/or agreed to cooperate. But...

'Would you like some tea?' Patrick enquired gently.

'Yes, please,' she answered almost inaudibly.

It was not necessary for him to do so but he left the room to organize it. I knew the reason for this: it was now my turn.

'Do you know about all this?' Irma said to me. I told her I did.

'You're his working partner.'

'That's right.'

'What's he really like?'

'He won't let anyone hurt you but will make you tell him the truth even if it upsets you far more than you are now.'

After this had sunk in she said, 'It's terrible about Imelda. We weren't that close but she was my sister.'

'Was it ever suggested that she might come and live with you?'

185

'No, she'd have hated London. I once stayed with her for a short while when she had a flat. She loved Bath.'

'Only there was talk that she'd written a letter to someone saying that she was.'

'This is all news to me. Please tell me what happened to her.'

Although our conversation could be overheard in the adjoining room anything she told me would not be allowed to be used in evidence unless I engineered it so that Patrick obtained the same result and it was recorded.

I said, 'Her body was found in a house in Bath that belonged to her boyfriend's aunt.'

'What, Dave's place?'

'That's right.'

'God,' she muttered and was silent for a few moments. Then she said, 'I didn't like him very much. I only met him the once and all he talked about was money.'

'Did he have anything to do with Martino?'

'Of course not! Nor did Imelda. They never even met him. I can't believe she's dead. She was a good person. Always helping people. She worked with old folk. Did you know that?'

'Yes, I did. Are you sure Martino, or someone connected with him, didn't know about Imelda?'

'Positive. Anyway, why would Martino want to hurt my sister? I know he's a crook but he used to be fond of me before he went inside and Italians love their families. God, I've been a fool, haven't I? So that little shit Tony's got a wife.'

That made two of us who thought so then.

186

'When did he come on the scene?' I asked.

'Only a couple of months ago. He was all smiles and charm and seemed an escape out of the dead-end life I've got. He bought me presents...' She broke off and her face twisted angrily as she realized how he had used her.

'*Is* he going to kill Martino?'

'He told me Martino was going to kick me out of the flat. He pays the rent, after all. And that they had a feud that went back years and years. I don't know really. Sometimes men are all talk.'

'And you're quite happy for him to kill him?'

'No, not really. Despite what I said the other day. I'd quite like Martino to kill Tony now. It would serve the bugger right.'

'The trouble with guns is that sometimes innocent people are hurt.'

'I know. Perhaps we could fix up one of the dragons to get him.' She smiled to herself broadly.

'Or you could turn Queen's evidence and Tony'll end up behind bars.'

'He'd get me when he was let out though, wouldn't he? Or pay someone else to.'

'You'd get police protection. You will now. You don't think you'll be allowed to walk back in there without the weapons, do you?'

She sighed. 'I'm in a real bloody mess, aren't I?'

Patrick returned with two teas for the females and reseated himself.

'Come to think of it, I met Dave's Aunt once,' Irma said, not thanking him and in a world of her own. 'It was before Imelda worked in the same

187

nursing home as Miss Bennett was in. You had to call her Miss Bennett, never Hilda. If you ask me she was going a bit potty already.'

I said, 'You mean this was before she went into care? Where was she living then?'

'In a little flat in one of those warden-assisted developments. Her own house was too damp and dirty to live in apparently. Imelda said it was only because she'd been too mean to spend any money on it. She didn't like the woman at all.'

'Did Miss Bennett dislike her?'

'She hated everybody. Bonkers normally, if you ask me.'

'But not her nephew.'

'Yes, according to Imelda, she hated him too.'

Patrick cleared his throat. 'Shall we continue?'

'Oh, yes all right. But I'm still not going to tell you anything.'

'This raid that's been planned,' Patrick said slowly. 'Is it tomorrow?'

'How many more times do I have to tell you that I'm not saying nothing?'

I was expecting the pressure to go up a notch, when he would suddenly cease to be friendly and there would somehow, inexplicably, be a veiled threat. But he merely smiled and asked, 'How's Tony's minder?'

Irma laughed. 'Julio? He had to be carted off to A and E and of course they wanted to know how he'd done it. Tony pretended Julio couldn't speak English and couldn't say someone had knifed him as the police would've had to be informed so he made up some story about him being drunk and spiking himself on an iron railing. They were there for nearly five hours. Talk about hopping mad! I didn't find it funny then but I do now.'

'Good,' Patrick said absent-mindedly, apparently finding something of interest to look at on the wall behind her.

'For a policeman you're very good at knife throwing.'

'Thank you – but I wasn't always a policeman.'

'I didn't think you was. You said you'd killed Tony's Luigi. Is that true?'

'All the main points of what I said the other day are true.'

'Tony's even madder about that. I think he said he was another cousin.'

What I had been waiting for happened. Patrick slammed his hand down on the table, making the cups and saucers bounce and Irma jump out of her skin.

'Why are you protecting these bastards when one or both are planning to rob, kill and maim?'

'I knew Martino had this big job planned but didn't know about shooting up a police station,' Irma shrilled.

'What on earth did you think they were going to do with all those guns?'

'Well, frighten people, I suppose.'

'I don't think you cared a damn as long as you got to Italy with Tony.'

'OK, I didn't!'

'Then you're just as bad as they are, aren't you?'

'No, I'm not. I just want a new start in life.'

189

'Paid for with other people's blood.'

'That's a horrible thing to say.'

He bared his teeth at her in a ghastly smile.

'You're horrible too.' Irma dragged her gaze from him to me. 'You said he wouldn't hurt me.'

'He hasn't,' I said but knowing perfectly well what she meant. The look in his eyes was scaring her silly.

She leaned on the table with both arms, braced herself and spoke directly to him. 'Look Mr Horrible, you're sitting there not saying so but I know something nasty's going to happen to me if I don't tell you everything because you're running out of patience even though this is supposed to be some kind of police outfit. But if I grass on them they'll get me sooner or later. So both ways I'm as good as dead, aren't I?' Her voice started to break.

I said, 'No, Irma, you aren't. As I told you just now you'll be protected, given a new identity. They won't be able to find you.'

Patrick shot to his feet, making her jump again. 'She's wasting my time,' he rapped out. 'Time for a change of tactics.'

'No!' Irma cried. 'No, look, stop it! You've got me really scared now.'

He made for the door.

'Don't go!' she pleaded. 'Please. Tell me how I'll be looked after and then I might—'

Patrick went out of the door, banging it resoundingly behind him, that and his footfalls echoing away down the corridor.

Irma burst into noisy tears. 'Please get him back,' she sobbed, hands over her face. 'I hate

190

him but I'm so frightened and—' The rest was lost in sobbing.

I drew my chair closer. 'We don't have to get him back,' I said quietly. 'Tell *me*.'

She peered through her fingers at me, her eye make-up all runny. 'You won't let him...?'

'Absolutely not,' I solemnly promised.

Completely oblivious to the fact that he had made her tell the truth by upsetting her far more than she had been already Irma gave me absolutely everything we needed to know.

Charm, retreat and then pounce. I sat mulling over this interrogation technique in Greenway's office just under three-quarters of an hour later. He had sent somebody to fetch fish and chips, the three of us having discovered that we were ravenously hungry. The other trio had disappeared – I would love to say 'scuttled off' but it was not true – presumably to brief their respective teams.

'I reckon they'll risk going ahead with it,' Greenway said through coping with a hot chip in his mouth.

'They might,' Patrick said, 'Especially as she reckons she only brought about half the weapons that were originally there, having helped Martino's second-in-command stow them away in the first place. What's been put out to the media?'

'That a woman driving that car was involved in an accident at a road junction and was very seriously injured, no actual time or location mentioned. Her identity isn't yet known as the

vehicle burst into flames just after she was pulled from it by passers-by, destroying her personal
belongings. The police think weapons or ammunition had been carried in the car as several
minor explosions were heard. D'you think
that'll fool them?'

'If it doesn't I don't know what else could
have been said. Whatever happens, the woman
has to disappear for her own good.'

'The price for her story being that we can't
charge her with anything,' Greenway said.
'Turning Queen's evidence and getting a lesser
charge isn't any good, not with people like the
Capellis' mob. They might even try to get her
before it came to court. Someone'd just wait
until she's freed from prison and then gun her
down.'

'They may change the time of the raid,' I said.
'Just to be on the safe side.'

According to Irma one thirty the following
afternoon had been chosen as it was reckoned
that most shoppers would be at lunch, this not
because of less risk to people round and about
but in the hope that not many hale and hearty
folk would be present who might be tempted to
'have a go'.

'When then?' Greenway said, fixing me with
his green stare. He does sometimes seem to
think I'm psychic.

'Opening time might give the same street
conditions,' I replied. 'But surely there'll be
police on site all day anyway.'

'Yes, several as shoppers, two in the jewellery
shop pretending to be assistants – they're there

192

now getting a crash course so they look as though they know what they're doing – others in the office upstairs whose job it'll be to protect the shop staff if and when the raid happens. What more can we do?'

'Have any blokes who might be mobsters called at Irma's place in a car and the registration's been noted?' Patrick asked.

'At least a dozen different men have been observed going in and out of the flat in groups of three or more. I believe her when she said she doesn't know their names because, as she told Ingrid, Tony Capelli nearly always got rid of her by telling her to make everyone tea or coffee. Some arrived in an old van, others on foot. But they'll steal one or two vehicles for the actual job.'

'I'm aware of that,' Patrick said. 'But who was the old van registered to?'

'A builder who had part-exchanged it three years ago for a new one. It had a cloned tax disc too.'

'So we'll just have to wait for them to mobilize,' Patrick muttered. 'I wish you'd allow me to be one of those hanging around in the arcade.'

'As I said before it's too risky. Capelli knows you. Besides, that part of it's not really my responsibility.'

'He wouldn't know him,' I said. 'Promise.'

Greenway's chin jutted. 'I suppose you want to be in on it as well.'

'It's safe to assume that the gang'll have done a little homework and made a mental note of those who normally hang around the area; *Big*

193

*Issue* sellers, traffic wardens and people like that. They'll be jittery and keeping an eye open for strangers who could be undercover cops so lone men poking around with brooms or leaning on walls reading newspapers will be treated with suspicion. A couple is always easier to blend into a public place. Besides, Patrick would probably be a better shot than anyone else present if the gang opened fire.'

The Commander thought about it. Then he said, 'Richard Daws said it would take fifteen years off my life just to have the pair of you around.'

'Did he really?' Patrick said eagerly.

'Go on, sod off. Get some sleep. Do what you want but for God's sake don't tell the Met I sent you.'

I was wondering if Martino Capelli was right in there somewhere and his cousin was now so much carrion with his throat cut for real this time.

'You don't have to take me along,' I said to Patrick a little later in our hotel room. 'I was just flying the flag.'

'I'm working on it,' he responded. 'And there's no time to plan anything elaborate.'

'We could really do with having a look at the arcade now.'

'You're right. But isn't it one of those places that have gates that are locked at night?'

'I don't know.'

He exploded out of his chair. 'God, talk about losing my edge! I've lost it! Who would know?'

194

'Either of those two guys at the meeting whose responsibility that part of it was surely.'

'I didn't take their mobile numbers.' Patrick undertook some inventive swearing.

'Leyland will have them,' I broke in with. 'Did you get his?'

'There seemed little point seeing he hated my guts.' He took his invective off into the bathroom.

Apologetically, I rang Greenway.

'DCI John Murphy's the one you want,' he told me. 'The one with red hair. He'll know. Good idea to go and have a recce if the place is open at this time of night. Hang on and I'll give you his number.'

I soon had my answer.

'There are gates which are opened at eight a.m. and closed at midnight,' I reported. 'It's on two police beats and a security company keeps a watch on several of the shops. DCI Murphy, who's in charge of the operation, tells me he'll be on standby locally tonight to supervise surveillance but refused to go into details. He has no objection if you want to have a look round now but doesn't want to see our faces there tomorrow.'

'He won't,' Patrick said. 'Coming?'

I was never quite sure why I took the Smith and Wesson out of the room safe and put it in my jacket pocket.

# THIRTEEN

The arcade was not what I had expected and obviously fairly newly redeveloped, the elaborate Victorian wrought iron pillars and supports in the roof restored and painted dark blue, the stonework cleaned and repaired. There was a wide entrance and as one went farther in everything became very modern and was on three levels with a below ground level courtyard furnished with tables and chairs where customers could choose between an Italian restaurant, a wine bar and a café, the first two of which were still open. The whole place was strongly reminiscent of Shires Yard in Bath.

Hinchcliffe and Atterberry's – established, according to ye olde sign over the door, in 1799 – was on a corner site almost facing, and not far from, the entrance where another corridor with smaller shops crossed it at right angles. There were steel roller shutters on the large windows, as there were also on several of the high-class fashion and leather goods outlets. Another restaurant, *Les Fleurs*, was, judging by the chatter and clatter, doing a good trade on the upper, terraced, level. Otherwise, only a few people were around, window shopping, probably mostly coming in to shelter from the drizzly night.

'I suppose we could have a snack while we're here,' Patrick said when we had drifted from one end to the other checking where other access points and fire exits were while playing the game of trying to spot the undercover cops. My money was all on a Chinese man and his girl-friend who were wandering around and Patrick was sure they were a man making a call on his mobile in the courtyard and another, a chef, who was at present standing outside the restaurant having a break to cool off.

'Are you hungry then?'

'I'm always hungry when I'm working.'

'What time is it?' I asked, having left my watch behind.

'Ten fifty-five.'

'If you're right about Murphy's people they're nowhere near the raid's target – which could be under surveillance from Martino's lot right now.'

'Probably not, but you have to move around, behave normally in case, as you say, there's someone keeping a watch out for *you*. And don't forget, there'll be unmarked police cars cruising around.'

I wandered back towards the main entrance, Patrick staying where he was, and took several deep breaths of damp, exhaust-tainted air, fine rain on my face. Traffic lights were reflected in the wet, greasy-looking roads with scarcely any vehicles to obey them: Londoners seemed to be staying indoors because of the weather. Odd then to see someone go through a red light.

I turned and called, 'If this mob's going to

shoot up West End Central afterwards then presumably they're hoping to disappear somewhere instantly, preferably going abroad.'

'No doubt something like that's on the cards.'

'Then they'll need instant funds, not a pile of jewellery they can only get rid of through a fence.'

'Diamonds are *the* international currency.'

'Point taken, but we passed a cash machine on our way from the tube station – about five minutes from here. How many JCBs do you normally see belting along around here at night jumping the lights?'

He came at the run. 'No harm in checking.'

We heard the huge impact when we were still about a hundred yards away. An alarm bell pealed followed by the wail of a siren but this appeared not to signify a police car as it was stationary, merely another bank security device. Above the racket there was the distinct sound of a couple of shots and as we reached a street corner two terrified women ran virtually into our arms. Patrick unceremoniously gathered them up and bundled them through the doors of a fast food eatery we had just gone by. A man and a young boy were just behind them and were similarly dealt with, Patrick shouting at them all to stay inside.

We took quick peeps around the corner. It was a weird scene, such traffic as there was had stopped, the bucket of the JCB being used to smash and crunch its way into the wall of the bank with the ATM in it like some crazed prehistoric monster. Then, a small flat-bed truck of

198

some kind came speeding up, travelling the last fifty yards or so half on the pavement, battering into a car that was in the way, knocking over street signs and scattering litter bins. It was spun round and reversed until it was quite close to the main entrance of the bank. All this activity was being guarded by four men, three seemingly carrying hand guns, another with a sub-machine gun. They had had to move aside for the arrival of the truck, the one with the machine gun firing a burst at a motorist who had left his car and was running away. The shots smashed into everything; vehicles, road signs, shop windows, all the while people screaming as they stampeded away. The man escaped uninjured.

'Where's bloody Murphy's law?' Patrick bellowed, the Glock pistol in his hand. 'Stay here!'

In the next second he had gone. Already having the Smith and Wesson in mine I ignored the instruction. There was a flurry of shots and the man with the machine gun nosedived to the pavement, the weapon still firing as he fell. The one on his left went over backwards but I did not see what happened to the third as I had rolled into the cover of a metal litter bin that had escaped the truck and took out the fourth, who was firing in the direction of where I thought Patrick might be right now, behind a group of concrete flower tubs.

I decided that my responsibility lay in disabling the lorry so potted the windscreen and two of the tyres nearest to me. Thus encouraged I followed this up with a shot to discourage the digger driver that whanged off the cab superstructure and killed a street light. The two men in the truck abandoned ship and would have run off had it not been for two people who ran past me shouting 'Police!' and tackled them to the ground. Sirens blared in the distance.

The driver of the JCB extricated the vehicle from the mess he had made and, bouncing over rubble, jerked forward into the main road, the driver shaking the bucket to rid it of more detritus. He endeavoured to turn right but there was no room to manoeuvre so veered around to the left and after twenty yards or so wrenched the vehicle around in the road, crashing into street furniture and a parked car. Bucket lowered it then headed straight for where the two who had apprehended the lorry driver and his accomplice had just started to cross the road, hauling them off to meet a rapidly approaching police van. They ran to get out of the way but one of the suspects tripped and fell flat, almost pulling over the man who was holding him.

I dared not shoot in case the digger careered out of control to cause mayhem and death on the other side of the road. Then, unaccountably, it swung hard right and thundered into the truck. For a moment it looked as though the latter might overturn but it thumped down again, trapping the bucket underneath. The digger stalled and juddered to a halt.

Gingerly, I raised myself a little. People, hopefully police, were arriving but cautiously, crouching behind parked vehicles, obviously not knowing how many would-be robbers were left. I could not locate Patrick for a moment but then saw that he was in the bank doorway with someone I presumed was gunman number three whom he had disarmed. As I watched he brought the man out, one hand tightly in the material behind the neck of the other's sweatshirt.

'SOCA!' he shouted to the four winds. 'You can all come out now.'

DCI Murphy was one of the first to appear. 'I thought that was a pretty good response time, actually,' I heard him say to Patrick.

He was given a big, bright smile. 'In that case, congratulations. Would you like this one?'

'I shall need you to make a statement.'

'We both will. In the morning. To Greenway. You can always read it afterwards.'

I joined them, and Murphy left with his prisoner after giving me a curt nod. Any further conversation was impossible at the moment because of the alarm bells and ambulance sirens so I went with Patrick as he moved from one wounded or dead man to another, trying to identify them, or rather find out if they were either of the Capelli brothers. None appeared to be.

The man with the sub-machine gun was very dead and, as Patrick said to me later and not for the first time in his career, you simply cannot risk them being able to use a weapon like that again. The one I had hit was wounded in the leg. I always aim low even though this also is risking them using their weapons again and killing someone. I always incur Patrick's anger over this – 'it's unprofessional' – but causing the kind of pain and loss of blood that I was witnessing now is bad enough.

The digger driver, a grossly overweight individual, was found to have suffered a fatal heart attack.

'Right,' Patrick said, having conferred with the paramedics in attendance. 'We're now superfluous.'

'The two who arrested the men in the lorry were the Chinese man and his girlfriend,' I told him when we had put a little distance between ourselves and the scene so we could speak fairly normally.

'Just as I thought.'

He was deliberately being annoying so I merely commented, 'There weren't enough mobsters here to do the job properly.'

'No. No Capellis either. I agree, it's odd.'

'So are they still going to hit West End Central, only tonight, or the jewellery place tomorrow as planned or was this another outfit entirely?'

Patrick paused on a street corner and gazed around. 'Pass, although I lean to the latter. But the police personnel at both places should be prepared for anything and it's not up to me to try to teach Murphy his job. I have no intention of riding shotgun for the Met for the rest of the night – it's not my brief.' The wonderful grey eyes rested on me briefly. 'And what do I do now? Mike's told me to do as I like, hasn't he?'

'I think he meant just tonight,' I pointed out.

'Yes, tonight. I shall go and look for Tony Capelli.'

'That's if he's not dead.'

'That would be a great pity.' He stopped speaking and then looked at me again.

'I know what you're going to say,' I said. 'You want to go alone.'

'Ingrid, you look all in – terrible. You've had a nasty crash and this job's not worth killing yourself for.'

'This is about Capelli ordering Luigi to kill James and hitting Joanna instead, isn't it?'

Patrick nodded. 'I know that neither of our friends is safe until he's dealt with, one way or another. He'll want to settle what he regards as old scores. He's like that. He'll want to take out Carrick, then Joanna, then me. Thorns in his flesh. His failures.'

'But surely then you'll have the rest of the Capelli clan after you.' I could see that even talking about it was reigniting the anger he had felt at the time.

'It's unlikely. James told me. It was Martino's brother in Italy who tried to finish him off last time. His own family. He'd done things at home that brought utter disgrace to them.'

'One way or another?' I queried.

'No, I'm going to kill him.'

We went to our hotel together where Patrick made sure that I was safe and comfortable, told me only to open the door of the room in answer to one of our special knocks and then moved to leave. Then, chuckling at his own forgetfulness, he came back and kissed me, his parting remark as he went out of the door, 'That was good shooting by the way.'

In the ensuing quiet I flopped on to the bed, the cursed writer's imagination churning out what the aftermath might be.

This was how it all ended. He went out of the door and she never saw him alive again. All that kind of pathetic piffle in third-rate women's fiction that nevertheless haunts me when Patrick goes off on his own. It seemed like hours that I sat there brooding about it but my left behind watch insisted it was only five minutes.

'This isn't fiction,' I said to my pale, miserable-looking and scabby reflection in the dressing table mirror.

Five children.

'Oh, God,' I whispered. 'What shall I do?'

I prised myself off the bed and went into the bathroom where I swallowed two of my painkillers plus two of the pills Patrick carries with him and takes when he needs to stay awake. Then I reloaded the Smith and Wesson, put some more ammunition in my other jacket pocket, slammed out of the room and tore after him.

He could always bring me back and chain me to the loo.

A piercing whistle rent the calm of the foyer as I hurried through it, the kind that some men use to summon taxis. I gazed around wildly and saw the source of it sitting in a little bar near the entrance doors. When I breathlessly arrived I saw that he was drinking strong black coffee.

'Ah,' Patrick said.

'You're a pig,' I panted.

'I thought it would be a good idea to hang around for a little while as you always follow me and this is one job where I'd prefer to have you under my nose right from the start.'

'That's about the most pompous thing you've ever said to me.'

'True though.'

'I seem to remember getting you out of really sticky situations a couple of times.'

He smiled infuriatingly. 'Coffee?'

'No, thanks, I took a couple of your wide-awake pills.'

'You're only supposed to take one.'

'I didn't bother to read the label.'

'Ingrid, you've done this before! I can distinctly remember you dosing yourself up with a god-awful brew concocted by some harridan in Hinton Littlemoor, one of her "rural remedies" or other such rubbish.'

'Your mother gave it to me. It was called *Essence of Flowers*.'

'Yes, mostly home-grown poppy juice!'

After I had admitted to experiencing a floating away sensation – we had been undertaking rooftop surveillance at the time – he had poured the rest of it down the kitchen sink.

While it was naive to assume that Tony Capelli would be calmly 'at home' in Romford that was where we headed initially, to lurk and watch. Despite what Patrick had said, I was of the opinion that he would make every effort to arrest him. If not, it had been the Italian who had made death threats first.

There were lights on in every room at the rear of the flat, clearly visible from our position in the small car park, that is, wedged in a dark corner near the inevitable stinking bins. The

205

outside door of the apartment was actually ajar but there was no movement within, no shadows criss-crossing the curtains.

'Was that raid a feint?' Patrick whispered. 'A few expendable thickos sent off to keep the Met busy and make them think the threat's over?'

I said, 'As we've already discussed, it's obviously not practical to raid a jeweller's at night because everything's in the strongroom, never mind the steel shutters over the windows. Unless you go and grab a senior member of staff and force them to open up everything, that is.'

'I don't think they're that organized. It would probably be early tomorrow morning just after the place has opened.'

'Leyland won't be too pleased if you grab Capelli first.'

Patrick's teeth flashed white in the gloom as he grinned at me. 'That's all part of the fun.'

We had not entered the area through the drive-in from the main shopping street but via a pedestrian access to another road with smaller shops and a public library where our taxi had dropped us off. Patrick had silently drawn my attention to a car with two men sitting in it parked nearby and then flung an arm around my shoulders and generally acted tipsy, almost causing me to lose my balance. But surely Leyland would not really have given out the descriptions of two members of SOCA with a view to warning them off. Would he?

Several minutes went by during which we did not speak and precisely nothing happened. Then Patrick broke the silence by saying, 'You know,

I'm still not happy with the idea of allowing these mobsters to commit a crime so they can be arrested. It's quite likely innocent people will be hurt or killed. The police might even screw up and they'll get away.'

'You might have to let the other bloke get on with it for once,' I murmured.

He did not respond for a moment, then said, 'Is this my oracle speaking?'

'Yes, it is.'

'We might have to pick up the pieces.'

'*We* won't have to pick up anything. SOCA wasn't created to sort out any potential disasters the Met might have.'

'But as I've just said, people might be killed!'

'Remember what Daws once said to you? "No more tilting at windmills." Stick to what you're meant to do or *you* might be the one who ends up injured or dead because of a misplaced crusading instinct and an erroneous belief that someone who's been in special services knows best.'

'Bloody hell! How long have you wanted to say that to me?'

'Years. May I make a suggestion?'

'I have an idea you will anyway.'

'You want Capelli. But in my view, he could already be dead. I think we should wait. See what these people plan to do, if anything at all now Irma's not returned. Let the Met do what's necessary and if he's alive and well and they fail to catch him then you'll have your chance.' When Patrick said nothing I continued, 'You were planning to storm in there when everyone

207

was catching up on a little sleep, weren't you?'

'I do believe I was,' he muttered. 'Right now actually.'

'Ignore me if you want to.'

'I loathe this man, Ingrid.'

'I know you do but please don't allow it to rule your common sense. Remember what you said to me about gunning for terrorists and gangsters in Northern Ireland and elsewhere? Something along the lines of the satisfaction being in the planning, tracking down, the fine weapon to hand, the outwitting of someone who employs vigilant and vicious weapons-carrying minders, etc. etc. To burst in there now would be un-professional and messy.'

'You're absolutely right, of course,' he sighed.

We waited.

Seemingly a couple of decades later and when I was of the firm opinion that all oracles should be bagged up and reconsigned to Greek mythol-ogy, four cars arrived at the kind of speed that suggested their drivers had some serious pur-pose in mind. They swung around and formed a half-circle at the bottom of the iron stairs that led up to the flats like prairie wagons preparing for an attack by the Sioux. In comparative silence at least eight men then ran up the stairs and entered the flat.

'Could it be undercover cops?' I hissed.

'Not unless they're playing a very strange game. And if they have arrest in mind they wouldn't have turned up in unmarked cars.'

The grandmother of all gun battles erupted, one of the flat's windows seeming to explode outwards under a hail of bullets.

Patrick went, shouting over his shoulder, 'For God's sake stay hidden until I tell you it's safe!'

Those remaining in the cars started firing at him as soon as they saw movement, shots pinging off everything nearby. I had no intention of countering my instructions this time but it was important to give those firing something to think about so I ran forward using the parked cars as cover, and, when in range and from the shelter of someone's people carrier, performed my usual target practice on the vehicles' tyres. Reloading, I then remembered my training and, bending low, shifted position, just in time as it happened, hearing the crash of breaking glass behind me.

OK then, we wanted no one being cowardly by remaining in cars where they could take more shots at Patrick. I did a little light strafing of rear windows and very soon doors on the far sides of the vehicles were being flung open and those within baling out. I realized they might come in my direction. If so, good, I was not staying around. Moving quickly I scuttled off to my right, away from what a man would probably refer to as 'the action', and in the general direction of where I thought Patrick had gone.

Over on the far side of the car park I paused behind a large concrete pillar, one of several that supported an overhead structure of some kind to the rear of a shop, and crouched down, peering around it. People were lining the windows in the other flats staring out. The firing was more sporadic now, men furiously shouting at one another, in Italian, I thought. There was then another shot

209

and a man staggered out of the door and pitched headlong down the stairs.

'You bastard!' someone inside yelled.

There was then another shot and a horrible scream followed by several shots in quick succession. The ensuing silence was broken, for the second time that night, by the howling sirens of approaching police cars.

Watching, I remained where I was. Moments later a short, tubby figure cautiously appeared in the doorway but dived back inside again when someone took a shot at him. Seconds later two people were silhouetted against the light, one holding the other in front of him as a shield, the impression being of a gun rammed in the man's back. It made no difference, there was a burst of fire and the one in front toppled down the staircase, no doubt riddled with bullets.

'The idiot should have put the light out,' said a voice softly close by, from behind another pillar.

'I was convinced you were inside,' I whispered, feeling weak with relief.

'I thought I'd wait and see who wins. With any luck the Met'll use their loaf and do the same, although I reckon this lot'll jump ship like rats when the law finally arrives. What the hell are they doing – stopped at traffic lights?'

'Who do you reckon arrived with back-up? Martino?'

'That's a fairly safe bet.'

'The drivers of the cars are still around somewhere.'

'Two are and that's who's doing the shooting. You must have winged one of them as he's under

210

the stairs not feeling too good. Another came this way and is now in that black bin over there marked non-hazardous waste.' Patrick chuckled cold-bloodedly. 'Now I know exactly where you are I'll go and find the other two. Please keep right out of the way.'

He went away again.

The police arrived with a flourish like a scene from *The Bill*, marksmen from a firearms unit immediately taking up positions. After this flurry of activity everything shivered into an uneasy stillness although I was sure I could hear groaning inside the flat.

Then a man appeared in the doorway. 'I'm the only one not dead or badly injured,' he called, leaning against the door frame.

He was answered by a voice amplified by a megaphone. 'Armed police. Come down, arms up and lie face down on the ground.'

He limped down and lay there, close to the two bodies.

I could imagine senior officers conferring and it was not difficult to guess where their considerations would lie. Informers had said that these mobsters were intent on shooting up a nick so this might be a ruse and they were now going to make do with a mobile unit instead. I did wonder how many of those indoors were fit for such activity after all the firing. On the other hand they were not the SAS and quite a high percentage of the shots had probably missed. There was also the chance that this latest development was merely a time-wasting exercise and the remainder of those still mobile were now

211

escaping by climbing out of the windows at the front on to the wide canopy above the shops and making their escape. I sincerely hoped a watch was in place out there.

All at once and as if my reasoning had weirdly made it happen there were shouts somewhere at the front of the building and the sound of shots. Seconds later yelled orders from the man with the megaphone sent several armed personnel pounding up the stairs, a couple peeling off to grab the prone suspect first to virtually sling him into the arms of other colleagues, another group running through the opening towards the main road. More yells, more shots. Then, comparative silence again.

A policeman appeared in the doorway of the flat, went back inside after a couple of doors had been slammed and then reappeared.

'Well?' asked the megaphone.

'I think we've sorted it, sir.'

# FOURTEEN

I left the security of the pillar and cautiously looked around me. I could not see Patrick but did not really expect to as the lighting in the area was poor, besides which in the present circumstances he would make a point of not being anywhere where he could be spotted. Then, fleetingly, I did see him as he crossed a space between

212

the line of parked cars. He had someone with him. I headed for where I thought he might end up, at the line of police vehicles. All the time more were arriving.

'One of the drivers got away,' he was saying to DCI Leyland as I arrived, handing over the man's handgun. 'You'll find another, unconscious, in the black rubbish bin over there and a third beneath the stairs, wounded – that's if he hasn't done a runner by now.'

Leyland saw me, looked through me and said to Patrick, 'So how come you're here?' Whether it was because of the erratic lighting from vehicle headlights I was not sure but the man looked haggard.

'I want Tony Capelli.'

'You can't have him.'

'Only to arrest him. You can have him immediately afterwards.'

'The answer's still no.'

'It's of no consequence to you surely.'

'What's it all about?'

'Personal reasons.'

Leyland half turned away. 'Bugger off, Gillard.'

'Is he here?'

'Until I've been inside and assessed what's happened out the front I can't answer that.'

'Do you know what he looks like?'

'Er – no.'

'Then you might need me to identify him.'

'I don't need SOCA here at all. Leave.'

He was then forced to give priority to the people who were clamouring for his attention.

Patrick, who had already parted with his prisoner, tucked an arm through mine and steered a course away from the group, between the cars and, taking a slightly circuitous route, over towards the stairs. The flashing blue lights of ambulances pulling up in the road outside – there was no room for them now at the rear – reflected eerily off walls and windows, feet pounded pavements, the sound echoing, the general effect almost surreal. Beneath the stairs the wounded man had been found and the two bodies were being examined for any signs of life. We paused by these but neither appeared to be the Capelli brothers.

'SOCA,' Patrick snapped to the first person we met at the top of the steps, producing his warrant card. 'I must warn you that the carved wooden dragons in there might conceal booby-traps that could well have been reloaded since I was last here.'

'Do you know about these things then, sir?' asked the man, looking alarmed.

'Yes, I do. May we come in?'

We entered. There was a strong draught, presumably coming from the open windows at the front. One glance at my immediate surroundings told me that scenes of crime people would be here for a long time. The place was shot to pieces; bullet holes everywhere, torn fabrics, pictures and ornaments reduced to splinters and shards. Amazingly, there appeared to be no spilt blood in the hallway and only one body was in sight, just inside the door of the first room we looked into, that of Martino Capelli. I would not

214

have known this if Patrick had not told me as he looked nothing like his younger brother. He had clearly not expected to die, the look of surprise forever frozen on his dark, heavy features.

'If everyone would just stay exactly where they are for a moment,' Patrick said loudly. 'While I check for anti-intruder devices.'

Personally I thought that if any of the dragons was going to do its stuff it would have done so by now but, hey, we were in, weren't we?

From where I was standing in the doorway I heard someone out of my line of vision laugh quietly as Patrick went over to what I remembered to be the biggest dragon of the lot, almost as tall as he was. When he discovered the hidden compartment in the front of the neck and the tiny weapon it contained there were muttered exclamations of surprise.

'It failed to go off,' Patrick reported, tipping the ammunition out on to the carpet. 'Do all stay in this room while I examine the others.'

Two or three sobering minutes elapsed while he went from room to room.

There was a sharp crack.

'Are you all right?' I yelled.

'Yes, it fired as soon as I touched it,' he replied from one of the bedrooms. 'Bloody dangerous things, especially as it wasn't activated.'

Leyland arrived, breathing hard. 'I thought I told you two to bugger off.'

'Patrick's just disarming the dragons,' I told him.

Predictably, he prepared to lose his temper.

Patrick appeared. 'Sorry, there was no time to

215

find gloves so my prints are on them. Although most of them were switched off I've removed and left all the weapons and ammo on the floor. I suggest you get firearms people to deal with them.'

Leyland said nothing and marched into the living room. 'That's Martino Capelli,' he said, giving the body the most brief of glances. 'How many more are indoors?'

He was told that one slightly wounded man was in the bathroom, under guard, vomiting, there were two dead bodies in the kitchen and a door to what was guessed to be a separate lavatory was jammed or locked, someone presumably inside. Leyland then gave them the information that the rest had tried to escape out of the windows and had been, or were being, apprehended.

'No one hiding under the beds?' Patrick offered from where we were standing to one side.

'Search under them,' the DCI ordered his team and they filed out through the door into the adjoining other living room from which there was access to the rest of the flat without going into the hall. 'Break down the door of the bog,' he shouted after them.

'So who's going to shoot first?' Patrick queried mildly.

Leyland glared at him. 'They know what they're doing.' His mobile rang and he answered it.

I went back into the hall. Patrick came with me but I noticed that he kept a watchful eye on

Leyland from near the doorway. Distressing noises were still coming from the bathroom, which was around a corner at the end of a short corridor, the bedrooms off it.

'There are drawers under the beds,' I whispered. 'No space for anyone to hide.'

'So there are,' Patrick responded.

'D'you reckon Tony Capelli's the one in the loo?'

'I don't think so. His poisonous aftershave tells me he's—'

The door of the large built-in cupboard right behind the DCI then smashed open and two men erupted from it. I saw they were armed and that was all before Patrick gave me a violent shove and I sprawled on to the floor. There were several shots, deafening indoors.

'– a lot closer than that,' I heard Patrick finish saying. 'Are you all right, guv?'

On all fours, I travelled to the doorway and looked in, just as the others poured in through the other. Leyland had obviously dived for cover behind a huge sofa – it had borne the brunt of the attack – and was now emerging, a little pale. Two men lay dead on the floor, both shot in the head. One was Tony Capelli. I had to look away.

Patrick put the Glock back in its shoulder harness and went to look down on the corpses. Although he had spoken in light-hearted fashion to Leyland there was no hint of triumph or contentment. He had saved the DCI's life and that was all.

The next morning I got the impression that

Greenway was so delighted that he would have Patrick's report of the night's activities put in a gold frame and hung on the wall of his office. Handwritten too, the operative's scribe being too worn out to oblige the night before – it had been two thirty by the time we got back to the hotel – while it was still fresh in his mind and he not too familiar with my laptop. So I had slept the deep sleep of the exhausted, not even hearing him come to bed but seeing him just before closing my eyes sitting at the desk cum dressing table, the lamp on it the only illumination. The light shone on a grave face, a little careworn now but very much the man I had fallen in love with at school. If Alexandra was still out there she wasn't going to have him.

'I have to say there *is* a certain degree of choreography here that, understandably, you haven't mentioned,' the Commander said slowly, tapping the sheets of paper before him. 'You thought there was a strong chance that Capelli was in the cupboard in the living room where you were all standing. Why didn't you draw Leyland's attention to your suspicions?'

Patrick took a sip of coffee. 'He was being uncommonly resentful about our presence and that, and tiredness, were affecting his judgement. I had an idea his lip would curl and he would open the cupboard to prove me wrong. And die on the spot, together with any number of those with him. It was important to de-clutter the immediate area to avoid collateral damage.'

Greenway's slightly battered from playing Rugby features split into a big grin. 'You know,

218

I really love the way you one-time soldiers talk. The Met'll just adore their crack response team being referred to as clutter at a crime scene. I might even put it in *my* report.'

Patrick effected a courtly 'as master wishes' gesture.

'What would you have done if they hadn't burst out of the cupboard?'

'They had to. They'd run out of air. I knew exactly how big it was because I'd taken a look inside at our first visit.'

'It was fine shooting.'

The word 'clinical' had crossed my own mind.

Patrick said, 'Ingrid dealt with a significant amount of rubber and compressed air last night too.'

'And I'm sure I was responsible for the man driving the digger at the bank raid to have a heart attack,' I said unhappily.

'Don't distress yourself about it,' Greenway said. 'He'd had two already and the docs had told him that if he didn't lose weight and stop drinking ten pints of beer a day he wouldn't survive a third. He didn't.'

'Do we know if the bank job was a ploy to make the Met think that was the real target and not the jewellery raid?' I asked.

'It wasn't. They were different mobsters who largely hang out in Southend thinking for some reason that they're safe there. This is the most ambitious job they've ever attempted as they usually stick to top of the range car theft and drugs dealing. But the armed foursome were freelance, well known to us and hired for the night. *They* won't be bothering us for a while, one of them now permanently in the really warm slammer.' Greenway harrumphed with laughter. 'As to the jewellery shop, it's under heavy, if discreet guard, but probably not many of Martino Capelli's lot are left standing to do anything even if the boss hadn't been killed, perhaps by his cousin.'

'This really was Martino trying to reclaim his patch then,' Patrick said.

'Oh, yes, it was a turf war all right.' Greenway consulted his computer screen. 'Five were dead in the flat, including Martino himself, four wounded, one badly. Four were uninjured, one of whom was stuck in the window of the toilet, trying to get out, the other three either having given themselves up or stranded on the canopy over the shops. Outside at the rear, you apprehended two, Ingrid slightly wounded another and a fourth escaped. The Met think they know who he is.' He glanced at Patrick. 'Tony Capelli was killed along with a man who appears to have been his minder. We don't yet know his name. You met them. Do you?'

'No, he was his *new* minder,' Patrick answered. 'The previous one tried to kill me but was clumsy and cut himself on my knife.'

The Commander made a note of this, a smile tugging his lips. Then he said, 'There were a couple more who were arrested, with others, who were trying to escape at the front and had shinned down drain pipes. It's still in the melting pot as to who actually worked for who as it would appear that Tony Capelli had poached

220

some of his cousin's followers.'

'Are they talking?' I asked.

'Some of them are. The usual thing, mostly bleating that they were threatened and coerced into doing as they were told. But that, as you know, has more than a grain of truth in it.'

'Your plan of letting Martino Capelli out of prison a little early came off then, sir,' Patrick said quietly.

'Yes, but like both of you, and despite what impression I might give, I regret the loss of life. The redeeming factor is that no members of the public or police personnel were hurt, or at least, only a constable who managed to shut his hand in a car door. A few egos might have taken a hammering though.'

And here he did laugh.

Almost all the rest of that day was taken up with the aftermath. I wrote a report of my own while Patrick went with Greenway to the two crime scenes, the Commander naturally wanting to see them for himself. After snatching a bite of lunch they went to a mortuary where Greenway, together with several other officers from the Met, was able to positively identify a couple of the bodies, the desired object of the exercise as some of the gangs' members had assumed stolen identities. All this took hours and by the time Patrick got away following another session of debriefings at HQ I was back at the hotel, having spoken to him a little earlier by phone.

'We're on a long weekend's leave so home tomorrow,' he announced as he came through

221

the door. 'Are you feeling rotten again?' he went on to enquire, seeing that I was sitting on the bed with my feet up.

'No, I'm fine,' I answered. 'Just enjoying the sheer novelty. I never have time to do this at home.'

'We must talk about your new writing room. Over dinner. God, I'm starving.' He threw off all his clothes and disappeared to have a shower.

Jeri Ryan, an actress in *Star Trek, Voyager*, which Matthew watches avidly, has the most superb way of questioningly twitching an eyebrow that I have ever seen achieved by a woman. I performed one of these, only mentally, right now, slipped on the one and only dress I had brought with me and applied a little make-up and perfume.

'It's perfectly achievable,' Patrick said over a pre-dinner glass of wine in the hotel bar. I had said not one word when he had ordered one for himself as well as he was due to see his specialist in a week's time, who on the previous visit had strongly hinted that he would lift the alcohol ban.

'What is?' I said, knowing perfectly well.

'Your writing room. We had that small room created off the kitchen that used to be the old coal store with the view that the kids could have their computer in there and use it for homework. But it didn't work out.'

Before he could go on I said, 'That was your idea and it didn't work out because even though Matthew and Katie – which is who we're talking about here – get on brilliantly together they do

222

need their own space and both now have their own computers. Which are in their bedrooms.'

'Perfect then. You can have it to write in.'

'Have you been in there lately?' I snorted. 'I already know the answer to that, no. Well, I can tell you, it's just about full and now a utility room. It houses the tumble dryer that wouldn't go in the kitchen, your parents' new chest freezer that wouldn't go in *their* kitchen, plus any number of boxes and crates, some of which contain your stuff, that haven't been unpacked yet.'

'Can't all this be changed?'

I looked at him over the rim of my glass. 'No.'

'Look, I have been trying to think this through for you.'

'I've already thought it through all by myself, thank you. I'm buying the house in Bath.'

Patrick took a fierce swig of wine. 'But Alex has put in a higher offer.'

'I've put in a higher, higher offer. And, don't forget, she's shortly going to end up behind bars.'

He just looked at me.

'You don't get it, do you? This woman was responsible for my having the prang and—'

'We don't know that for sure yet. Nor about any of the rest of it.'

'Then let me have your defence thesis by nine tomorrow morning, double spaced, written on one side of the paper only, no more than ten thousand words.'

'Ingrid...' Unusually, words failed him for a moment. 'You never used to be quite as stormy as this.'

223

'That might be because no one's ever tried to take you away from me before.'

There was a longish silence before Patrick grinned ruefully. 'Perhaps you're getting more like me.'

'That's perfectly possible seeing we've spent so much time together,' I murmured. 'Shall we eat?'

But he still just sat there looking at me. Then he put out a hand and lightly stroked my cheek. 'I really love you, you know.'

I realized that I had been terribly thoughtless about something and took the hand. 'No police or members of the public were hurt as a result of you killing several mobsters yesterday. Are you all right?'

'I was wondering when someone was going to ask me that.'

'I'm really sorry.'

'Yes, I'm all right – it was the job, and either them or us.'

James Carrick showed commendably more sensitivity when we met him and Joanna in the Ring o' Bells in Hinton Littlemoor the next evening for dinner. I was wondering how the business of the Gaelic diatribe would affect the evening but should not have worried, both men miming extreme terror on first clapping eyes on one another and then bursting out laughing. The subjects of work or our participation in any shoot-outs were not even mentioned until after we had eaten and were relaxing over coffee in the snug.

'I wish I'd had a pud now,' said the glowingly pregnant Joanna in a faraway voice.

'I'll fix one for you,' Patrick offered, getting up.

'No, really,' she said, going pink.

'They do a mean treacle sponge with home-made custard.'

'Oh ... all right. But I'll go and order it. I might change my mind and have the apple pie and cream instead.'

'Thank God she made a hundred per cent recovery from the Scottish nightmare,' James said fervently when Joanna had left the table.

'Tony Capelli's dead,' Patrick said in an undertone. 'You won't have to worry about him any more.'

'So I understand. The names of those known to have died were on internal memos yesterday. I heard a Met DCI almost got himself filled with lead.'

'He'd probably been on duty for the best part of two days without much of a break and was just about done in. So when he told me to bugger off I stayed around.'

Their gaze met and Carrick understood and nothing more was ever said about it.

Although the case was not mentioned that same evening I knew that Carrick had had to release David Bennett as there was no proper evidence to link him with the death of Imelda Burnside. Tests were still being carried out on her remains and until these came through all the DCI could do was tell him not to leave the area. I made a mental note to phone and ask him if

225

anything had come of the discovery of the knife and truncheon in the garden over the wall.

A couple of weeks went by. Patrick returned to work to apply himself to his self-styled role of 'Chief Inquisitor of Those Left Standing', as Michael Greenway had significant unfinished business with the late Martino Capelli's criminal empire. I stayed at home and tried to write. I began to make progress with this, forced into it by the news from James that the little house in Cherry Tree Row was no longer a crime scene. I contacted the estate agents only to be told that the solicitors acting for the owner were stalling and that other people had shown an interest in viewing the place. Alexandra appeared to have gone off the map, which, in the circumstances, I thought was understandable. I found myself beginning not to care about the house, a fair price to pay perhaps if it meant I would not have to think about the wretched woman again.

The car was returned to us and I had to make myself get in it and drive to Bath station to meet Patrick off a London train. Not being able to recollect what had happened was still upsetting. I was having nightmares about driving a tractor down an almost vertical road in a mountainous region in heavy rain and braking to no effect so perhaps my subconscious knew exactly what had gone on and imagination was adding a few frills.

'Developments,' Patrick said, breaking off to give me a quick kiss. 'In connection with Stefan's knocked out front tooth and associated bloodstains. The DNA matches that found on a woman who was raped and an attempt made to strangle her in a back lane in north London two years ago. A couple of off-duty firemen heard her screams and ran to assist. She survived but her attacker got away. The police know him as Steven Harris but he also calls himself Stefan Jabowitz when he's assuming a foreign persona, a sort of dark glasses and leather coat look.'

'Presumably he got the job as handyman at Boyles House using that identity.'

'And has apparently been known to use others.'

'Is SOCA looking into this now?'

'We are, and since that prison room was discovered he's been tacked on as a suspect in connection with other cases where women are forced into prostitution. Needless to say, a warrant's out for his arrest.'

'The cops were a bit slow then seeing as he's been as large as life in Kensington for some time.'

'Looks like it. By the way, that photo of Alex you took by accident didn't make any waves. It really doesn't look as though she has a criminal record.'

'Has anything come up in connection with that character I met in Boyles House?' I had looked through mugshots to no avail and a facial image had been created using E-FIT, again with no result, the only possible match already serving a sentence for attempted murder.

'Nothing. But as we both know, it's easy for people to change their appearance.'

'Will it cause friction between us if I ask you

227

if Alexandra has contacted you again?'

'No, and she hasn't,' Patrick answered shortly. I changed the subject.

# FIFTEEN

For some reason I recovered from my writer's block, or whatever it had been, and reacquired the ability to concentrate. This coincided with my imagination giving up on producing night-mares, instead obediently producing up to around a thousand words a day and I made good progress with the novel. Regrettably, I deliberately pushed the horrible demise of Imelda Burnside to the back of my mind and it was James Carrick who first made contact in connection with his murder investigation.

'Sorry if you're working but I thought you'd like to know about the truncheon,' he began. 'Forensics has finished with it. It's been cleaned up and has a Queen Victoria crown and the letters CP stamped on it, which stands for the City of London Police. It's of a type that was used in the late nineteenth and early twentieth centuries and although there's no divisional stamp – they only used those after 1910 – there is a badge number. The truncheon was issued to one Constable Jack Davison and a lot of poking around later I've established that he was Miss Hilda Bennett's great-grandfather.'

'Oh, well done! David Bennett's great-great-grandfather then.'

'And the knife *had* been used to sever the murder victim's head. There was quite a bit in the report about traces of neck glands but you're probably having your morning coffee so I won't go into details. Ironically, putting the items in the plastic bag had helped preserve the blood and fragments of bone and other stuff trapped in the serrated edge of the blade so extracting DNA was no problem.'

'What about the human blood in the soil sample?'

'That too contains the victim's DNA.'

'It does rather point towards these things being handy in the house and Bennett having killed her there, doesn't it?'

'Yes, I'm about to have him brought in again and lean on him heavily.'

Ten minutes later my mobile rang.

'Please forgive my bothering you,' said the celestial tones of Alan Kilmartin. 'But I'm in a real quandary.'

'I do tend to be a quandary wrangler,' I said with a laugh.

'I hope you're fully recovered from your accident – only it wasn't, was it?'

'No, but I have, thank you.'

'Which makes what I'm about to say even more awkward and I shall understand perfectly if you put the phone down on me.'

'I won't,' I promised. Ye gods, what was he about to propose? A fortnight in Mustique?

'It's about Alex.'

229

'Go on.'

'She rang me last night, late, saying that my number was the only one she could remember. She sounded very distressed and then the call was cut short.'

'People have numbers in their phone's memories though surely.'

'She wasn't on her own phone. I got the impression she didn't have it with her.'

'Was she sober?'

'I don't *think* so. Her voice was slurred anyway. But I've never heard Alex like this before. If what she said is correct she's in some kind of trouble.'

'What did she want you to do?'

'We didn't have a chance to talk because, as I've just said, the call was cut short.'

'Can you remember exactly what she said?'

There was a short silence while he tried to remember. 'She said, "Is that you Alan?" and I told her it was. Then she said, "You must help me." Then she cried a bit. I urged her to tell me what was wrong and she said, "I've found a phone that works in this bloody place and your number's the only one I can remember. If I—" That was all. Someone might have grabbed the phone – or hit her because there was a thump before the line went dead.'

'I wonder what she was going to say before she was interrupted.'

'I've been asking myself that. Perhaps she knew the number of it and was going to ask me to tell her where she was – find her even. I don't know. I don't know what to think.'

230

'Have you contacted the police?'

'That's part of the quandary. I've no evidence to give them that she's really in trouble. And it's exactly the kind of stagy thing she'd do to get even with people.'

Like pretending to be Carrie with the flu so I dashed off home in order to get rid of me, for example, not to mention what happened afterwards.

'Sorry to present you with a bit of a problem,' Kilmartin went on when I remained silent. 'But when you said your husband worked for SOCA ... I just felt I ought to do *something*.'

'I'll give Patrick a ring,' I told him. 'Don't do anything until I phone you back. It might not be for a while if I can't get hold of him.'

I put the mobile back on my desk and muttered a few Patrick-style expressions. The woman kept coming back like bad drains. It went without saying that every last atom of my being wanted to consign her to whichever hell she had got herself into, which was most likely a surfeit of alcohol or even drugs. But Alan Kilmartin was a very nice guy, was worried and I am not the kind of person to do nothing and lie by telling him that moves were being put in place to find her when they were not.

'Barnsley Sand and Gravel,' Patrick said when I rang him.

'It might not have been me,' I pointed out.

'I knew it was you. I've downloaded some new ringtones that are different, and suitable, for everyone in the phone's memory.'

'So what's mine?'

231

'A moo.'

I heard Michael Greenway chuckle in the background.

'You obviously have loads of time on your hands so here's something for you to think about.' I told him the story.

'I suppose the call could be traced,' he remarked when I had finished. 'Please ring Kilmartin back and ask him to let me know the number of the phone that he received the call on.'

This I did and then went back to work. I heard nothing more about it until the evening, when, as it was Friday, I collected Patrick from the station.

'The call came from a semi-derelict building, an old Inland Revenue office block eventually to be demolished in Woolwich,' he said in response to my query. 'With Mike's permission I had a search made of the place but nothing was found. But there were signs of the building having been inhabited quite recently by squatters, or whoever, and, significantly, abandoned women's clothing. There were no phones around but it's a big building with rubbish everywhere so one might have been overlooked at some stage. These findings were referred to the people working on the vice gangs cases and I understand they're going to conduct a search of their own and possibly get forensics involved.'

'But even if Alexandra was playing tricks on Alan she wouldn't normally be in a derelict building in Woolwich surely. And if she was there in connection with a sex trade business she has she would hardly draw attention to it. Alan did say though that he thought she'd been drinking. Or is she really that stupid?'

'I wouldn't have thought so. That particular phone line's dead now too – as it should have been in the first place.'

'So what on earth's going on?'

'You tell me. Do your oracle thing.'

'I'm too biased to give you an honest answer,' I muttered, concentrating on Bath's horrendous traffic.

'Bias is of no use to SOCA.'

'Don't be so bloody pompous!' I yelled at him. 'OK, Alex is shallow, ignorant, spiteful, silly, jealous, on occasions crass, and vastly insecure. She's also fun to be with, larger than life with a great sense of humour, but, above all else, vulnerable. It doesn't balance out, does it? – so everything nasty that happens to her she deserves. *That's* bias.'

'I meant that I was too personally and emotionally involved, that's all,' I snapped back.

'Look, I really do need you to think this through. It's important.'

I turned into a residential road and, against all the odds, found somewhere to park. Then I said, 'It's most unfair to expect me to do that when I'm *driving*.'

'We can't risk having a blazing row at home.'

There was a tense silence.

'I know now why you want that house,' Patrick sighed, opening his window for some fresh air and lapsing into silence.

'It's called privacy,' I said. 'All right, this

horrible old bat the oracle speaks. Given the circumstances of the call there are several possibilities and I don't have money on any of them. One is that because Alex was drunk, or, at least, under the influence of something and was in the building in connection with her illegal business, she just thought she'd wind Alan up, being too sloshed to care or realize the risks of what she was doing. The phone packed up. *Or,* she was in the building ditto, and because of being even more sloshed or under the influence was scared stiff having genuinely forgotten almost everything about herself except Alan and his phone number. But she dropped the phone and then accidentally trod on it. *Or,* her business has got out of hand, she got a bit drunk and panicked, wanting Alan to make everything all right again as he's good at that. But she then suddenly changed her mind and slammed the phone down. *Or,* a perfectly legitimate little agency was infiltrated by vicious nasties who brainwashed her into thinking there was a lot more money to be made in running brothels using the girls she got from abroad. It all went swimmingly for a while until she realized exactly the kind of nightmare she'd got herself into. She wanted to bale out and planned to move to Bath, might have even tried to go to the police, but was forced to carry on and is now, having made herself a thorough nuisance to various someones, a prisoner. She was drugged but tried to ring Alan only for the phone to be snatched from her, yanked out of its fitting and chucked out of the nearest window. You could get someone to have a look for the

234

phone as there might be some useful fingerprints on it.'

Patrick was by no means gaping but his face was wearing an expression that this oracle found immensely gratifying. Then he reached for his mobile.

Amazingly, this last theory paid off, at least with regard to the finding of a smashed old-fashioned-style telephone on the top of dumped rubbish on the ground outside the building. Unfortunately, subsequent tests would establish that half of London's fingerprints plus a generous amount of tom-cat pee were on it. At the time though the discovery narrowed down the areas those doing the detective work ought to search first, that is, rooms on the side of the building that faced west. Someone immediately remembered that a group of broken windows with blinds hanging out of them had been in rooms where women's clothing had been found and they all traipsed back to the seventh floor – the lifts were not working – and began their search, which was still ongoing.

One did not have to be very clever to know that Patrick was all ready to go and look for the woman but did not like to broach the subject with me. He would be aware that he would not be able just to set off without being given some kind of mandate by Greenway. In the *carte blanche* days of MI5 when he had virtually been his own boss matters had been different but to a resourceful man this merely meant that a different approach was now needed. And pray that his wife wouldn't mind too much?

'The quandary file is getting fatter,' I commented later that evening, Patrick in a world of his own, preoccupied with tactics.

'What? Oh ... yes.'

'You want to go and find Alex.'

'Not just her, the others as well. It somehow makes it worse when you know someone who's involved.'

'I'm sure there are people working overtime to put plans in place to find out where they're being held. There are probably several groups of women.'

He grimaced. 'Yes, but with all due risk assessments completed and health and safety clauses taken into consideration, plus a reminder to personnel to take a woolly and a clean hankie.'

'You're doing your ex-special services soldier knows best thing again.'

He smiled in a distracted way. 'I can't help it.'

'Then give Greenway a stunning plan of action that he simply can't turn down.'

Patrick got to his feet and restlessly paced the room. 'Ingrid, you should know by now that I don't do stunning plans of action. Like your books, it's mostly made up as I go along. All I know is that I want to go undercover, and with the deepest malice aforethought, find these bastards and stop what they're doing.'

'Start with Fred at Boyles House. Terrorize information out of him – I'm sure he knew a lot more than he told me.'

Patrick paced some more. 'It's Greenway

though. And you're right: plus everyone else who's working on this. If I go off-piste it's a slap in the face for them.'

'You could ask. Mike might be reluctant to order you in because you've been ill.'

This Patrick did, phoning the commander there and then, at home. He was briskly told to be patient: as he was already well aware, a painstaking search of the building was being carried out and forensic people were involved. As he also should know this took time and any results of tests even longer. There was no point in rushing off without the benefit of knowledge as this might hazard the safety of the women even more. Greenway finished by saying that he hoped to see him first thing on Monday morning when the first outline results should be ready and then went on to remind him that he was an adviser to SOCA, not 007, expletives deleted.

'Not good enough,' Patrick muttered, having seemingly reported this riposte to me just about word for word. Then he threw himself back into his chair and said, 'What I really could do with is a member of the Vice Squad.'

'You have one: James.'

'He *was*.'

I carried on reading.

Carrick arrived at the rectory about half an hour later – he lives fairly close by – and admitted that Joanna having decided to have an early night the invitation to have a dram had appealed, a lot.

'It's not just about whisky,' I warned him as both men came into the living room, Patrick

237

having answered the door.

'It never is,' the DCI lamented. 'When people lure Scotsmen with strong drink they usually want them to dig out their *skein dhu* and polish up the *claidheamh mór.*'

'Do you really have a claymore?' I asked.

'Regrettably, no.'

'Dad has his great-great-great-uncle Bertram's sabre that he used when he fought alongside General Gordon at Khartoum,' Patrick observed when they each had a glass in their hand.

'Did an English sword save him against spears?'

'No.'

'Thought not.'

'Have you questioned David Bennett?' I asked.

'He wasn't at home and a neighbour said he thought he'd gone away. If he doesn't turn up very soon and has done a runner I shall put out a warrant for his arrest.' He surveyed Patrick appraisingly. 'What do you want me to do?'

'I need insider knowledge from snouts, undercover people and all relevant parties as to where women, including Alexandra Nightingale, are being kept prisoner, having been very recently moved from somewhere else, by people running some kind of vice ring.'

'She's being held captive?' Carrick said in astonishment.

'It would *appear* so. She rang her one-time boyfriend from a derelict building in Woolwich. It's being searched now and, like the place in Boyles Road, there are signs of recent habitation and discarded women's clothing.'

Carrick turned to me. 'You thought she was running something like that.'

'It looks as though something's gone horribly wrong.'

'Could it be a con though? – the woman appears to be a real besom.'

'Even *I* can't imagine she'd go to the lengths of getting inside a potentially dangerous building due for demolition just to get her ex in a flap.'

'Greenway says wait until forensics come up with something, perhaps Monday,' Patrick put in. 'If they know that the police aren't far behind them these people might kill the evidence and take the first plane out.'

'Do we know anything at all about them?'

Patrick gave him what information there was about Stefan Jabowitz, aka Steven Harris, adding that nothing was known about the man who attacked me at Boyles House, the other man called Fred who worked there nor anyone else who might be involved.

'Trying to sort this out yourself is all very well but you're not working for MI5 now,' James pointed out soberly.

'Sorry, I'm really fed up with people saying that to me. Richard Daws recruited me for SOCA because he thought I had something to offer. Greenway's lost sight of that fact.'

'He might actually be dead worried that you'll overdo it and be ill again.'

'Ingrid said that, but I'm fine now. Are you going to help me, or not?'

'It's a while since I trod the streets of London.'

'I'm sure your buddies up there still keep you abreast of events in case any scumbags head for the West Country.'

Carrick took an appreciative sip of his single malt. 'Getting on the phone right now wouldn't be a lot of use and I don't have mobile numbers for the people I'm thinking of, who might not even have mobiles anyway. We'd have to go there and drag them out of their rat holes, those who are still alive and not in prison or helping with enquiries, that is.'

Patrick looked at me.

'This is your operation,' I said.

'I was going to say that I don't think you ought to come with us.'

'No, this time I'm quite happy for you to go without me,' I replied, not entirely truthfully. 'You can both watch out for one another. I shall be here if you need me to do anything.'

'We can take my car,' Carrick said. 'Unlike SOCA advisers I can't afford a big posh motor.'

'Are you sure?' Patrick asked him. 'I'd have a problem driving yours but you could drive mine.'

'A Range Rover's too conspicuous for the places we're going. It would be gone as soon as we'd turned our backs. D'you want to set off now?'

'After an hour's kip perhaps.'

'I shall need to go home for some rough gear and to tell Joanna.'

Then, after exchanging sorrowful glances they

240

both sighed and carefully poured the rest of their whisky back in the bottle.

I went to bed, for some reason needing to distance myself from what was going on. The only way I can explain this is to compare men like Patrick – and James for that matter, who worked undercover when he was in the Vice Squad – to cats; when you let them out they go to the wild side. This does not usually manifest itself when we work together although on the occasions when it has, when events have turned very nasty indeed, it can be the stuff of nightmares. It is perfectly true that the presence of women has a gentling effect on their menfolk but, frankly, they do not necessarily want it. Not if they are to get the job done. Therefore, I did not want to be around when Patrick collected an overnight bag from the Range Rover and put into it anything else he might need because he would be that other person, the one with the murderous glint in his eyes.

That he was upset by what appeared to be happening to Alexandra I found perfectly understandable, it would be ghastly for any woman. It was a relief not to feel remotely jealous about Patrick's decision, my only reservation being that if it did turn out to be a hoax then I would indeed yearn for her boiled-down bones to be fed to hyenas.

They went: I heard Carrick's car return and then depart again. Selfishly, I was rather hoping they would achieve something meaningful before the weekend was out or I would have some difficult explaining to do to Commander Greenway. At this point I must have dropped off to sleep for I awoke with a start, nerves jangling, when the phone rang at just after midnight.

'Has he gone?' Greenway asked.

'Yes,' I said.

'I'm learning, aren't I?'

'He has DCI Carrick with him.'

'That's good news. Don't worry, if they're not back by then I'll get on to Carrick's boss first thing on Monday and tell him I've requisitioned him for a job.'

'Can you do that?'

'Dunno, I'll find out. Please let me know what's going on – the last person Patrick'll contact is me.'

I found myself admiring Greenway enormously.

# SIXTEEN

The next morning, having not really slept after Greenway's call, I mentally consigned writing to a bottom drawer and threw myself into domesticity and innocent family matters, beginning by giving Carrie an unexpected day off. Perhaps Patrick had been right and I was trying to cut myself into too many pieces already, never mind taking on restoring a house.

'I wish I could go with Unc— Dad on some of

his assignments,' Matthew said wistfully when he, Katie and Justin were having their breakfast. Vicky had woken early, as she tended to, been given a bowl of porridge sweetened with honey and promptly gone back to sleep on the sofa in the living room.

'I want to!' Justin yelled through a mouthful of boiled egg.

'Don't shout,' Katie scolded. Lately, she seemed to have taken it upon herself to curb his noisier excesses. I found this quite amusing, and helpful, but made no comment – that's what big sisters are for, isn't it?

In an unfamiliar and happy mumsy glow I joined them with my buttered toast around the big farmhouse kitchen table saying to Matthew, 'It's not like the police shows on TV, not just exciting chases and always getting their man. Quite boring for most of the time really.'

'I know. But I could help him. Someone my age wouldn't be noticed by crooks if I was watching a place. They'd say, "It's just a stupid kid." I can do stupid.' And proceeded to look very stupid indeed, setting Katie laughing.

'Tell Mum how you found out who had pinched Tom's pens and stuff at school,' she urged. 'Just by staring at the boy you thought had done it until he panicked and threw them back.'

'You just have,' Matthew whispered. 'It's nothing to brag about.'

This shook me to the core. It had never entered my head that he was like his uncle. No, stupid me; he looks very much like him at that age, as family photos prove and while Elspeth always

243

says that Justin is exactly like his father as a child, being noisy, a show-off and naughty, here was another version, the clever bit.

'You have to be very good with people,' I said. 'Know when suspects are lying, be able to get to the truth, be sympathetic with victims of crime but a bit horrible to people you know are guilty.'

'He went off with DCI Carrick last night, didn't he?' Matthew went on, raising an eyebrow questioningly in the direction of one of my pieces of toast. 'May I?'

I gave it to him and got up to make some more. So he possessed that mannerism as well.

'I heard a car and looked out. I like James,' Matthew went on. 'He did say I could call him James. I just wish I could have...' His voice petered out unhappily.

'They'll have gone somewhere nasty,' Katie said matter-of-factly. 'Otherwise they wouldn't have gone in the middle of the night.'

'How do you know they weren't driving to London for a rugby match at Twickenham this afternoon?' I enquired.

Matthew shook his head. 'There are no matches there today.'

'You thought of that then?' I went on to ask, hearing the incredulity in my tone.

'Yes, we were talking about it this morning. We know James plays rugby. He's going to coach me when I start playing, but it can't be that.' Matthew regarded me brightly. 'So they went to London?'

'I can't discuss it with you, I'm afraid.'

'That might have to be today's mystery then,'

244

Katie announced.

'You have mysteries?' I said, feeling that showing an interest would mitigate my negative response.

'We work on them most days,' she answered. 'But if they're not solved quickly they can go on for weeks until we either get an answer or put them in the question mark file.'

'Mysteries such as what?' I wheedled.

Eyes bright with enthusiasm she said, 'Did you know that the man who digs the graves with that machine thing has a girlfriend and they smoke pot in the hut in the churchyard where the grass-cutting tools are kept?'

'No,' I said evenly.

'We think they do other things in there too.'

*'Katie!'* Matthew hissed.

'And there's a wholesale butcher's delivery-man...' She broke off and asked Matthew, *'Wholesale?* Is that right?'

'Wholesale,' he confirmed.

'Who often parks his lorry by the pub, takes a whole load of meat in and comes out with crates of beer and several bottles of whisky.'

'That must have a perfectly logical explanation,' I said.

She was unabashed. 'Right now we're working on the case of the man in the black Mercedes who's been just sitting in it at the top of the village.'

I went cold. 'When did you first notice him?'

'Just before you had your accident. Then he disappeared. But he's back now, we saw him yesterday on the way home from school.'

245

'I suppose you didn't get the registration.'

'We did. I'll get the case file,' Matthew said and left the room.

I must have looked at Katie a bit wildly for she said, 'We're very careful when we're operating. Just stupid kids, hanging out.'

Matthew came back with a red folder, explained that they were colour-coded depending on the perceived degree of potential seriousness – only he didn't use such long words – and opened it to reveal a single sheet of neatly printed information.

'May I have a look?' I asked.

He passed it over.

Noted down were the dates and times when they had seen it, where the vehicle had been parked, and the registration. Fantastically, there was also a description of the driver as he had got out of the car to stretch his legs.

'This might be important,' I said, trying to sound casual. 'Is it all right for me to take a copy of it?'

They were delighted.

'And you must promise me, really promise, that you won't, under any circumstances, go near this car again or even watch it from a distance. If it does have a bearing on a case Patrick told me about then you'll very likely risk the outcome of the investigation. Is that clear?'

'Yes,' they said in unison.

'Promise?'

They promised.

'We'd better make it the rubbish dumping in the lane job then,' Katie was saying as they left the kitchen. 'Look for names and addresses in it. Oh,' she put her head around the door. 'If we just happen to spot the car when we're around do you want to know?'

'Don't happen to be anywhere near where it was. And wear my gardening gloves if you're handling rubbish.'

Feeling a bit weak and picturing broken glass, used syringes, razor blades and tin cans, I glared at Justin who immediately stopped what he was doing, smearing spilt egg yoke more widely over the front of his clean-on teeshirt.

'Ever seen Daddy do that?' I asked grimly of him.

He nodded solemnly and then gave me Patrick's lovely smile.

The description did not match that of the man who had attacked me in Boyles House so, whatever the truth of Alexandra's past or present circumstances, she was a three-yob woman, at least. This one was fifty to sixty years of age, grey-haired but balding, of medium height and had appeared to be wearing a lot of gold jewellery. I sent the information listed on the sheet of A4, exactly as it was, to Greenway's work email address, there was no point in bothering him with it at home. I knew that his mobile was never switched off except when he was on holiday, presumably taken on an Antarctic ice shelf, but was determined to contact him only as a last resort. Having access to vehicle records I set about finding out to whom the Mercedes belonged. Anything I found out could be relayed to

Patrick.

The car was registered to one Romano Descallier, his address in Berkshire. I ran the information through crime records and discovered that this gaming club and wine bar proprietor – he owned several businesses in London – had served twelve months for demanding money with menaces in his youth but had since matured sufficiently to be charged with tax evasion, GBH, of which he was cleared on account of witnesses failing to turn up in court, a hit and run offence for which he lost his licence and served two years, culminating in driving whilst disqualified and assaulting a police officer. This case was still on the book as he had jumped bail.

'So he's another one who's fallen through holes in the system,' I muttered.

After checking on my family, Mark asleep in his pram in the garden just outside the window, Vicky awake but still on the sofa in the next room playing happily with her three Teddies, Justin in the dining room with me crawling around the floor with toy cars and spittily making all the sound effects, the elder two presumably picking over someone's rubbish, I rang Alan Kilmartin.

Why did my heart still thump madly every time I heard his voice?

'Did Alexandra ever mention a man by the name of Romano Descallier?' I asked when we had exchanged greetings and I had told him that Patrick and the Met police were working on the phone call he had received from her.

'Yes, she did. He was one of her clients.'

'He may well be involved. Do you know what kind of staff she supplied him with?'

'A butler, a nanny, I *think*, plus other people like gardeners and cleaners. It seems he was very fussy – always sacking his staff on excuses that Alex said were downright flimsy.'

'It doesn't sound as though she liked him.'

'He infuriated her but – and I might be quite wrong here – I think, on the quiet, she came to quite fancy him, perhaps on account of his being loaded.'

I filed that snippet away and said, 'Do you know if she ever went to his house?'

'We both did. We were invited to a Christmas bash one year.'

'Look, I know you're terribly busy but—'

'I'm not, it's Saturday and anyway there's nothing pressing.'

'Would you write down what you can remember about this man, his home, any family, everything you noticed, and email it to me?'

'It might be easier for me to come over – that's if you don't mind. I can do you a drawing of the place and a rough plan of the room layout as well if that might be useful to the police. He insisted on showing everyone round – a complete poser if you ask me.'

'Please do, but as Patrick's parents have gone out for the day I have full charge of five children.'

'Oh, I like kids.'

I then went into panic mode over what I could give everyone for lunch.

\* \* \*

I need not have worried. From the moment he walked through the door carrying a large cardboard tube that contained sheets of drawing paper everything was in hand. First, we lunched on jacket potatoes with various fillings and salad followed by what was left of a large home-made chocolate gateau that Elspeth had won in a village raffle and had begged me to help them finish. Then, while I quickly tidied up, Alan Kilmartin spread a few sheets of paper on the kitchen table, together with some professional felt-tip pens in the most fantastic colours I had ever seen and got the three eldest busily designing their dream houses. Having already told me that his two sisters had babies he then dandled Mark, who had been squalling, on his knee. Vicky, bless her sweet little soul, was still having a quiet day, had eaten a large lunch and was, once again, asleep on the sofa.

We took our coffee, and Mark, into the dining room where I cleared a corner of my desk and Alan got to work.

'How do you write in here?' he broke off to ask. 'There must be far too many distractions.'

'With difficulty,' I answered.

'You ought to have your own space.'

'That's why I wanted to buy a house in Bath. Unfortunately, you-know-who had seen it first. I've lost it now, she put in a higher offer.'

'Don't give up hope. She often sees something she decides she wants even more and drops what had been the latest toy. Unless she's an innocent victim in all this she'll end up in court and

250

probably won't need it anyway. Nasty of me, I know, but I rather hope she gets locked up.'

What he had said would be a rough sketch was turning out to be what looked to me like a finely executed and detailed plan.

'Please be very careful over this Descallier character,' Alan said a couple of minutes later. 'Since you rang I've been thinking about what went on that evening and have decided that my conclusions that he was merely a poser with very poor taste was because I had been looking at him through the bottom of a champagne glass for a lot of the time. There were some dodgy-looking people there with whom he seemed to have some kind of understanding.'

'What else went on that made you suspicious?'

'It was just the atmosphere. Convivial on the surface but with not too pleasant undertones. Meaningful looks, Descallier sending people off on some crrand or other with a scowl and a jerk of his head, a general feeling of unease – hard to describe actually.'

An argument, Justin shouting, again, having broken out in the kitchen, Kilmartin left the room before I could move and I heard him point out that drawing offices were very quiet places and any real problems should be referred to the dining room. Silence fell.

No one, he went on to tell me, had been intro-duced to the guests as a wife or partner and no children or very young people had been present. There had been plenty of young women around though, some of whom had given the impression they lived there. The house was large, modern and situated close to Windsor Great Park.

'Is your husband planning to break into this place and that's why you want the information?' he went on to ask lightly.

'I don't think so, but he might when I tell him about it.'

Later, when he had gone, I rang Patrick and left a message, his phone being switched off, which I had half expected. There was no response until quite late in the evening when I was able to relax, Carrie having returned and happy to carry on with her duties.

'We're in a pub,' was Patrick's first piece of news.

'Fancy that,' I said.

'We deserve a pint and something to eat. James broke all the speed limits except where there were cameras and we got here in time to take apart four one-time or active pimps who he knew about before they crawled back into their sewers. Another two were in prison and the last was dead. We didn't learn an awful lot but got the whereabouts of an old warehouse that's known to have been used to conceal female immigrants, legal and otherwise, and went there. The place is deserted but it's obvious that people have been living there quite recently. Boyles House was mentioned by one man but he didn't know any details. We'd called there on the off-chance on the way but Fred doesn't work nights. Then we had a kip in the car and now we're fuelled to follow another lead, an address in east London that someone swore is being used for what was described as a holding pen. What's this about something the kids have found out?'

I had not previously gone into details but did so now, finishing by saying, 'In my view this would be a more profitable line of enquiry. This man could be the boss. He followed me to Warminster, and now he's back. Matthew and Katie saw him the day before yesterday.'

'I don't like the sound of that. I'll ring you back when I've spoken to James.'

Quite a while went by before my phone rang again.

'Understandably James doesn't want to get involved with breaking into a private house without a warrant,' Patrick said. 'And I'll have to get Greenway on board, ditto. We're going to have a nose around the place in Chingford that I mentioned just now and then, if that doesn't lead anywhere call it a day. James will then drive back home and organize some surveillance around Hinton Littlemoor. I'll go to my club and contact Greenway. Would you email me the drawings and plans Kilmartin drew up?'

'I can't, they're on A3 paper, too big to scan in to our machine. I'll bring them.'

'There's every chance that Descallier, or one of his minions, will follow you.'

'He might not be around at four in the morning if I leave then. If he is, or someone else is standing in for him and tails me I'll just shoot out his tyres.'

'No, I think you should concentrate on losing him – we don't want this character to know we're really on to him.'

253

It was nice to know that he took my threat seriously.

Brave statements apart I still tended to unlock the Range Rover with fear gnawing at my insides. I had been keeping it parked as close to the house as possible so that if anyone approached it during the night the outside security lights would come on. Still not being able to recollect those few minutes of my life made it worse and every time I went anywhere near the vehicle I checked that there were no tell-tale drips of brake fluid on the ground beneath it.

Those still abed had been warned of my early departure and as the tyres crunched over the gravel of the drive I wondered if Matthew and Katie were now awake and this would be their new mystery. Perhaps Mike Greenway would permit us to show them a small part of SOCA's HQ next time we took them to London.

No black Mercs were parked in the High Street of the village and no one appeared to follow me. I had been on the road for over an hour, the sky lightening, before I saw a familiar black shape in my rear mirror. I was on the outskirts of a village and immediately turned left into a small housing estate where I did a U-turn and then parked, facing the way I had come in. Switching off the ignition and lights I waited.

Five minutes went by. Light traffic whooshed to and fro on the main road but no one came into this quite little enclave, not even a dog barked. I set off again, prepared for the vehicle to be similarly parked in a side road while the driver

254

waited for me to pass. A few miles farther on I had not seen it and began to relax, chiding myself for having got in a mild flap over what had obviously been another black Mercedes, hardly an uncommon vehicle.

Patrick's club – a low-key, but frankly, sumptuous affair for ex-officers who have been severely injured in the course of duty – is in Chiswick and I got there just in time for breakfast. This, and my arrival, had previously been arranged, the club being sufficiently old-fashioned to prefer members not to have females arrive out of the blue. I had asked on a previous visit if ladies who fitted the criteria were allowed to join and had been told they were: it was just that there weren't any. And no, the place isn't one of those stuffy establishments where old fogies sit around dozing, waiting to die. Behind the scenes it is a meeting place, the heart of an information network, a grapevine, for MI5, MI6, covert police departments, including SOCA and Special Branch. Most of the people who go through its doors are not members at all, but, like me, 'visitors'.

Patrick, who keeps a change of clothing on the premises as a certain standard of dress is expected, was waiting for me in the entrance hall, actually a large room furnished with armchairs and sofas with a coffee bar in one corner. When I first glimpsed him, standing by a table reading the headlines of one of the morning newspapers placed upon it, my heart turned over, as it usually does. Here, surely, was the other side of the coin to the man who had gone away just over

255

twenty-four hours previously with murder writ large in his eyes. But not so, I saw when we were close: his smile when he looked up and saw me was genuine but he was as taut as a bowstring.

'No luck then?' I said, after I had signed the visitors' book at reception and we had exchanged a quick kiss.

'Yes, in a way. I'll tell you about it in a minute. Were you followed?'

I handed over the drawings in the cardboard tube that Alan Kilmartin had left behind for me to use. 'There was a Merc behind me at one stage but it hadn't followed me from the village. And this man or his henchmen can't possibly wait for me to go somewhere around the clock.'

When we were seated in the dining room; heavy blue brocade curtains, gold-coloured carpet, marble fireplace, chandeliers, discreet bar, Patrick signalled to the waiter. Then he said, 'I've been on to Greenway with your info. Descallier's hot. Friend of Cabinet ministers – on the quiet – financier of political parties, whichever one best suits his inclinations, racehorse owner and on nodding terms with minor royalty. There's no question that any vehicle registered to him – and it would have been driven by an employee – could have been remotely connected with what happened to you as it would retrospectively be reported stolen as he's a chum of a couple of top cops too.'

'We have a problem.'

'Quite.'

We ordered our breakfast and then I said, 'I know he has a criminal record.'

256

'Yes, as long as your arm, under different aliases and in different countries.'

'I can't understand why he's bothering himself with what would appear to be taking over Alexandra's business.'

'It's the contacts he'd be after. And people like him have their dirty fingers in so many pies, employing so many bit players who are terrified of them that it becomes almost impossible to trace crime back to the man at the top. Like Martino Capelli, only worse.'

'I take it then that Special Branch is already working on this.'

'Any number of branches are.'

'Are there undercover people inside the house?'

'According to Greenway, no – too risky. I shall take these plans to Mike.'

'What about the couple of top cops?'

'Being watched – and due for retirement.'

'Which makes it stalemate as far as we're concerned.'

'We could go and have a look at the place.

# SEVENTEEN

Shackled, as it were, by different protocols to those of MI5 we could only pause outside a pair of magnificent gates, one corner of the house just visible down a curving drive as it was screened by trees. One of several such, fairly new, properties, it was situated near the entrance of one of the public, but gated, roads that run through Windsor Great Park.

'Nothing to see,' I murmured.

'But someone's just driven either in or out,' Patrick said.

'How d'you know?'

'The gates were a few inches from shutting as we came round that last bend.'

His mobile rang and he handed it to me to answer.

'Sorry to bother you at the weekend,' said Alan Kilmartin's voice. 'But I've just had a another weird call from Alexandra and I thought I'd mention it to your husband first as you said he was working on it.'

I asked him to hang on, relayed the message to Patrick and he pulled off the road on to a woodland track. I could gather little from what was said as he mostly listened and spoke little. After the call ended he sat pensively, staring at nothing through the windscreen.

'Well?' I ventured after half a minute or so.

'He's had this call, similar to last time, with Alex saying she's managed to get to a phone and giving the impression she's being held somewhere against her will. As before, the call was cut short but this time she screamed before the line went dead. I'd better let Greenway know so he can organize a trace.'

The Commander said he would immediately do so and was sufficiently fired up to ask us to meet him at a local country house hotel in Englefield Green. (We discovered at a much later date that he lived in north Ascot.) He was wearing what my father would have described as 'best gardening togs' and had bits of leaves in his hair which made me think that his wife was probably away from home.

'I hope you appreciate I wouldn't be taking the weekend off if this case was my sole responsibility, which it isn't,' he began by saying. 'But...' He left the rest unsaid, gazing over what was before him. Then, 'I'd like to talk to this architect...' He glanced up questioningly.

'Alan Kilmartin,' I said. 'He used to go out with Alexandra Nightingale, who's been making these phone calls.' I gave him his phone number which he noted down.

'There being a possibility that Descallier's involved with the people trafficking cases we've been working on is new,' Greenway said, still perusing the drawings. 'So my instinct is to act. But I do have to respect what other outfits have been working on for some time even though

259

they've been at it, in my view, for far too long. When this finally does get blown apart there's going to be a lot of what the farmers call muck flying around and a couple of our beloved political masters are going to lose their jobs. I think that's the main reason for the delay. I shall send these off to the other departments involved to demonstrate that I'm sharing intelligence but how, or if, they'll be used is anyone's guess.'

'Do we know what this man looks like?' I asked. 'I forgot to ask Alan about that.'

'I've seen a mugshot,' Greenway answered. 'But it was taken some years ago. He's of medium height and build, greyish sort of complexion, pale blue eyes, light brown thinning hair, no visible scars. An ordinary-looking bloke, really.'

The trace came back very quickly, an old warehouse on a wharf at Deptford.

'But how does such a place still have landlines?' Patrick said impatiently, Greenway having imparted the news.

'I was just about to elaborate,' he was told. 'Presumably, it doesn't. The building's due to be converted to upmarket apartments, starting Monday, tomorrow, and the call was actually made from a Portakabin office hired by the developers. We won't know any more until someone's been round there.'

This he organized and there was another wait.

'I simply can't believe that Alexandra's in danger,' I said quietly to Patrick when we were on our second pot of coffee. 'Two calls almost the same is too much of a coincidence.'

Patrick merely grunted. Me, right from the beginning I had thought it a whole barrel of stinking red herrings, the work of a spiteful woman all too keen to get her revenge on one man who had dumped her and another who had given her a piece of his mind and made her pay the bill. I was about to risk pointing this out but Greenway spoke first.

'Think of the scorn of the media if we raided the place to look for trafficked women and found nothing,' he said slowly, head back, eyes seemingly studying the ceiling.

'What, this house?' Patrick said, gesturing towards the drawings. 'Bloody hell! You don't think they're actually being kept there now, do you?'

'Not necessarily. But if this woman ... she is the one who has the hots for you, isn't she?'

'So it would appear,' Patrick said stiffly.

'Forgive me for asking but have you told her where to get off?'

'I have.'

'It fits. What revenge, eh?'

A few minutes later Greenway had a call with the information that the Portakabin at Deptford had not been locked and there were no signs that anything had been disturbed. The phone was being examined for fingerprints but even though it had only recently been installed was greasy, as someone put it, "As if a bloke was eating fish and chips with his fingers while using it." The warehouse itself was still being searched.

'That's it,' he said. 'We can't do any more right now.' He surveyed the pair of us. 'You know

261

what I'm going to say right now, don't you?'

Patrick said, 'You're about to forbid me on pain of death from going anywhere near Descallier's place.'

'D'you reckon you could get a few bugs in there?' said the Commander with a crafty grin.

'If I know anything about Special Branch there's probably a ton of them planted already. And what's this about not messing around with any other departments' scenarios?'

'Cold feet?'

'Don't be ridiculous.'

'What would you do if you were still head of your own outfit at MI5?'

'I had almost complete freedom then.'

'I'm aware of that.'

'And licence to kill.'

'I know that too.'

'But you haven't thought through the implications. If there was strong evidence that this character was keeping women prisoner on the premises I'd have gone in there and if I met resistance from any number of gun-toting minders, henchmen, whatever, I'd have started a small but useful war.'

Greenway looked at me as if for verification but before I could utter a word, said, 'There isn't strong evidence.'

'Then we stay out.'

'Good,' Greenway said, getting to his feet. 'Just testing.'

Patrick took a deep breath and let it go very slowly.

* * *

An hour later, when we were having a light lunch, the Commander received a report on the search of the warehouse. Women's clothing had been found on the top floor and one enterprising soul was of the opinion that although obviously old and creased, the garments were actually clean. With permission, whoever it was intended to call at all the nearest charity shops as soon as they opened the following morning to try to discover if they might have been the source.

'The clothing you found at Boyles House had been worn, hadn't it?' Greenway asked us.

I told him, yes, filthy.

'Do we know what condition the stuff was in at the building in Woolwich?'

'Not yet.'

'This has every appearance of being a hoax,' Greenway muttered. He glared at Patrick. 'Has this female the kind of mentality to do something along these lines?'

'Frankly, yes,' Patrick replied. 'But it doesn't mean that she's a willing player. There's more to this than a hoax. For a start there's the irrefutable evidence that a car registered to Romano Descallier has been following Ingrid and the driver might be responsible for tampering with her brakes. I have to say in using such a potentially traceable vehicle they took a huge risk which perhaps demonstrates how arrogant, or stupid, or both, the man is. As we already know Descallier was a client of Alexandra Nightingale and a room she was ostensibly using as an office – it wasn't – at Boyles House had another, concealed, room at the rear where people had obviously been imprisoned.'

'She could be working with this man.'

'Or had her business forcibly taken over.'

'Where does she live?'

'In a studio flat in Bayswater. DCI Carrick and I went there but there was no one in.'

'You broke in?' I enquired, keeping my cool, all this being very new news to me.

'I felt it important to do so. We used the fire escape and I got in through a window,' Patrick said impassively as though answering an enquiry from the Commander. 'Carrick stayed outside as was right and proper. I fully expected to find her there and that her first call to Kilmartin was a trick. She wasn't at home. I did a quick search for any evidence that might point to where she could be but found nothing. There was only one message on her phone; from a woman friend wondering when they could meet and have coffee together.'

'Wasn't she supposed to be house-hunting in Bath?' Greenway said.

'She was, and looking for a business premises of some kind.'

'Stefan, or Steven, was,' I corrected.

'He could still have been controlling her. Her recent behaviour's suggested she was either drinking too much, which we witnessed, or taking drugs. That might be the control they have over her.'

The memory came into my mind of Alexandra marching into the hotel foyer, eyes flashing, furious. Could the glitter in her eyes have been real tears and not just anger? Could her demeanour be put down to being on a knife-edge, on the verge of breakdown? I resolved to give her the benefit of the doubt until the real story emerged.

'We can do nothing more right now,' Greenway said. 'I'll see you in the morning.'

He left.

I looked at Patrick and Patrick looked at me.

'Well?' I said.

'He's left the plans behind.'

'So I see.'

'I'm desperate to get inside that place.'

'There will be very sophisticated alarm systems, far more sensitive and modern than anything you encountered at MI5.'

'You think I didn't do any training when I joined SOCA?'

'You mean they showed you how to deal with such things?'

'SOCA didn't. Private training, a refresher course. From a bloke who served under me, now puts 'em in and owed me a favour. He gave me a gizmo.'

'A sort of remote control, you mean.'

'Umm.'

'That was something else you didn't tell me about.'

'There was not a lot of point in telling you I'd been to Alex's flat as I drew a blank. If there'd been some kind of result I would have shared it with you.'

Sometimes you just have to let things pass.

The pair of us remained sitting there. Then Patrick said, 'I ought to stick to what I told

265

Greenway – despite him leaving these drawings behind as a heavy hint.'

'So do I.'

'I'd prefer to go through Alex's flat much more thoroughly before making any more moves.'

As a precaution Patrick had driven down a boggy forest track at speed, plastering half the vehicle in mud, including the number plates. Just outside the car park of the country house hotel we were waved down by the obviously eagle-eyed crew of an area car: to have an obscured registration plate is, strictly speaking, illegal. Patrick showed them his ID and they became interested and extremely friendly.

'Know anything about that house on the corner by the gate into the park, the one next to where one of her Majesty's trees has recently been blown down?' Patrick asked casually.

'Only that we're supposed to keep an eye out for people hanging around nearby,' one of the men replied. 'Some big noise or other lives there. He probably plays golf with the Chief Constable.'

His colleague nudged him warningly.

'Oh, don't worry about me,' Patrick said. 'Just drifting around.'

'It's only because the top of the tree took out a section of their boundary fence,' said the same man with the air of someone who knows better. 'I keep meaning to walk down to see if they've had it fixed yet.'

'When did this happen?'

266

'Around ten days ago.'

We took our leave and duly drifted off.

'Sometimes things drop right into your lap,' Patrick said.

'We're giving priority to searching the Bayswater flat,' I reminded him.

It was situated, like thousands of others, on the very top floor of a terraced Victorian house. In case Alexandra was at home Patrick first rang the door bell. When there was no response we went down a side way at one end of the row of houses that led into another narrow lane that gave access to the rear. But not vehicular access: everyone had to park in the street. The backs of the properties were the usual muddle of added-on bathrooms, kitchen extensions, conservatories, garden sheds, bins, children's swings, and rubbish, each one surrounded by a brick wall of medium height, some topped with trellis for extra privacy. We were making for the seventh one from the end.

There were gates in the end walls, the one we wanted open and falling off its hinges. Unlike most of the others that I had glimpsed in passing the garden was hardly able to deserve the name, consisting mostly of long grass and weeds with hugely overgrown privet hedges. I thought no one was about and then as we walked down the path and approached the back door a middle-aged woman emerged.

'What do you want?' she asked, no doubt grumpy because of having been caught with her hair in rollers. 'I don't know you.'

'Police,' Patrick said, waving his ID in her direction. 'Have you seen Alexandra Nightingale lately?'

'Who?'

'Alexandra Nightingale. She lives in the top flat.'

'Oh, *her*. No, not for ages. But that's nothing new. She's only around sometimes. Doesn't speak, you know.'

'Have you seen her with anyone here?'

'No, I've hardly ever clapped eyes on her at all.'

'There's concern for her safety and she's not answering the outside bell. Perhaps you'd be good enough to let us into the front hall so we can see if she's at home.'

'But if you've already tried ringing her bell—'

'We have keys,' Patrick interrupted quietly.

The woman led us through her untidy, drab, fishy-smelling home and without another word let us out through the front door. It banged resoundingly behind us.

'You'd never believe this was a fashionable part of London, would you?' I said in a loud voice.

Patrick uttered a noise not unlike a cat fight and made for the stairs.

'You said you'd climbed in through a window before,' I remarked.

'With difficulty and not in broad daylight,' came the reply. 'I know we don't want any more children but it was an extremely tight squeeze.'

I'm afraid I giggled.

It could have been the last laugh, ever.

* * *

Patrick's skeleton keys quickly dealt with the locks on the door of the top flat.

'Alex?' he called. 'Are you there?'

There was utter silence within.

We entered. The door opened directly into a large studio room. It was attractively furnished with two sofas in a pretty shade of deep pink, a coffee table, a workstation with computer and, along one wall, there was a divan bed covered with a throw that matched the sofas. In a corner was an Alan Kilmartin designed kitchen unit exactly like the one in his office. Further exploration revealed a separate shower room and toilet, the window of which was not properly latched, presumably the one Patrick had climbed through – I saw what he meant, it was only around sixteen inches wide – and a couple of large built-in cupboards mostly full of clothes.

'There's usually a door on to a roof area—' I was saying as several men burst through exactly that having thrust aside a concealing curtain. The room filled with them.

'Go!' Patrick shouted to me. 'Go on! Go!'

The last, and latest, rule of engagement: Ingrid does not get involved if there are these odds.

One of them was already standing between me and the front door. I employed my usual recipe for this and kicked him where it hurt most, dashed past the stricken and gasping result and out on to the landing. Half a house-sized oaf was waiting there so I repeated the exercise, missed but he shimmied out of range, overbalancing

269

slightly thus giving me time to belt back inside and into the toilet, slam the door and lock it. I was trying to shut my mind to the hell that was taking place in the main room.

Already someone, no doubt Oaf Two, was trying to kick the door in. I stood on the toilet seat, opened the window wide and started to wriggle through it. If a six foot two bloke of slim build could get through it then so could I. But I am not so slim and my bosom was still generous after having Mark. The door was bouncing in its frame. Then it crashed inwards and the moron tumbled in with it. This provided the impetus I needed and with an involuntary shriek of pain as I felt I was skinned fore and aft I half fell out of the window, almost getting hung up on one foot, and landed in an untidy heap on a platform of the fire escape a couple of feet below. There had been a sound as of a sack of bones hitting concrete as my pursuer cannoned at speed into the loo.

Moments later I was dashing down the stairs. The car was several streets away and I was praying that no one was lurking in the side way. To be on the safe side and having run down the garden I turned the other way, hoping the little lane did not come to a dead end. That was all I thought about, that was the rule, one half of the partnership must come to no harm in these circumstances: not only could they get help but because of the children.

The path came to a T-junction and I turned right, desperate to avoid ending up in the same road. I tore on. Then I was running between the blank side walls of houses again, my footsteps echoing hollowly. Bursting out on to the pavement in another street I stopped dead. There were plenty of people and traffic about, no one suspicious-looking. I carried on running, knowing roughly where I was and feeling for the spare car keys in my pocket. We always carry a set each in case of emergency.

Almost setting off the alarm in my haste I threw myself into the vehicle and started it, freaking out in case they had spotted the car, mud or no, and Oaf Three was somewhere nearby. No one materialized and I tried to calm down as I drove away. Breaking all our rules I returned to the road where Alex's flat was and braked hard at what I saw, causing the driver of the car behind to blare his horn. I pulled over, into the entrance to a car wash, ignoring his obscene gestures as he drove by.

Outside the house two cars were double-parked, several men in various states of disrepair getting into them. Of obvious injuries among the limps and winces, one appeared to have a nose bleed, another was holding his arm as if it was broken and a third, Patrick, was being supported by two others and, as I watched, he was tipped unceremoniously into the back seat of one of the cars. The vehicles were driven in my direction so I shot into the car wash, causing another driver to sound his horn.

The traffic was too heavy for me to be able to follow them but I did have allies.

Michael Greenway was out of breath slightly as though he had had to run to where he had left his phone. 'He's what?' he demanded to know. 'Sorry, the bloke next door's started a mower and I can't hear you.' A few seconds later, 'Right, that's better.'

'Patrick's allowed himself to be taken,' I said again. 'For heaven's sake get someone to watch the entrance of Descallier's house for two cars going in. Now. I got the reg of one of them and half of the other.' I gave them to him, repeating them when Greenway had hurried indoors to find pen and paper.

'I'll get on to it right away and ring you back.'

This he did when the car wash staff were getting a little restless at my continuing and profitless presence.

'It's a dreadful risk,' was his opening comment. 'Suppose they've no intention of taking him there? They might just put a bullet in his head.'

'He'll be banking on them wanting to find out why we were in the flat – how much the police know. I have an idea he'll then play on one advantage he has – that several criminal and terrorist organizations have put a price on his head. He's worth a hell of a lot of money to a crook.'

'How much?'

'A million dollars is being offered by one outfit.'

'Bloody hell!'

I went on to give him a full account of what had occurred.

'Do you have a base?' Greenway then went on to ask. 'Where are you staying?'

'We were at Patrick's club last night. But I don't think partners are allowed to stay there without members being present.'

'In the circumstances you shouldn't be in the city on your own. Go back to the place we had lunch – I'll book you a room there and fix it that someone's around to watch your back. I'll get on to people involved with the investigation and we'll go from there. Shall I meet you at the hotel at around six? Meanwhile I'll call you as soon as I know if those vehicles turned up.'

It was as if someone else had conducted this conversation and concisely reported what had taken place that afternoon, another person, not me, not the one half off her head agonizing over her husband's safety.

# EIGHTEEN

It being Sunday and everything police-wise short-staffed and manic – at least, that is what the man said – I ended up by having a Commander as bodyguard, Greenway himself. But the fact that he seemed preoccupied when we met told me that there were undercurrents in all this, he was working on something. I already knew that both the cars I had seen had entered Descallier's property but whether there were listening devices in the house or not Greenway had not revealed. I had to know.

'You would tell me if planted bugs had picked up ... well ... things you perhaps wouldn't want to upset me about,' I said.

He emerged from his reverie. 'You mean screams if they were torturing him?' he replied gently.

'Yes.'

'The phones are bugged but there are no mikes in the place. I don't actually know if anyone's listening to mobile phone conversations but did make it clear that I wanted every last piece of useful intelligence relayed to me immediately. Those indoors might be suspicious that the land-lines are being monitored because no calls in or out have so far mentioned visitors – not even any remarks that might be construed as containing code words. Personally I don't think any of them – except possibly Descallier himself – are bright enough to go in for things like that.'

'They won't be expecting any more visitors,' I said.

'And you think they might be getting some?' he enquired coolly.

'A section of the rear boundary fence was brought down a short while ago when an oak tree in the royal park was blown down. I checked before I came here as to whether the fence had been repaired. It hasn't. That might make what you're planning a little easier.'

He stared at the floor for a moment, his big hands clasped together and then sighed, 'You're a mind-reader.'

'Not at all, just a student of human body language.'

'I think it's important to have a very low profile look at this place. Especially in view of the fact that this character seems to have a lot of clout. Going against the rules, I know but I've never achieved anything by sitting on my backside on the sidelines.'

'I'll come with you on one condition.'

'Hell fire! I wasn't going to take you at all.'

'You have to and I was going to have a look round anyway. I'm the only one who can work with the way Patrick does things.'

'Ingrid, he could well be hurt and incapable of doing anything.'

'Those are my terms,' I told him.

'Look, I might not have a bloody price on my head but I've been involved in some pretty hairy cases along these lines.'

'And I promise I'll never tell *anyone* you went into a serious criminal's HQ with only a subordinate's wife as back-up in the most unprofessional and reprehensible fashion. *And* that you were actually *her* back-up.'

He gazed at me, open-mouthed.

'Not a soul,' I assured him.

'Ingrid...'

'You'll have to do exactly as the pair of us tell you.'

Any doubts he might still have been harbouring – and again I was admiring the man enormously as what I was asking of him was very unreasonable – appeared to be allayed when we met again in the hotel car park at a little after ten thirty that night. He was duly attired in dark clothing, a

275

navy blue Met action kit of some kind. I was similarly dressed in tracksuit and black trainers and had the Smith and Wesson snugly in its original shoulder harness that I had adjusted to my size. This was no time for handbags. Just to be on the safe side Patrick's spare knife was in my pocket.

'I have to know if you're armed,' I said.

He shook his head. 'No.'

'Patrick's Glock 17's in the Range Rover.'

'Best not to. I'm not a great shot.'

'Please carry it. At least you'll have it if it's needed.'

This took a few minutes as I had to fiddle with that harness as Greenway is broader than the usual wearer.

'We'll take your car,' I said.

The night was still and fine with no moon. Perfect.

I had no doubts at all about Greenway's reliability and desperately needed his presence although wondering if this intention of his was a little highly irregular macho stuff; an attempt to rescue the somewhat dark and deadly ex-MI5, ex-undercover army officer from the crime-lord's stronghold. And, ye gods, if he flopped somehow he would never be able to look Patrick in the eye again and from his point of view their working relationship would be in tatters. Two objectives for me then, assuming the man in my life was still alive.

We left the car in the road outside a pub and walked the half mile or so towards the park entrance. Although there was no moon the sky was not completely dark due to reflected urban lighting and we were able to walk on a wide tree-lined grass verge using the flash lamp I had brought only when there were no passing cars to illuminate our way. I did not think anyone would spot us as we moved as close to the trees as possible, the only likely hazards being walking into a low branch or tripping over one of the very low post and log fences that bordered the road and drives to private houses on either side.

'No one knows you're here?' I said.

'No, I've my pension to think about. Look, this might be a really daft idea but did he have his mobile on him?'

'Yes.'

'He might not have had a chance to turn it off.'

'He can't have done.'

'Why don't you ring him and pretend to be his mother or someone like that and see what happens? You might catch someone on the hop.'

This I did and it was answered at the fourth ring.

'Patrick?' I said without giving anyone a chance to speak first. 'It's your mother. How are you, darling? I haven't heard from you for ages. Where are you?'

Silence but for breathing noises, not Patrick's, probably. Then, whispering. A few seconds later, staggeringly, Patrick came on the line.

'Hi, Mum,' he said, his voice sounding weak.

I repeated most of what I had already said.

'Sorry not to have kept in touch,' he replied. 'Yes, I'm fine but in a meeting right now so can't talk. Where?' he asked as though I had

277

asked him that. 'Oh, Frinton. It's very smart.'

The line went dead.

'Not much to learn there then,' said Greenway, who had been standing close in order to overhear. 'Other than he's still alive.'

'Well, recognizing voices apart, he knew it wasn't his mother to whom he was talking, but me,' I told him. 'He calls his mother by her Christian name, Elspeth, and she never calls him darling. The phrase "in a meeting" means he's seriously outnumbered and "Frinton" is our code-word for "fearful" as in fearful of a successful outcome. "Very smart" means –' my voice caught in my throat – 'they've beaten him up.'

'Do I call out the troops?'

'I'd never presume to advise you about things like that.'

'No, but your oracle thing?'

'They'd have plenty of time to shoot him dead while the police were breaking down the front door. But you must know that my priority is Patrick, not nailing Descallier for his murder.'

'I'd rather stick with yours until something better presents itself.' After we had walked in silence for a few moments he said, 'I didn't tell you the truth just now. Richard Daws told me to have a go at getting Patrick out without making any waves and keep quiet about it.'

'Why?'

'No idea, but he obviously highly values the man. Perhaps he somehow feels responsible.'

'Daws is a bit more hard-boiled than that. He might be hoping Patrick does start a war if he has a little back-up.'

'And thinks this character will do less political damage dead? Obviously I would not be at all happy if that was the truth. SOCA wasn't set up to get rid of the politically inconvenient.'

'Well, hopefully not,' I said dryly.

We did not speak again until we had entered the park and turned sharp left on to the rough grass. Some hundred yards ahead of us was the huge fallen tree. The park authorities had begun to cut it up and the top, where it had crashed through the fence, had been removed and dragged away. Also from my earlier visit I knew that quite a lot of damage had been done, not just to the six foot tall high-quality wooden fence but to shrubs and a small tree within the grounds of the house, which appeared to have been split in half.

'Keep walking,' I said. 'There's a section of fence that's really been flattened just ahead.' The fact that, so far, no repairs had been effected pointed to the unlikelihood of guard dogs roaming around.

When we reached the gap I took hold of Greenway's sleeve and he halted.

I listened. On the lightest of breezes the night sounds were brought to us; the faint hum of traffic and the occasional closer car, planes high overhead, the rustle of leaves, an owl hooting. Then I heard voices coming from the direction of the house still concealed by the vegetation. It sounded as though people might be talking outside.

My main concern right now was that I had a big man with me who had the potential to blunder around like an elephant with a headache. This turned out to be a groundless worry for when we advanced a couple of minutes later, picking our way over the brash and wood chippings, the voices no longer audible, he turned out to be almost as silently moving as Patrick. On my unspoken suggestion, having navigated our way through the wreckage into an undamaged part of the shrubbery, we bore right, following the boundary fence. In order to remain quiet progress had to be extremely slow.

After what seemed like hours we reached a slight outward curve in the fence and then, a matter of ten yards farther on, another that met it at right angles. I had Patrick's tiny torch with me and risked using it for a few seconds. This fence was lower but I did not dare shine the light over it in case it was spotted by those indoors. We had no choice but to follow it even though it meant we were going closer and closer to the house before I really thought it safe to do so.

Quite quickly we reached an opening, a rustic archway that appeared to lead into whatever was over to our right on the other side of the fence. I was in front and turned to halt Greenway by placing a hand on his chest, leaving him there while I investigated what was through the arch. A few yards in I met a wire mesh fence: it was around a tennis court screened off from the rest of the garden. I went back and got the Commander to follow me. If we could go this way to get nearer without being detected...

I was trying to concentrate and not think about Richard Daws' involvement but this was difficult. Had he been worried that I would go in alone if no police action appeared to be forthcoming? He knew the way Patrick worked too. He also hated corruption in high places, being a high place sort of person himself. I could only think that rather than just getting Patrick out quietly he wanted the whole thing blown wide open, the pair of them having had a small part in bringing down a government once before after the Home Secretary of the time had condoned the setting up of a 'school for terrorists' to catch some of the world's most wanted criminals. Encouraging such people into the UK had had disastrous consequences.

'You've stopped,' Greenway breathed into my ear, perhaps wondering if I was losing my nerve.

'I'm thinking,' I whispered crossly.

'Sorry, ma'am.'

I set off again and, as we were shielded by the fence from the house, risked using the little torch. We were following a grass path and soon came to another opening. I peeped though it and saw that a side wall of the house was only a matter of yards away across a driveway that I guessed accessed garages, this proving to be correct when I leaned out a little further to have another look. There did not seem to be any point hazarding ourselves in walking in such an exposed position.

'Go back,' I said.

He made no demur and we retreated until we had reached where we had gone though the archway, carrying on through the shrubbery. After a few minutes of painstaking progress,

281

Greenway having indicated that I should again lead the way, it became possible to glimpse lights through the foliage. Then, suddenly, a wide expanse of lawn was before me, nothing between us and the house but a fairly large tree over to one side. I went smartly into reverse, treading on one of Greenway's toes and then stood motionless, he looking over my shoulder as I carefully parted the greenery so we could see more clearly.

There were a lot of lights on in the house and, directly before us, French doors into a living room which were wide open, the light streaming out on to an extensive patio furnished with tables and chairs, large potted palms and some kind of built-in barbecue. Judging by the voices people were in the room beyond and, as we watched, three men came out through the doors. They were silhouetted against the light for a moment. Was one of them Stefan and another the beer-bellied moron who had attacked me in Boyles House? Not coming in our direction they approached the tree, one side of which, away from us, was in deepest shadow. They spoke but seemingly not among themselves but to the tree. One man laughed, moved into the shadow and I heard a soft thump followed by another, indeterminate, sound. Then they all laughed. As they strolled back towards the house and I went into the light I saw that two of them had drinks glasses in their hands and were walking unsteadily. Yes, possibly Stefan and beer belly.

Quickly, I turned, almost bundling Greenway out of my way, and set off back towards where

282

we had entered, moving as quickly as I dared. I knew he was following me but was not about to explain my reasons right now. Back in the shrubbery by the main boundary fence, actually the rear of a wide border, I went right past where we had entered until we were in the area nearest to the shadow side of the tree.

'What are you doing?' Greenway whispered when I paused for a moment.

'I have a very, very nasty feeling about that tree,' I said before setting off again.

To his credit he did not press me further, just padded softly to the rear.

There was a sudden burst of loud laughter from indoors and I paused again for a few seconds before moving off. A darker shape materialized in front of me that turned out to be, after I had practically cannoned into it, a gazebo. I slid around the side of it, risked a second's flash with the torch into the interior, and then went in, drawing Greenway in with me when I sensed him slightly losing his bearings in the opening.

'Stand still,' I breathed. 'There's a teetering pile of folding chairs right behind you. Please stay here while I have a recce.'

He patted my shoulder by way of acknowledgement and I walked out on to the deep shade of the lawn. The tree was before me, a large darker blob, against the brightness of the light being shone across part of the lawn from inside the house. I could see no detail. When I reckoned that the nearest lower branch was a matter of feet from where I was I stopped and listened. I could hear nothing.

Then I heard a soft creaking sound as of stretched rope and the short hairs on the back of my neck prickled.

I went in the direction of the sound and walked right in to someone, someone who was hanging from the tree and judging by the way we touched, revolving slowly. Swiftly, I conducted an examination, discovering that his feet were only a matter of inches from the ground and that he was hanging, thank God, not by his neck. The lower part of his right leg was not flesh and bone but I already knew who it was : you tend to know your husband even in the dark.

Patrick appeared to be alive but unconscious.

Trying to remain calm I went back over to the gazebo, making a hissing noise when I guessed I was nearby.

'I can just see you,' Greenway hissed back.

'He's hanging from the tree,' I told him.

Greenway swore under his breath.

'By his wrists,' I amended.

I was all ready for trouble, sure that we would now be detected. Again, I risked a quick flash with the torch, mostly to avoid braining ourselves on the branch, not very thick, that was bowed down under its load. Swiftly, and somehow managing in almost complete darkness, Greenway hoisted me up and succeeded in supporting me with one arm and taking most of Patrick's weight with the other while I cut through the rope using the knife. It was very sharp but still seemed to take for ever.

'I've got him,' Greenway grunted when everybody went groundwards and the branch whoosh-ed up to its normal place giving me a hearty slap on the face with twigs and leaves on the way.

We half ran back to the gazebo. I stood in the doorway to try to prevent any stray beams of light escaping having given the torch to the Commander in order that he could assess Patrick's condition. When the patient suddenly sat up with a choice expletive he got a large hand clamped across his mouth. Even when this was removed and he had doubled over, trying to cope with the pain, he carried on swearing very, very quietly. I did not think he knew we were present or that he was no longer in criminal hands.

Greenway realized this too and we changed places. I thought mild shock tactics might work, knelt down and kissed that part of his face that was not curled into the agonized ball, as it turned out his right ear. The swearing ceased.

'It's me,' I said into the ear. 'And don't thrash about, we're in a summer house in enemy ter-ritory.'

He was still in terrible pain. I shone the torch beam quickly on his hands and they were livid with huge welts around his wrists from the rope. Gently, in the dark again, I massaged the life back into his fingers.

'We must go,' Greenway said.

Patrick started, not having realized he was there. Then, his voice hoarse, probably because it would prefer to scream, and speaking in short bursts, he said, 'The women ... are in the indoor swimming pool.'

'*In* the pool?' I said.

285

'It's been drained and they're being held there at gunpoint. I think they're going to ... dump them somewhere and Descallier'll leave the country.'

'How do you mean, dump?' Greenway asked, also crouching down.

'There's was talk of a shipping...' For a moment Patrick could not speak at all, shuddering. 'Container,' he continued. 'There's no ventilation ... which is reckoned ... will solve the problem. But first...'

'First?' Greenway prompted.

'They're going to have some fun ... with them.'

'I'll fix me a raid,' Greenway said and his clothing rustled as he stood up and rummaged for his phone.

That was when the screaming started.

I went into a kind of mental limbo, shocked by the dreadful sound, and aware that Greenway was speaking quietly on his mobile after another fleeting use of the torch, no doubt thinking, rightly as it happened, that no one indoors would hear or see him with all that racket and 'fun' going on. Patrick got to his feet, staggered and dislodged a couple of the garden chairs but the clatter brought no reaction from the house.

'I'm not going to wait for reinforcements, which are on their way, but get in there and arrest some of these bastards before some woman gets seriously injured or killed,' Greenway announced.

'They'll kill *you*,' Patrick told him. 'There's at

least twenty of them in there.'

'They wouldn't dare,' said Greenway and set off into the darkness.

I tore after him. 'Think!' I implored him, using Patrick's time-honoured exhortation. 'Have some kind of plan first.'

'There's no time for plans.'

I grabbed one of his arms and hauled him to a standstill with sheer physical effort. 'Our terms!' I said, hardly caring if anyone heard me. 'You do as we advise.'

'Patrick's in no fit state to do anything.'

'Yes, he is,' Patrick's voice said from behind us. 'Just.'

'We ought to go in armed and you can't even hold a gun.'

'I can do anything when necessary.'

When driven to it, speakable and ... not so.

Without another word, Greenway handed him the Glock and I gave Greenway the Smith and Wesson.

'Stay safely out of the way,' Greenway said to me.

'No, I think we ought to find Ingrid some kind of protection,' Patrick said absently and headed off, weaving around a little, adding over his shoulder, 'You're right, there's no time for plans.'

Trying to shut my mind to what was occurring indoors I paused just behind Patrick on the patio as he stood to one side of the double doors, Greenway on the other. As we had approached I had glimpsed a couple of men slumped in arm-chairs just inside, probably two of the three who had taunted Patrick as he had hung from the tree. The shrieking and screaming was coming from somewhere within the house – it sounded horribly as though women had been released and were now being hunted down – but it was impossible from one quick look to ascertain how many other people were in this first large room.

Patrick bent and, fumbling, picked up something from the garden that turned out to be a fairish-sized clod of earth. He handed it to me and mimed what I should do with it. Lobbed in with some verve the lump burst wonderfully on the forehead of one comatose figure, yippee, Stefan, showering the pair of them with soil. They reeled from their chairs towards us, sozzled, were grabbed as they exited and then guided into a more certain state of oblivion, Greenway providing the fairly brutal means. Relieved quickly of weapons they were then consigned, with glorious indifference, into the prickles of an adjacent holly bush.

I found myself in possession of a short-barrelled .38 Smith and Wesson, with which of course I am very familiar, and thanked my lucky stars it was not what the US police refer to as 'A Saturday Nite Special' a cheap, badly made weapon, similar to the kind of thing inside Martino Capelli's dragons and likely to blow up in your face.

'This is official,' Greenway said to us just before striding into the room. 'We're here to arrest them. If they resist...'

Was it my imagination or could I hear sirens over the din?

'Did you bring any handcuffs?' Patrick asked in conversational tones as we hurried through the room, bright and opulent, which was empty of people but for another inebriate in an armchair who appeared to be out cold.

'No,' Greenway replied.

'Pity.'

'Yes, it means we might have to shoot them anyway,' the commander observed cold-bloodedly. 'God, I *hate* this kind of crime!' he ended up roaring as we entered another room. 'Armed police!' he bellowed. 'Stand quite still or we'll shoot!'

Two men, one with his trousers down, dived for weapons in the pockets of jackets thrown over nearby chairs, were in receipt of a shot each and did not get up again.

'You all deaf?' Greenway shouted.

Everyone had dived to the floor and the women who had already been on the carpet grabbed what clothing they could find and crawled towards the sides of the room. I knew I ought to help them but they were reasonably safe if they stayed there. My role, I decided, was the traditional one, watching Patrick and Greenway's backs.

We were by no means through yet.

Someone fired and a bullet thunked into the wall somewhere behind me. After this events became confused, some of it so weird I thought afterwards that my memory was playing tricks. Had Greenway really picked up a man and thrown him, like a large log of wood at three others who charged at him through a doorway?

289

And when a man had come from behind us had Patrick clubbed him down with the Glock before he could fire? The room emptied and there was more sporadic shooting in other parts of the house.

Belatedly, I obeyed Patrick's swift gesture that I should go back into the first room and not long afterwards, a matter of seconds probably, it went oddly quiet. The drunk was still sprawled in his armchair and other than for him I was alone in the room. At that moment a vast noise erupted from somewhere out the front as the door was battered in. Sirens howled, vehicle tyres slewed on gravel, orders were shouted, tracker dogs barked, women started screaming again. Then a man appeared in a doorway and furtively crossed the room towards the doors into the garden.

'Stop right there,' I ordered, standing up. Only then did I notice the gun in his hand.

'I'm with the cops, dearie,' he said.

'No, you're Romano Descallier.'

'Not at all,' he said with a broad smile brimming with gold fillings and insincerity.

'I was given your description,' I informed him, 'Medium build, medium height, middle-aged but looking older, wishy-washy hair, pale blue eyes. Hobnobber with the rich and famous, criminal record as long as your arm but what it all boils down to is that you're just a nondescript old fart.'

'Bitch!' he spat.

'You're under arrest.'

His gun arm shot up but I got him first.

I loathe being called dearie.

# NINETEEN

I kicked the dropped weapon out of the way just as Mike Greenway came into my line of vision, the whole house now reverberating with the tramp of standard issue police footwear. He was triumphant but hurt, one sleeve of his sweater dark with blood which was dripping to leave a trail on the floor.

'You're about to be tedious by saying it's only a scratch,' I scolded. 'It isn't. Please allow me to do something about it for you.'

He caught sight of Descallier who was nursing a wounded gun arm and upon seeing the commander, fainted. 'You got him! Brilliant! I was beginning to think he'd got away!' He then subsided abruptly on top of the drunk in the armchair.

I shoved his head between his knees, closed and locked the doors to the garden, removing the key to prevent my prisoner from getting away and went off through the mêlée to find the kitchen where I rummaged – bugger forensics – until I unearthed a couple of new tea towels. With them I endeavoured to stop the bleeding from the flesh wound in Greenway's shoulder, having ruthlessly hauled the sweater off him to get at it.

'No one tried to arrest me just now,' I said chattily to try to mitigate the pain I was causing him as I pressed a folded tea towel on to the wound.

'They'd be raving mad if they did,' he said through tight lips.

'What?'

'Well you hardly look like a trafficked woman or one of Descallier's trollops, do you?' he went on with some asperity.

'You wouldn't know where Patrick is, by any chance?'

'I have an idea he's gone to look for that woman.'

I had forgotten all about Alexandra.

When the place soon became teeming with paramedics as well as everyone else I was able to leave the Commander in someone's care. I presented a cop who looked as though he might be in charge with the Smith and Wesson, together with the location of its real owner, plus friend, added that I was with Greenway and left him, a trifle bemused, in the entrance hall at the bottom of the staircase.

Ascending, I found myself on a spacious landing – or at least it would have been without so many police in it – like the hallway below almost a room in its own right. All eight doors visible from this were open, a quick tour on my part revealing that the views through them suggested that at least two led into suites. One of these I knew from Alan Kilmartin's drawing was Descallier's. It was sumptuously furnished, a shower room I glanced into in passing loaded with gold taps and other fittings, used silk-embroidered towels thrown down on the floor and into the bath.

'Looking for someone?' said a businesslike, smartly-dressed woman, presumably a CID officer, coming from within and forcing me to stand aside.

'Yes, Patrick Gillard. I'm with SOCA.'

'Another one! I wasn't even aware you were here, but do carry on. There's a female in there I think I'm going to arrest as I suspect she's Descallier's mistress. She's talking to a SOCA man she referred to as Patrick. What's your interest?' she finished by bluntly asking.

'He's my husband.'

'I'm envious,' was her parting remark as she walked away.

'I left a confiscated firearm with your man downstairs,' I called after her, having realized that *she* was in charge. 'I fired it twice in protecting my colleagues.'

'Thank you.'

They were in the huge master bedroom, Alexandra huddled up on the bed wearing a silky robe and her usual pout, Patrick leaning against an ornate chest of drawers that would have done Versailles proud. Gilt-framed mirrors were everywhere and the curtains were heavily draped velvet with huge gold-trimmed tie-backs. I began to see what the boss lady had meant; arms crossed, his shirt in tatters, his face marked, the welts on his wrists raw, Patrick was still the only thing in the room worth looking at.

293

'Oh, not you,' said Alexandra. 'Come to gloat?'

'Those phone calls you made...' I began.

'He's just asked me that. And I told him.'

'To get the police going to all the wrong places,' Patrick said. 'As we have recently suspected, with planted clothing and other stuff. But not Boyles House, that was a real prison, wasn't it, Alex?'

She improved on the pout, saying nothing.

'You were not at all keen when Descallier first suggested a partnership so you tried to do a runner to Bath,' Patrick continued. 'I'm guessing here, Alex, you'll have to correct me if I'm wrong. But first he waved a big stick in the shape of Stefan and then enough money and promises under your nose to make you change your mind. *And* got rid of the other bed-warmers that Alan Kilmartin saw when he came here with you that time. I reckon old Dessie actually fell for you in a big way, never mind your little business, which, let's face it, is a microdot in his empire. For after all, he'd already met you several times.'

'I wish they'd strung you up by your bloody *neck*!' Alexandra shrieked. She slapped her hands over her mouth for a moment. 'I – I didn't mean that.' She gazed up at him, tears welling in the beautiful eyes. 'Please, please help me. You could, easily. You have a lot of authority. I could see that you were going to be wildly successful when we first met.'

'I seem to remember that you colluded in trying to kill my wife,' Patrick murmured.

294

Authority, the boss, returned with a uniformed woman constable, and politely intimated that this really was her patch. We left the room. There was really nothing else to say but I still would have liked to ask a lot more questions.

'Thank you for your forbearance,' Patrick said at the top of the stairs.

'Any time,' I said with a smile.

'No, seriously, I was expecting you to take her apart.'

'Am I *that* stormy?'

He leaned on me a bit. 'D'you reckon anyone's got a couple of aspirins?'

It had, Patrick admitted later, gone badly wrong. One of his main objectives, to use subversion; hoping to engage with the workforce, nurse any grievances they might have and create dissent so there was every chance they would round on those in charge, had misfired. They all, it appeared, had big stakes in the set-up and were not just hired gunmen, thugs and bruisers. Worse, Alexandra had already told Descallier about us, that we worked for SOCA and were likely be on the case so there was no getting out of that. She had said she had the idea we would go to her flat and as luck would have it we had walked right into the group Descallier had sent round there.

It came out later that Descallier had been keen to delay any police investigation, which was getting uncomfortably close, but had not been remotely interested in selling Patrick to the highest bidder. But Patrick had at least, probably by his demeanour, made the man reluctant to kill

295

him, the years in prison, should he be convicted of all the criminal charges he had so far wriggled out of no doubt ratcheting up unpleasantly in the man's mind. So he had decided just to string him up to teach him a lesson and then dump him ignominiously somewhere. After they had disposed of the latest batch of women. Of these, although a couple were ill after their treatment, fortunately none had actually been hurt during the raid which was a relief to us.

Neither Patrick nor I were personally involved in the aftermath of the case, our only connection the leads provided by our connection with Alexandra that led all the way back to house-hunting in Bath. I found I despised her but pulled myself up sharp: how would I have reacted when given the same choice? Would I have settled for a stinking prison in case I told my story to the police or cooperated and have a life of luxury?

Using our first aid kit, I had applied analgesic, antiseptic salve to Patrick's wrists, which I had then bandaged. His hands were still comparatively weak and he was suffering from racking pains in the shoulders and a badly bruised face. I had no idea how he had managed to fell one of Descallier's gang, the man who had come up behind us and had been about to shoot Greenway in the back.

'You did a good job on the man with his trousers around his ankles,' Patrick said to me.

'I didn't kill him, did I?' I gasped.

'No, but he won't be going in for rape for a while, if ever.'

Oh, good.

To his disgust, Greenway had been carted off to hospital where, despite his protests, he was kept in overnight after being stitched up and then sent home the following morning with dire warnings as to what would happen if he opened the wound up again. This meant that his wife issued him with some kind of meaningful ultimatum and he did not go to work to conduct the debriefing with us that he had planned. I did not regret this at all: it had not really been our case.

Months later, Descallier and most of his associates, were given various prison sentences for people trafficking and other crimes that were on file, the Metropolitan Police generously giving SOCA a one-line mention in one of several reports.

And Alexandra? Her defence counsel played on her big blue eyes for all he was worth, portraying her as the naive, even a little simple, woman preyed on by the ruthless master criminal. She finished up having to do a few hundred hours community service, which come to think of it, was the best punishment.

But right now, we went home.

'We were little more than armed back-up to two cases really,' Patrick said to James Carrick a couple of days later when we met him for a drink in the Ring o' Bells. 'It's not what I joined SOCA to do but you can't pick and choose.'

I thought his views on our roles a little sweeping but made no comment, asking instead, 'How's the investigation into the head in the cupboard case going?'

Carrick pulled a face. 'I'm forced to admit that it's stalled. Despite establishing exactly who the victim was, Imelda Burnside, discovering the murder weapon, the old police truncheon and the knife that was used to decapitate the body, plus knowing that she had had rows with David Bennett, who has now admitted knocking her around, I have absolutely no evidence that he killed her. It would be a waste of time and money bringing it to court. All I can say for certain is that she wasn't killed in the house but the body was decapitated in the garden. That suggests she was killed out there too.'

'What does Bennett say about the truncheon and knife?' Patrick enquired.

'I showed them to him and he was emphatic he'd never set eyes on either of them, not even when he visited his aunt in the sheltered accommodation where she lived before she went into care. I can't say that I believe him but short of getting out the thumbscrews...'

'She was in another nursing home before the one she's at now,' I told him. 'One of the residents told me.'

'Not that it can have any bearing on anything but which one, do you know?'

'No, but she'd arrived in a green people-carrier with gold lettering on it. And I've just remembered, Imelda Burnside worked in the same nursing home where Miss Bennett was for a time. Irma told us. It could have been that one.'

'Did she say anything else that might be useful?'

'She said she'd met her once and didn't like

her. In her words, she was "bonkers normally", and hated everyone.'

'But seemingly not her nephew.'

'Yes, she hated him too.'

'Then why leave him the house?'

'Perhaps that was better than not leaving a will at all and it going to the State. I take it the woman has never married – I mean, some women revert to their maiden name when they're divorced – and there's no other family.'

'It might be worth finding out,' Carrick mused. 'Someone might know about the will and if David Bennett was had up for murder there might be a case for a challenge to it.'

We all confessed that we were a little hazy on the details of civil law and then went on to talk about something else.

'It doesn't add up,' I said to Patrick a few days later. He was having a long weekend.

'What doesn't?'

'When you really think about it, why would David Bennett, having killed Imelda in a rage, or whatever, then cut her head off and put it in a cupboard? The house was due to be his. He wouldn't want two stinking messes there, never mind the resulting hoo-ha.'

'To make it look as though she'd been murdered by some nutter and thus draw suspicion away from himself,' Patrick replied without hesitation.

'OK, but presumably he wants to make money on it, not live there. Who'd want to buy it?'

'Well, you do.'

'I did make the initial decision *before* finding the head,' I reminded him. 'And who, exactly, has put the place on the market? Bennett? How can he? His aunt's still alive.'

'She might have done.'

'She's not mentally capable.'

'You'd better ring Carrick with all that. It's not our problem.'

'It *is* my problem. I feel responsible.'

But men cannot understand such female notions and Patrick finished his coffee and went back into the garden to carry on mowing the lawn. I knew his hands were not yet really strong enough for the task but supposed that his thinking was that if he ignored how they felt they would recover more quickly. He was probably right.

James, whom I had already discovered was a more sensitive soul and whose problem it most emphatically was, thoughtfully heard me out.

'I can answer one of those questions because I felt I had to establish the truth myself,' he said. 'According to the estate agent Miss Bennett did put the house on the market but under the guidance of her solicitor. Perhaps she's known him, or her, for a long time and does manage to communicate with whoever it is.'

'Does she have to sell up to pay for her care?'

'I didn't ask that as it didn't seem relevant. That's the problem; the only person who might have a lot of answers is beyond reach.'

'I'm not being nosy, just thinking that if she is having to sell for that reason then if she lives for quite a while there won't be much left for her nephew.'

'Yes, but surely he can't be planning to finish her off.'

I almost chided him with, 'No, silly,' but said instead, 'She hates him, remember? If she left him the house rather than let it be forfeited to the Crown in the event of her dying intestate only for the money it fetches to trickle slowly away for her nursing home care – not that she might have any choice in the matter – she could be one happy lady thinking of him ranting and raving in his cupboard at Claverton.'

'It would probably serve him right. So where does that leave us?'

'Nowhere really now you've answered my question.'

'That's a shame as I could do with a break-through.'

I stared at the phone after he had suddenly rung off: he must be under enormous pressure to get a result.

'You know the head in the cupboard case we have down here?' I said to Michael Greenway after enquiring about his shoulder injury.

'I gather you'd wanted to buy the place.'

'That's not why I'm ringing you. I'm sure DCI Carrick's getting it in the neck for not having yet solved the murder and I was wondering if I can use my SOCA ID in order to try to give him a hand.'

'Has he asked for your help?'

'No.'

There was a short silence before he said,

'D'you have any leads?'

'No, if I did I would have shared them with him.'

'Patrick too?'

'No.'

'It would have to be in your own time.'

'Of course.'

'OK, you have my permission – off the record. Be careful though, David Bennett's not the main suspect for nothing; he's pretty stupid as well as being dangerous to women.'

My reasons were not entirely altruistic: the book had hit the wall again and sitting staring at a computer screen hoping for inspiration is always a waste of time. Greenway need not have warned me about David Bennett as I had no intention of going anywhere near him, that was Carrick's job. As I had said to Patrick, I could imagine the man lashing out in a rage and killing Imelda but not indulging, if that was the right word, in what took place afterwards.

Bennett had insisted that he had never seen the truncheon and knife before. I could believe it with the former as such an item is distinctive, but not the latter. What ordinary British man can tell one kitchen knife from another?

It was reasonably safe to assume that Hilda Bennett had had the truncheon in her possession when she was living reasonably self-sufficiently in the warden-assisted accommodation several years before moving to the care home that had the green people-carrier with gold lettering on it. Had she given it to her nephew and he was lying? It seemed likely. And if Imelda had

302

worked at that same home had she built up any kind of friendship, if that was possible, with the woman?

I delved into the Internet. Bath had around a dozen care and nursing homes but there were no details on the individual websites as to the nature, let alone the liveries, of any vehicles used to transport their clients or take them on outings. But having established where Miss Bennett had actually stayed it seemed pointless to ask questions as who would have known about her possessions? I began to realize why Carrick felt he was going around in circles. Perhaps if I rang the district nurse...

This no-nonsense Irish lady had proved to be a godsend just after Mark was brought home from hospital and had been difficult and colicky. She seemed to know everyone and everything about the neighbourhood and I wondered if her wisdom stretched as far as Bath.

'That'll be Amelia Davies House,' she said without hesitation. 'Very upmarket, very smart, big posh people-carrier that they use to ferry people about. They only take people who are fairly mobile and with it. Start wandering around the city centre in your nightie or beating up the other residents with your Zimmer and you're out, pronto.'

'I take it the place was called after a wealthy benefactress.'

'That's right, and she was a right old harridan apparently. How's the baby?'

'Blooming, thank you.'

'Good, he's a real poppet.'

303

I resolved to tell Mark this when he was around nine.

The nursing home was situated in Ralph Allen Drive and was a large house set in immaculate gardens. Right beside the main entrance the green people-carrier, almost a minibus in size, was parked. It was not the kind of vehicle to have room for wheelchairs, hence the need for residents to be reasonably mobile. I obeyed the sign for visitors to enter and go to reception.

'The *police*,' the young woman behind the desk gasped in sheer horror.

'This is just a routine matter,' I soothed. 'But it does involve a request for information about a woman who no longer lives here. Is there someone I can speak to?'

After a whispered exchange in an adjacent office I was shown in. A man who could have been anyone's bank manager was caught red-handed trying to tidy his desk by sweeping most of what was on it into a drawer, including a newspaper. The Racing Times? Page three boobs?

'I'm the director,' he said in lofty tones, slamming shut the drawer with the paper still sticking out of it. 'Rex Turner. What can I do for you?'

'I'll come straight to the point,' I told him, seating myself having shown him my ID and keeping a straight face with difficulty. In such moments do the self-important wreck their pretensions. 'There was a murder in the city recently in a house in Cherry Tree Row. You must have heard about it. The building belongs to a one-time client of yours who is now living in another nursing home. It would appear that the murder weapon is an item that was once in her possession and I'm trying to trace its whereabouts around the time she was here.' It was at that moment I realized I was doing nothing of the kind.

'Who would this person be?'

'Miss Hilda Bennett.'

His face betrayed nothing. 'You must realize that I can't—'

'You'd have to if it came to a court of law,' I interrupted.

He steepled his fingers and stared at them before saying, 'I remember her well. Her condition deteriorated rapidly and we could no longer have her here. In fact, she didn't want to stay. But I'm afraid if you want to know about certain of her possessions I can't help you as for various reasons we have quite a high turnover of staff and it's unlikely that whoever was dealing with her is still working here.'

'Did she become disruptive?'

He again hesitated before answering. 'You must understand that this is highly confidential.'

'Unless what you tell me is important to the case it won't go beyond this room.'

'Our first difficulty was that she made it plain that she detested everyone, staff and residents alike. Matters came to a head when she kept walking out.'

'Was this as a direct result of her illness or was there a real problem?'

'Her doctor thought it was a mixture of both.'

'Do you remember a woman by the name of Imelda Burnside working here?'

'How did you find that out?' he asked hoarsely.

'From her sister.'

'Look, if it emerges that—'

'The murder victim was on your payroll?' I finished for him. 'Not good for business, eh?'

'It's just that—'

'Mr Turner, this is a murder investigation. Was there a problem concerning the two women?'

He remained silent for a moment and then reluctantly said, 'There was. I believe Miss Bennett discovered that the Burnside woman was going out with her nephew. She was furious, shouting that she was common and after his money. But, you must understand, this was not instrumental in her wanting to leave.'

'No?'

'No. After words were exchanged the carer, Burnside, was consigned to other clients. Things settled down for a while. We just had to make sure they did not come face to face.'

'Surely Imelda was upset by this reaction.'

'Probably, but she cooperated with the new arrangements. There are always difficulties with people suffering from dementia.'

'When Miss Bennett walked out where did she end up?'

'Once or twice back at the sheltered accommodation where she had lived previously, then at that house you mentioned she owned, and on the last occasion the police found her wandering in Victoria Park. She had been missing for hours and I'm afraid that was when we told her nephew she had to be moved to somewhere where her needs were better served.'

'Was Imelda Burnside still working here after Miss Bennett left?'

'No, she'd left about a fortnight before this final episode.'

'Do clients have their own rooms or do they share?'

'They have their own. It's one of our advantages over other care homes.'

'And you visit them?'

'Not in their rooms. I chat to them in the lounges and they can request a private interview if they wish.'

'Did you *ever* go into Miss Bennett's room?'

He began to weary of me. 'Is this really—'

'Please answer the question.'

'Yes, I did. On the last occasion when she'd gone off on her own.'

'Did you notice an old police truncheon on display anywhere? It had belonged to her great-grandfather.'

'No.'

'Are you sure?'

'We don't encourage clients to bang nails in the walls.'

'It could have been anywhere.'

'If it was there I didn't see it.'

I thanked him and left.

# TWENTY

It has become important to me, whenever possible, to do my thinking at the scene of the crime and this time I was going to have to be very professional and detached. Making no reference to my previous offer on the house, I merely showed my ID to the woman in the estate agents, someone I had not seen before, and came away with the keys.

The weather had turned wet and gloomy as only the West Country can sometimes be and I anticipated that the little house would be even darker with the creepers and other plants rampant across the windows. Not so, I saw as I parked the car. Everything had been cut back, the shrubs in the front garden pruned, alas cutting off most of the flower buds, and the tiny lawn had been mowed, scalped actually.

There was a car parked right outside and the front door was open. Sounds of activity were coming from within and the tiled floor just inside the front door was wet. I already knew that the knocker was seized solid with paint or dirt so rapped on the open door with my knuckles.

Hot and bothered, David Bennett poked his head around a corner and then frowned deeply.

'What do you want?'

'I'm not here in any official capacity,' I said, wondering whether I ought to go away, right now.

'What capacity are you here in then?' he demanded to know.

'It was me who found the body. But I live locally and had already put in an offer for the place.'

He emerged, wet patches on his clothes, holding a dripping scrubbing brush. 'You can give me a hand if you like.'

'No, thanks.'

Coming right up to me he said, 'D'you still want to buy it?'

'I might. But someone's put in a higher offer.'

'As of yesterday I've got power of attorney. Auntie's worse, bananas, so it's me who decides. And no one's said anything to me about higher offers.'

'May I have another look round?'

'Please do,' he said eagerly. He stood aside but I indicated that he should lead the way. I was not going to turn my back on this man.

'The place was filthy.' Bennett said chattily. 'All the buyers seemed to have gone cold so I thought I'd better do something about it. The agent was a bit sniffy about the state of it too. Bloody great spiders. I got some spray stuff and polished them all off, I tell you.' He turned to leer at me. 'I know how all you ladies hate creepy-crawlies.'

I never thought that I would mourn the death of a spider.

Downstairs, I followed Bennett from room to room and was forced to admit that he had done a lot of cleaning. With the vegetation removed from the windows everywhere was now starkly light which unfortunately showed up the cracks in the plaster of the walls and ceilings and the woodworm holes in the floorboards. I saw with dismay that there was a large damp patch that I had not noticed before on the wall above the fireplace in the right-hand living room and when we reached the kitchen could hardly fail to notice that the dry rot, or whatever it was, was escaping from the cupboard under the sink and creeping across the bare boards of the floor. There was a lingering smell of decomposition.

'Needs a lot of money spending on it,' Bennett said gloomily. 'But it'll be great when it's finished. She never spent a penny on the place herself and it got to the stage where it wasn't fit to live in. She's always been odd, frankly.'

'That's what Imelda's sister thought.'

'Oh, she did have a sister then,' Bennett said in offhand fashion.

I leaned on the larder door, *the* larder door. 'Be honest with me. Do you think Imelda really wrote that letter saying that she was going to live with her or did someone else?'

'I think...'

'Yes?'

'Someone else might have done.'

'And you're positive you received it?'

'You said this wasn't an official visit.'

'It isn't, but if I'm to buy this house I need to know the full story, don't I?' I conjured a

310

jolly smile.

'Yes, it was left here, on the mantelpiece. But I'd never seen Imelda's handwriting so it's possible she didn't write it.'

'What kind of state was your aunt in just over twelve months ago?'

'Not too bad. But trying to leave where she was. She didn't like it there.'

'She found out you were going out with Imelda.'

'*Did* she?'

'Perhaps Imelda told her herself – she was working there.'

'Oh, yes, I suppose she was.'

'Apparently she was furious.'

'Auntie was like that.'

'Mr Bennett, didn't Imelda say anything to you about this?'

'Er, no, we weren't really speaking then on account of her still living here when I'd asked her to go.'

'And you'd had words.'

'Yes.'

'And you'd hit her.'

'No!'

'Funny, DCI Carrick said that you'd admitted you had.'

'Look—' Bennett began angrily.

'Are you covering up for your aunt? Did she so bitterly resent the fact that her carer – she'd been shouting that Imelda was common and only after your money – had lived here with you that she came here and battered her with her great-grandfather's police truncheon?'

311

Bennett stared at me.

'And then in her confused, no, crazy state, she found a knife in the kitchen and cut off her head, putting that in the cupboard upstairs and the body here in this larder. To get her revenge as well as give you a horrible shock. Because she hates everybody.'

'She might have done,' he agreed.

'I suggest that you know she did.'

There was a protracted silence before Bennett said, 'OK, she did. I'd had a call from the home to say that Auntie had gone walkabout again so I first called in where she'd been the last time, at the sheltered accommodation, no luck, and then came here. The place was in a real mess, blood everywhere. Auntie was standing like something turned to stone, over there by the sink. She was covered in blood too. The knife was still in her hand and she'd obviously been trying to wash the blood off it. She wouldn't speak to me.'

'Where was the body?'

'She must have already dealt with it. I didn't want to look for it, believe you me. I suppose I panicked. I gave her a coat of Imelda's and told her to take off her outer clothes so I could burn them. Then I took her back to the home and told them I'd found her just wandering around. They said that was the last straw, they couldn't cope with her any longer.'

'Then you came back, cleaned up the house, shifted out all the furniture and got rid of it having first disposed of Imelda's car.'

'That's right.'

'Why?'

'Eh?'

'*Why?* If you'd gone to the police without touching anything and told them the truth the outcome would have merely been that your aunt was sent to a secure mental hospital.'

'As I said, I panicked. I thought I'd be number one suspect.'

'Because of your criminal record for violence against women.'

'Yes.'

'What did you do with the car?'

'Sold it. It was mine. She'd only been using it.'

'A set of keys for it was found in her bag buried, together with her clothes, in the garden. Did you really think that you were going to succeed in making this woman just disappear?'

'I've told you – I panicked.'

'No, actually, you're lying. Forensic tests have proved that Imelda wasn't killed in the house, but probably in the garden which is where her head was cut off. *You* battered her to death and did what followed in order to shift any blame on to your aunt, the act of a deranged woman, should you subsequently find yourself charged with the murder. There was no letter saying she was going to live with her sister, who insists such a move was never mentioned. And that night when your aunt wandered off she was found by the police in Victoria Park.'

He was still staring at me.

'Imelda was quite a big, strong girl,' I continued, watching him carefully. 'Carers have to be in order to be able to lift people. Your aunt would never have been able to move her body,

313

even with the head removed, let alone wrap it in bedding and put it in the larder. You hit Imelda and when she ran into the garden to try to escape you killed her. On one of the rare occasions you'd visited your aunt you'd helped yourself to the truncheon, no doubt thinking it might be worth something and you could sell it. And that gave you the idea.'

'You can't prove any of this,' Bennett whispered.

'Another thing is that I'm still mulling over what you said just now about not knowing about offers on this house. Someone accepted my original offer and then went on to tell that estate agent to tell me I could have it for a lot less. In a panic then, were you in anticipation of your power of attorney? Sell the place with poor auntie not able to understand what's happening and then hightail it back to New Zealand with the money? I think you'll find that the police have a pretty good case against you.'

He came a bit closer. 'What if I did kill her? She was just a bloody nuisance – you're a bloody nuisance.'

'You admit it then?'

'Why not, just between us two. It is just you, isn't it? You haven't told anyone else what you think.'

He was blocking the doorway into the hall and I was hoping I could make it through the back door and get over the high wall in the garden before he could grab me. 'This isn't my theory. My colleague reckons you're guilty and, in roughly his words, you made the killing look as

314

though it had been done by some nutter.'

'Your colleague?' Bennett said blankly.

'Remember me?' Patrick said, appearing behind him. He gave me a big smile. 'I thought we could have lunch.'

Bennett moved quickly to stand by the back door, probably thinking himself now out of range and having visibly changed his mind about trying to bulldoze the newcomer out of the way.

'I heard most of what was said,' Patrick informed him. 'You've been tailed ever since you were first pulled in for questioning, Bennett, and the guy whose turn it was rang in pronto when the two of you were here together. Carrick rang me and will soon be here. It's his case and he can arrest and charge you.'

Patrick had already been in the city centre so had grabbed a taxi and arrived before the DCI, neither he nor James wanting to take any risks. Carrick arrived about two minutes later and we all went to the nick where I was requested to put the case as I saw it on record. Bennett meanwhile was apparently raging around a cell, shouting obscenities and promising what he would do to me should we ever meet again. I was beginning to think that Hilda Bennett was not the only one in her family to be mentally unbalanced.

'That was as good as a whodunnit play,' I said over lunch at The Moon and Sixpence. 'Your entry I mean. A Not Quite Inspector Calls. A bit over the top if you ask me.'

315

'Over the top?' Patrick echoed.

'You both pulling out all the stops to get there, just because I was talking to a suspect.'

Patrick laid down his knife and fork. 'Ingrid, you talking to suspects usually has the same effect as throwing lighted matches into a petrol tank. We didn't want you to go up with it.'

'How sweet.'

We both laughed.

'I'm not buying the house,' I said, the decision having just been made. 'I don't want it now. It was a dream that tarnished. I'd never be able to forget that poor woman and the way she died.'

At Patrick's suggestion we spent the afternoon at Bath Races, something we had never done before. It felt like the continuation of our short holiday, as though what had taken place since had never happened.

When we returned to the rectory it was in a state of turmoil, furniture in the hallway, piles of books everywhere, the smell of fresh paint pervading everything.

'There,' Elspeth said, 'you've beaten us all to it.'

'I did try to stay out as long as possible,' Patrick said to her.

I homed in on what appeared to be the centre of activity, John's study. The room had been stripped right out, the old wallpaper removed and Katie and Matthew were finishing off emulsioning the walls in two shades of apricot. Carrie appeared with some toning fabric with gorgeous flowers on it over her arm, curtains, I saw when I looked closer. She flashed a smile at me, touched the freshly painted wall over by the window to check that it was dry and mounted a stepladder to hang them.

'Is this *quite* John?' I tentatively queried.

'No, it's for you,' Elspeth replied. 'It's your new writing room.'

'For me! But—'

'He suggested it,' she said firmly. 'We have a spare bedroom that we simply don't need and it was high time this lot,' she waved vaguely in the direction of the stuff piled in the hall, 'was sorted out. We've found minutes of meetings going back over forty years that were here when we arrived! Plus newspapers that the church has a mention in, fishing magazines that he couldn't bear to throw away, even old choir robes all damp and full of the moth. It was all a horrible fire hazard. The room in the annex is plenty big enough even with the bookshelves moved in there and it's actually warmer for John now he's getting on in life. And I won't have to walk a quarter of a mile to tell him that his meals are ready. The only thing that has to stay is the safe we keep the church silver in. I hope you don't mind but we simply couldn't shift it.'

I went right in and gazed around. 'It's heaven,' I whispered utterly truthfully.

'He's in the annex,' Elspeth said, a little misty-eyed.

John looked up from reading a newspaper. 'Like it?'

I went over and gave him a kiss. 'Thank you *so* much.'

'You deserve somewhere quiet to work. And I

317

want to thank you too, for what you've done for Patrick. I'm convinced he would have gone right off the rails after his leg injuries if it hadn't been for you. He might even have gone the other way and turned to a life of crime. There's a dark side to him that might have taken over his mind completely.'

He would have made a very successful criminal though.